I0782307

MIKE DUKE

THE HOUSE OF SMARBA

THE HOUSE OF SMARBA

MIKE DUKE

The House of Smarba
Mike Duke

Published by Sinister Smile Press,
A Division of Crystal Lake Publishing
P.O. Box 637
Newberg, OR 97132
Copyright © 2023 by Mike Duke

Cover art by Kealan Patrick Burke of Elderlemon Designs

Trade Paperback ISBN – 978-1-964398-46-4

www.sinistersmilepress.com

CONTENTS

I'd like to dedicate this book to Ziva, my German Shepherd, who was my constant companion while writing this book in the months just after Covid hit when i was out of work on furlough and fighting depression. The love and joy she's given me over the last 13 years is beyond measure and I'll cherish every day I have left with her.

I'd like to give a big shout out to Lisa Lee Tone for all her editorial assistance and advice while preparing this book to submit to publishers. Also, big thanks to all the people who beta read this book. I greatly valued their feedback.

PROLOGUE – MAY 15

NATHAN AND DEBBIE LOCH DROVE DOWN THE WINDING back road leading away from the lakeside cottage where they had spent the weekend. It had been a delightful family vacation, even if it only lasted three days. Martin drew pictures in his sketchpad and hunted for salamanders. Bella played with her dolls and imagined she was a princess of the lake, with deer and rabbits acting as her forest dwelling attendants. And both children enjoyed swimming in the lake and fishing from the rowboat with their father. Debbie had reclined in a lawn chair by the lake, getting a tan and listening to a book she had been unable to find the peace and quiet necessary to indulge in while at home. Nathan was content to fish for the most part, whether with the children or on his own.

On their way home now, every one of them was relaxed. Both Debbie and Nathan felt reinvigorated with a level of positive energy they had not experienced in some time.

They should have known it was too good to last.

They passed two vehicles headed in the opposite direction—a Toyota 4Runner and an old pickup truck riding the 4Runner's ass. Those were the only vehicles Nathan had seen in the last half hour of driving. Right after they appeared in his side-view mirror, without warning, their minivan died.

It was like somebody pulled the plug. Radio and dash lights blinked out, and the power steering failed. Nathan squeezed the brake and looked for a placed to pull over. There was a driveway on their right, leading to a large house set back away from the road. A "For Sale" sign was posted in the front yard. Nathan strained against the wheel to turn the vehicle and pulled into the driveway, coasting to a stop.

"What's wrong?" Martin asked first. Their little Johnny on the spot, always attentive to any change in his environment.

"I don't know, bud," Nathan said. "It just died on me. Let's take a look under the hood." Nathan looked over at Debbie, who had opened her eyes and looked around when he stopped, still listening to a book. She pressed pause and pulled out an earbud.

"What's wrong?"

"Vehicle died," Nathan answered. "Me and mini-me are gonna take a look under the hood. When I ask you to, turn the ignition."

"Okay," Debbie said.

Nathan pulled the handle to release the hood latch, then he and Martin got out and lifted the hood to take a look. Nathan fiddled with the battery cables and asked Debbie to turn the key. She did. Nothing. The engine didn't turn over at all. Nathan looked around to make sure the alternator belt had not come off. It looked good. He pulled out his pocketknife and tapped the alternator to see if the light impact might jar it into action. He was no mechanic, but he thought he remembered hearing a friend say when the alternator is going bad, a good tap might get it to kick back in for a while. He asked Debbie to turn the key again. Still nothing.

"We're screwed, bud," Nathan announced. Leaning back, he made sure Martin was clear of the hood and shut it.

"Hey, Deb," he got her attention. "Can you call AAA? We're going to need a tow and maybe a rental car too."

The positive energy she had stored up during their weekend retreat seemed to drain out of Debbie as she sighed. She fumbled through the glove box, found the number, and punched it into her phone, but when she hit "Send," she realized she had no signal. None at all.

"What the hell?" she inquired of the cellular gods. She paid homage to them regularly. Her fealty could not be in question. *This is bullshit,* she thought as she tried again unsuccessfully. She leaned out the door.

"Nate. Check your phone. I don't have service. No signal at all."

Nathan scrunched up his face.

"What the hell? We had service the whole time at the lake, and now we're closer to the towers than before and there's nothing? That doesn't make a lick of sense."

He looked at his phone.

"Dammit! Me too. Nothing."

"What are we going to do, Dad?" Martin asked.

"I guess we'll have to walk up to this house and ask to use their landline, the old-fashioned way," Nathan answered, looking down at Martin. "C'mon, Deb," he called. "Grab Bella and let's go ask the nice people at the house to use their phone."

Debbie turned around. Bella was still snoozing in the backseat, oblivious. Debbie hated to wake her but decided things might go smoother if the whole family knocked on the door, rather than just Nathan and Martin. She exited the vehicle, reached in the back, and stirred Bella. Hefting her onto her hip, she joined her boys. Together, they walked up to the house.

Nathan rang the bell. After a minute, a man about their age opened the door, looking a little unsure.

"Can I help you?" he asked.

Debbie spoke up.

"We're so sorry to intrude, but our minivan died out of the blue. We're coming back from the lake and live about thirty minutes away. But our cell phones have zero reception for some reason. We need to call AAA. Can we borrow your phone, please?"

Nathan just smiled and nodded.

"Well, sure. Sure," the man said. "Come on in and follow me." The man led them to his kitchen, where a cordless phone sat on the counter. He handed it to Nathan. Debbie read him the number, and he punched it in.

"Can I get y'all anything to drink?" the man offered.

"Oh, thank you, but we're good," Debbie answered. "We still have drinks left over in the cooler from our weekend at the lake."

"Mommy," Bella said, "I need to go potty."

"Oh my," Debbie said. "Sir, I'm sorry to impose, but could I possibly take her to your bathroom? Poor thing woke up needing to go."

"Oh, sure," he responded. "It's right down that hall," he pointed, "second door on the right."

"Thank you so much," Debbie said and hurried toward the bathroom.

Martin cocked his head, his attention caught by an unfamiliar noise. His father was on the phone, and his mother had left the room. The man of the house appeared to be searching through the fridge. Martin heard something again. He thought it was a voice. Deciding to see what it was, he followed the sound back into the living room. He heard the voice speak clearly this time... from upstairs.

"Do you want to play?"

It was a boy.

Martin climbed the stairs. Standing at the entrance to what looked like a bedroom was a little boy who was about the same size as Martin. His back was turned.

"I've got a bunch of cool toys," he said to Martin, still facing away. "Do you want to play?"

Debbie came back into the kitchen with Bella next to her, hand in hand.

Nathan hung up the phone and set it down.

"Okay, good news," he informed Debbie. "AAA says they'll have a tow truck here in half an hour. They're also sending a rental here for us, so no uncomfortable rides squished in the front seat of a wrecker."

Nathan smiled, proud of having handled things. He generally despised talking on the phone. He was a "Is that textable?" kind of guy.

Debbie grinned and patted his head. "Good boy." Her momma radar kicked in right then, and she looked around. "Where's Martin?" she asked.

Nathan spun around, searching. "Crap," he said. "He was just here a minute ago."

Debbie stepped out into the living room as she called Martin's name.

Martin glanced over his shoulder from the top of the stairs and saw the scowl on his mother's face.

"Martin Loch!" Debbie said in a sharp tone. "What do you think you're doing?" She didn't give him a chance to respond because she didn't really care what he might say, to be honest. "Get your butt down here!" she commanded.

Martin looked toward the little boy's back.

"Sorry, my mom's calling," he informed the boy. "I've got to go. Bye."

Martin turned and scurried down the stairs in a hurry.

"Sorry, Mom," he said when he reached her. "A little boy asked me if I wanted to play with his toys."

Debbie's scowl softened, but she still scolded him.

"I understand, buddy, but you can't go wandering off in a stranger's house. One, it's not polite, and two, sometimes it's not safe, either. Okay?"

Martin nodded, and they walked back into the kitchen.

A blond-haired lady stood there next to her husband, wine glass in hand. She sipped and smiled at Debbie.

Nathan spoke up.

"Debbie, this is Marcus and his wife Blair," he said. "Marcus and Blair, this is my wife, Debbie, and my kids, Martin and Bella. Thanks so much for allowing us to use your phone and bathroom."

Debbie cut in to express her own thanks and compliment them.

"Yes, thank you so much! And you have such a beautiful house. I love it!"

"Oh, you're more than welcome," Blair said. She was about to say something else, but Martin spoke up, looking at Nathan.

"Their son asked me if I wanted to play. He said he has some cool toys. Can I, Dad?" Martin beamed with excitement.

Marcus and Blair exchanged a startled look. She gulped the wine down, emptying her glass.

"Well, bud, that's up to his parents. We do have a half hour to kill."

Nathan turned to Marcus and Blair, who were both trying to hide some new discomfort.

"Um...well..." Blair began when Marcus turned quiet as a church mouse. "He's...um...not well!" she finally spat out. "He's running a little bit of a fever. You should probably wait in your van."

Blair tried to offer a congenial smile, but her face strained to do so with little success.

"Well, you don't have to tell me twice," Debbie said. "We don't want the kids to pick up any bug. Thank you for all your help, though."

With that, they exchanged goodbyes, and Debbie and her family walked back to their vehicle.

A half hour later, both the tow truck and rental arrived minutes apart. The tow truck driver decided to try starting the minivan. To Debbie and Nathan's surprise, it started right up without a hitch.

Nathan cocked an eyebrow and looked at Debbie.

"Weird."

"It seems to be running fine, now," the tow truck driver said. "You still want me to tow it?"

Nathan thought for a second and decided he didn't want to take any chances.

"Yeah," he answered the driver. "Go ahead and tow it to Vic's garage. He's the mechanic I normally use. I'd like to have it checked out anyway."

"Can do, sir," the driver responded.

"We'll follow you and cross load our stuff there," Nathan said. "Don't want to hold you up here."

"Okay, sir. I'll see you there."

Nathan and the family loaded into the rental car after signing some papers. The rental guy climbed in with a coworker who had followed him there. They watched the tow truck driver load the minivan onto his vehicle and strap it down, then they all drove off.

"I can't believe they want to sell that place," Debbie said aloud, as much to herself as to Nathan. "It's beautiful."

Martin glanced back at the house as they pulled out of the driveway. He saw what looked like the silhouette of a little boy staring out a window on the second story. What he could not see was the boy's mouth moving as he spoke to his real father.

"He's the one, Dad."

November 2, All Souls Day – The Day of the Dead

Debbie woke around noon. She had gotten up and seen Martin off to the school bus, then crawled back in bed to weep, pray, and remember her daughter Bella.

It had been over five months since the funeral. She was losing her mind and depressed. And today, the day people remembered the dead, was hitting her like a sledgehammer. She lay in bed thumbing through an album of pictures on her phone. Photo after photo of her darling daughter, so vibrant and full of joy, a joy she diffused into the world around her, into the people she contacted, every day of her terribly short life, cut down before it had time to really begin.

She noticed the pendant her daughter wore in many of the photos. They had bought it for her when she was three while at an amusement theme park, in one of those little stores that sells all types of pewter statues and other fantastic oddities. The pendant was round, made of silver, and had a Pegasus carved out of it. Bella loved the flying horse with wings spread wide. Later, she wanted a Pegasus t-shirt, and when she started kindergarten, she wanted her lunchbox, backpack, and school folders to have a Pegasus on them as well.

After the accident, Debbie and Nathan, as well as the police, were unable to find the pendant or the chain it hung from. They searched the crime scene thoroughly, but no luck. It pained Debbie without ceasing, like a knife twisting deep within her heart or an empty abyss pulling at her, sucking the life from her soul. Not only had Debbie's daughter been taken from her, but somehow, one of the items she would have held most dear in remembrance of Bella was also stolen from her.

Tears flowed at the thought of her loss, the outrageous insanity of it all.

Bella was cut down by some man in an old-ass pickup truck. A hit and run. Debbie was not positioned where she could see a tag on the suspect vehicle that day—the day a stranger ran over her daughter in the middle of the street, right in front of their house...right in front of her, while she stood on the steps of their porch, screaming, then sprinting like a cheetah for her daughter's limp form, the bloodstains on Bella's white sundress spreading as she approached.

Debbie's memory was questionable at best during the days that followed. The truck was not her mind's focus at the time of the accident, and her brain did not hold firm to those details. In fact, the only clear recollection she possessed was of all things relating to her daughter's body. Bella was throwing frisbee in the front yard. She accidentally threw it too hard, released too late, and the frisbee flew out of the yard and landed in the street. Before Debbie could say anything, the girl ran to the edge of the pavement. Debbie would swear on a bible her girl looked both ways before scurrying out into the middle of the street to retrieve her toy. She picked it up and looked at her mother, her eyes twinkling. Debbie never noticed the vehicle approaching. She simply saw Bella's torso and face flatten against the grill of a pickup truck, then rebound through the air in front of it. Debbie's eyes tracked her daughter's trajectory until Bella's body struck the ground. Her limp form was just beginning to tumble like a rag doll when the truck ran her over, a tire from each axle bouncing off her frame like a speed bump.

Thump. Thump.

In an instant, her baby girl was dead, and the truck was gone. The white sundress Bella wore lay disheveled on the asphalt, hiding the mangled body of her daughter at a distance...but not up close.

When the officer asked her for a description of the vehicle, Debbie struggled. She could say with certainty it was a truck, and after much effort at recollection, she was convinced it was an old pickup truck, possibly quite old, yet in good shape. She said the man was white, in his thirties, and had the bearing of someone who was wealthy. But that was the best she could do. She was unable to identify the make and model.

She assured the officer at the scene if she saw the truck again, she would recognize it, without a doubt. The man driving too. Despite her inability to offer a description of any value, Debbie was adamant their images had been burned into her brain.

The officer seemed less than confident in her assertion, and with little to no real description to go on, they were unable to locate Bella's killer.

In the coming weeks, Debbie was desperate to remember, to provide some helpful clue. Days after the accident, she dreamed the truck was faded blue, but upon waking, she could not say it was true with any confidence. She sat and stared out the window at the exact spot where her daughter died and tried to envision the incident. Once, she even bought some peyote and sat there looking at that same spot, praying for some pertinent details to come to her. But nothing of any help ever occurred.

At the end of her tether, Debbie visited a psychologist who was certified in regressive hypnotherapy. After two sessions, she managed to draw a picture of the vehicle. She was not as good an artist as Martin, but she had some raw talent. The investigating officer looked at it and did a little research. He said it appeared to be a pickup from the late sixties or early seventies. The problem was Chevrolet, GMC, and International models during that time all looked similar. There was no way to differentiate for sure.

So, despite Debbie's success, her hopes were crushed beneath the boot of an indifferent universe once more. Or at least, that's the way Nathan saw it. He would not taunt her with such a statement, but she knew that's what he believed. In his eyes, the universe yawned at their misery. In fact, it had not even noticed their tragedy until they roared with rage and tears at an imaginary God above and all that was and is and might ever be. And even then, when it did notice them then, Nathan was sure it was no more than an elephant catching a glance of an ant scurrying from a mound before its foot crushed the entrance flat, along with the ant.

Despair embraced Debbie, invaded her soul, and transfused joy for a bleak, bitter perspective on life, rendering her unable to lay hold of any merry prospects for her future. She tried to envision something positive, anything, yet even when she focused on Martin and tried to forge plans of a life in which she watched him grow up, she was only able to imagine calamity, destruction, and unanticipated tragic accidents like that which stole her Bella. It filled her with anxiety. She began to smother her son with an overbearing motherly protection that any child would find difficult to tolerate.

But her Martin was a special boy, and he loved his mother. He tolerated her overprotectiveness and did all he could to comfort and console her.

This made life more tolerable for a few weeks, but then she started seeing the truck that killed her daughter and the man driving it as well. At first, she saw them on the street in front of their house, but later on, she spotted them nearby in the downtown area as well as multiple other places. She called the police the first two times, reporting the vehicle, but when they arrived in the area, they were unable to locate it.

The third time, Debbie jumped in her minivan and pursued the vehicle, but after turning down a side street, she was unable to find it.

On the fourth time, she pursued it again. This time the truck turned down a street that ended in a cul-de-sac. Debbie had slammed a fist into the steering wheel and screamed, "I've got you now, motherfucker!" as she held her cell phone in the other hand. It was on speaker mode with the police dispatcher on the other end as she gave the lady a moment by moment course adjustment for the police to find her.

But when she reached the end of the cul-de-sac, the truck was nowhere to be found. She looked in every driveway. Insisted the police check every backyard and garage. And they did. But they found nothing. Nothing. The officers looked at her like she was hallucinating or flat-out batshit crazy. They advised her she should return home, then climbed in their vehicles and left.

Distraught, angry, disturbed, and bursting with a dreadful depression, Debbie headed back to her vehicle, but as she rounded the front end, she noticed something on the pavement glistening in the beam of her headlights. A pinprick of curiosity stabbed at her brain, bidding her to go investigate. She listened and walked over to the object, where she squatted down to get a better look at it.

Debbie gasped. Her fingers reached down as if locked in a slow-motion prison, stretching toward the shiny item, an item she knew all too well. Part of her brain accused her of seeing things again, but she refused to listen. She kept reaching for it until her fingers touched the metal, pinched the ends of the pendant, and lifted it up for closer scrutiny, a metal necklace hanging from it.

The Pegasus was clear as day. It was Bella's. Debbie had no doubts whatsoever. She turned it over, inspecting the entire thing. She gasped again, startled by what she saw.

There was a word and some symbols engraved on the back. Nothing had been there before, but now, along the outer rim of the pendant's backside, were the letters *S M A R B A*. On the inside of the circle of letters were some interlocking symbols. A tiny circle with three lines extended out and down from it. Each of those lines ended with a tiny circle. If she had drawn a line connecting the circles at the bottom, it would have looked like a three-dimensional drawing of a pyramid. At the top, just below the peak of the pyramid, on each side, a single line drew outward on an ascending angle. It was difficult to tell what the symbol at the end of those two lines might have represented. To Debbie, it kind of looked like an old German Iron Cross, except it was missing the bottom component. At the same time, the symbols reminded her of three trumpets positioned at ninety-degree angles relative to each other.

Debbie didn't have a clue as to what the symbol was or what it meant. She turned it back over and looked at the Pegasus.

"This is my daughter's," she said aloud. "It's here. Where the truck disappeared. I don't know what the *fuck* is going on, but I am *not* crazy."

She clenched the pendant in her hand, stood, and hurried back to her vehicle. Slipping it into her shirt pocket, she got into her car, started it up, and drove back home. She decided the police would only think her crazy if she showed them the pendant. They might even think she had held onto it the whole time. Once in her house, she stashed the pendant in her dresser drawer. She decided not to tell Nathan about it, as well. She knew his belief system, or lack of one in anything that couldn't be explained by atoms and evolution. She didn't think he could handle it and remain open minded.

Either way, after that night, the police department decided she was losing it. Nathan even started to think so. Debbie's assertions about seeing the truck seemed pathological at that point, based on the evidence at hand. Nathan never called her crazy to her face. He'd never do that. But he feared for her sanity as he watched her downward spiral.

Debbie saw the pickup truck and the man's familiar face on numerous occasions after that day, but she never called the police again. Never told Nathan. Several more times she got in her vehicle and pursued, only to lose it time after time. Occasionally, she questioned her own sanity, and each time she had to return to her dresser drawer, pull out the pendant, hold it, inspect it, and give herself time to affirm the object's tangible existence.

Eventually, though, Debbie realized, real or not, the truck was becoming her Moby Dick, her obsession. Her mind was not healthy while she continued to chase the white rabbit like a greyhound on race day, following the lure down a hole she might not emerge from one day. Debbie gave up on the chase, gave up on hope, gave up on her own quest for justice.

It seemed her lot in life was torture. Tantalizing, teasing visions offering a resolution to her dreams of vengeance, which, in reality, were nightmares. Nothing more. Nothing less. Horrible, agonizing nightmares strangling the life out of her soul. She struggled to be a mother, a wife.

Debbie looked at another photograph and resisted the temptation to walk into the living room and stand next to the front door. And right then, on the Day of the Dead, she finally said, "Enough. I can't take it anymore. I can't look out this goddamn window another day."

When Nathan arrived home after work, she informed him they were selling the house and moving. He seemed as if he might argue at first, but upon seeing her neck was stiff, her chin set like flint, and her eyes were on fire with a determination he was all too familiar with, he realized arguing would not be a prudent course of action. He relented. It was what she *needed* to let go and get on with life.

"Okay," he said. "Where do you want to move to?"

She sipped a glass of wine and smiled. It was the first genuine smile he'd seen from her in weeks, maybe months.

"I did some house hunting online this afternoon. Remember that house where the minivan broke down?"

 DECEMBER 1

LITTLE MARTIN LOCH RAN UP THE STAIRS LIKE AN eight-year-old boy on fire, unable to contain the excitement coursing through his body. New house, new bedroom, as well as a big yard and numerous acres of forest that belonged to their family now. The nearest neighbor was almost a mile away as the crow flies, and the lake they vacationed at was only a forty-five-minute drive now.

As he cleared the steps two at a time, one hand gripped the hard wood railing with each step as the other flew an X-Wing fighter. He vaulted onto the second floor and tore into the first room on the left, his room.

"Whoa!" he yelled, skidding to a halt. "This room is HUGE!"

The house was old and quite large.

"Martin!" his mother called out from the first-floor entrance. "Where are you?" Her voice was anxious, her tone and pitch elevated with fear.

"I'm in my bedroom," Martin hollered. "Holy cow! I could fit two king-size beds like yours in here and still have room left over. This is awesome!"

"Wait for me, honey. I'm coming."

"Debbie," Nathan said, "don't smother the boy. It's safe."

Debbie ignored Nathan's advice and hurried up the stairs to find Martin gawking at his new room. It was beautiful. Hardwood floors, double-door windows, and a deep ledge with a cut-out nook and space for a reading chair. The ceiling was tall but sloped down on a forty-five-degree angle toward the far right side, the width of a full-size bed. Martin was already picturing the set-up for his room. His bed would go under the sloping ceiling, and he'd put up posters above where he'd lay. They'd place his dresser across the room next to the bathroom door and a desk for drawing and doing homework against the wall where he entered the room.

"There you are." Debbie huffed and breathed hard, a bit winded from rushing up the flight of stairs. She spun Martin around to face her and gripped his shoulders with a ferocity bred by illogical fear. "I told you not to run off," she admonished him with a firm shake. "I told you to wait up!" She shook him again and waited for him to respond.

Martin froze like a deer in headlights. He'd seen his mom worked up in the last six months, but this was the first time she was physical.

"Did you hear me?" Debbie shook him with a force bordering on violence. Martin's eyes grew wide and jiggled. The X-Wing fighter fell and struck the floor. "Don't. Do that. Again," his mother commanded, shaking him with each word to emphasize the intensity of her feelings.

"O-o-okay, Mom," Martin stuttered. "I'm sorry."

He stared into her eyes, looking at her as if she were a stranger and hoping she wouldn't rattle his brain anymore. After several seconds, Debbie released her grip and stepped back. For a moment, her face betrayed a sense of shock and shame at her own actions, but she turned away and moved to the window. Martin watched her walk away, then picked up his toy and continued to look around.

He opened the closet door and peeked in.

"Holy cow! Mom, this walk-in closet is huge!"

Debbie startled at Martin's initial exclamation and whirled about, only to see him safe and sound at the closet entrance. He stepped in and reached up to pull the string and turn the light on.

"This is so cool," he muttered to himself. The closet was about six feet wide by four feet deep. He spotted a small door inset on the back wall, roughly three feet by three feet. Martin knelt down to inspect it, the excitement of discovery making him feel almost giddy.

He lifted a small metal hook from its latch and pulled the door open. Inside was a small room. It was empty but more spacious than he had expected. Maybe five by five and close to four feet tall. Not quite tall enough for him to stand upright.

Martin heard the creak of the floor behind him as his mother moved. He quickly shut the door and hooked the latch. Standing in a hurry, he stepped out of the closet and shut the door. He couldn't have said why if pressed, but he yearned for a silent space, a place of his own away from his mother. A secret place to hide.

"Um...you like your room, Marty?" Debbie asked, not sure how to recover from her outburst.

"Yeah, Mom. It's sweet!"

"All right, kiddo. How about we bring in all your boxes and then go into town and grab some ice cream? Sound good?"

"Uh, yeah, Mom," he answered, a bit confused after earlier. "That sounds great! Is it a High's?"

Debbie pursed her lips and nodded.

"Yes!" Martin pumped his fist in the air. "They've got the best ice cream! Can I get an orange sherbet freeze? Please?" Martin's eyes begged his mother.

"You bet you can...*after* we bring up the boxes. So, let's get to work. 'Kay?"

"Yes, ma'am!" Martin set down his X-Wing fighter in a safe corner, saluted his mom, then ran out the door and downstairs.

Martin finished bringing in his things and made sure to hang up all his clothes in the closet first. Then he filled the floor with shoes, boxes of toys, and other junk, conveniently hiding the door to the hidden storage area in his closet. Once complete, he was ready for that trip to High's.

TWO WEEKS LATER –
DECEMBER 14

The dream was full of vivid details, a level unusual for Martin. The images were crisp and real, possessing a tangible quality. A catalogue in his hands seized the boy's fancy and reeled him in. As he stared down at it, Martin felt the heft of this sizable tome of merchandise, the multitude of thin, glossy pages alive with gifts galore inside, sent to him by some mysterious purveyor of dreams. Dreams this wonderful directory promised to make reality.

The cover was a picture of two toddlers sitting under a Christmas tree—a boy and girl, both blond—opening a gift. The girl was dressed in yellow pajamas. A doll dressed in all yellow sat next to her. The younger brother wore baby blue pajamas. The word "SEARS" was printed over part of the picture.

Martin watched hands that didn't feel like his own grab the catalogue with a greedy zeal, then place a thumb on the outer edge and let the pages speed by until toys appeared. Stopping, the fingers fumbled to backtrack to the beginning of the toy section. From there, Martin observed numerous toys of all sorts, many of which he was struck by an overwhelming desire for. He stopped and retrieved a folded piece of paper and pen. The hands opened it and laid it on the opposite page of the next toy he saw that drew his attention. He picked up the pen and added the name and page number of the item to a growing list, already stretching three quarters of the way down the page.

As Martin sat in the closet perusing the catalog, two of the walls began to undulate, as if a wave were moving up and down them, until their surfaces shimmered and transformed. Like a curtain being pulled back to disclose what lies backstage, so the walls dissipated, revealing a gateway to another place. In an instant, the walls were no more, and in their place, stretched out before him, lay an African savanna. Red oat grass swayed beneath a wind he did not feel, and the setting sun caused the golden plain to glow with such a rich hue it blazed as if on fire itself.

Something moved in his peripheral vision. Something in the savanna. Martin's eyes jerked toward the motion, his body startling, but the potential threat had already vanished. For a moment, Martin thought he'd seen a lion in the distance, but then it was gone, its beautiful mane and yellow fur blending in with the golden grass moving to the rhythm of the breeze. A feeling of discomfort rolled over him like the wind itself and then was gone. His eyes spotted a mechanized wind-up robot toy in the catalogue and were dragged back into the market of endless joys arrayed for his perusal.

Lost in its wonders once more, Martin continued to observe the budding march of commercialism, recording one toy after another on the list.

When he woke, Martin felt a distinct sense of discontent. He needed those toys, even though he could not recall any of them specifically.

The following night, the same dream occurred, except this time, he remembered a few of the toys. There was a creature with a pliable yet muscular male body and skin of a deep green hue. It possessed a reptilian-like plastic head. The name on the box said "Stretch Monster." There was also a game with a large plastic great white shark. Its mouth was hinged and held in place by rubber bands. Several items were placed inside, weighing the lower jaw down in an open position. Martin had particularly vivid memories of one toy. He saw the name "Mighty Men" and "Monster Maker" printed on the box. This toy had a large base and came with numerous plates. They had raised lines and were divided into head, torso, and lower body. If Martin laid a piece of paper over the plates and used colored pencils to shade over them, it would reveal the design beneath. By mixing and matching the different plates, Martin could create heroes or monsters. This one he liked most of all.

Martin remembered one other thing as well.

A lady whose voice did not sound like his mother's. She called him Malachi.

DECEMBER 15

When Martin woke, he found a piece of paper on his nightstand. The names of the toys he dreamed of were scribbled on it, along with a corresponding page number. Oddly enough, the handwriting did not look like Martin's, not quite. He folded it up and dropped it in his nightstand drawer. Martin got ready for school without giving the note another thought and went downstairs.

Walking into the kitchen, he pulled his chair up close to the island just as his mother scooped three pancakes onto his plate next to some cheesy scrambled eggs.

"Eat your eggs first, Martin," she admonished him.

"Yes, ma'am," he said while putting a slab of butter on top of the fluffy stack of goodness. He topped it off with the hot maple syrup his mother had heated in a pot of boiling water.

Martin grabbed his fork and shoveled the eggs down as if he were a Hoover vacuum cleaner. He sipped on the orange juice, then dove into the pancakes while they were still hot. His father walked in wearing his typical work uniform—black slacks and a white, long-sleeve shirt. Today was dark-blue tie day. Nathan poured a glass of orange juice for himself and Debbie and sat down at the table while she dished up pancakes for the two of them.

Nathan picked up the bottle of syrup, and his face twisted, the wetness on the bottle jarring him from his routine. He stopped to inspect it and noted the label was disintegrating. Much of the sticker had peeled off, and the remainder was soggy.

"Honey," he began, "why don't you just use the microwave to heat the syrup like most of the modern world?" He chuckled as he said it.

Debbie cocked an eyebrow and glared at him for a moment.

"You know I don't like to use the microwave for everything. Besides, that's the way I grew up with my mother doing it…and I never have to worry about burning my mouth with a hot spot."

Nathan sat the bottle down and lifted both his hands, palms out in a sign of surrender, then cut into the pancakes.

"You do you, baby," he told her and smiled.

"Bella liked the syrup that way best," Martin said matter of fact as he skewered a big mouth full of pancake with his fork and dragged it through the standing syrup on his plate. "And I do too."

Debbie stiffened at the mention of her dead daughter and turned back to the stove. Nathan cut his eyes at Martin, who paid no attention to either of them or the impact of what he said. His sole purpose appeared to be fondly recollecting a habit of his sister. Nothing more.

"She liked for you to put her glass in the freezer overnight too," Martin commented. "She thought it made the orange juice taste better."

Martin smiled at the idea.

"Maybe I should try that," he said and stuffed more pancake in his mouth.

Debbie's rigid body seemed to indicate she was tortured by the conversation and desperate for it to end.

"Um, thanks for cooking this morning." Nathan changed the topic of discussion. "I've got a big meeting at eleven, so I probably won't get a chance to eat lunch until around one o'clock."

"Oh, sorry," Debbie said, wiping at her eyes. "That sucks. What's the meeting about?"

"We're brokering a major merger," he told her. "Lucrative doesn't do it justice. If this deal flies, I'm getting one big-ass bonus."

A broad smile spread across Nathan's face and excitement twinkled in his eyes.

"You got any plans today, Deb?" he asked, trying to distance her from thoughts of Bella, then shoved more food into his mouth and chewed while waiting for an answer.

Debbie sat down across from him at the table and took a bite of pancake. She chewed methodically, and when she swallowed at last, she followed up by taking two sips of orange juice.

"No idea, huh?" Nathan asked, looking at his plate, the excitement in his voice draining away.

"Actually," Debbie responded at last, "there's still a load of boxes and stuff that need to be put away from the move. I plan on getting as much of that done today as I can."

Nathan's face brightened a bit.

"Excellent!" He took another bite and looked at his son. "How 'bout you, sport?" he mumbled toward Martin. Debbie cut her eyes at him, and he swallowed. "What's going on with you? Anything good?"

"I've had some cool dreams," Martin said through a fork full of pancake filling his mouth.

"Martin!" Debbie scolded him. "Don't talk with your mouth full."

Martin covered his mouth and said, "Sorry."

Debbie shook her head. "Men," she said. "You're all just a bunch of barbarians...even the cute ones in suits." She scowled at Nathan for a moment, then winked.

Nathan looked at Martin.

"What kind of dreams, bud?"

Martin made sure he swallowed all the way, then answered his dad.

"I've been dreaming about all kinds of toys the last couple of nights."

"Toys, huh?" Nathan asked. "Nothing unusual about that. Christmas break is almost here. Santa's checking his list twice by now."

"Dad, you're silly," Martin said. "I know Santa's not real."
Nathan chuckled.

"Well, then," he asked Martin, "what kind of toys are you dreaming about? Anything we should add to the list of possibilities?"

"I hope so, but I haven't seen these toys anywhere."

Nathan stopped and looked at Martin, his face scrunching up in confusion.

"What do you mean, you haven't seen them?"

"I just dreamed about them," Martin said. "Never seen them before. But they were really cool."

"So, you made them up in your dream?" his mom asked, her curiosity piqued now.

"Not exactly. They were in a catalog I was looking at in my dream."

"A catalog?" Debbie pressed. "What type of catalog?"

"Not sure. I just know it said 'SEARS' on the cover and it had a huge section with all kinds of toys."

Nathan stopped chewing and stared right at Martin.

"What did you say?" he asked, not even trying to cover his mouth.

"SEARS, Dad," Martin said matter of fact, "and I think it had Christmas Wish Book on it too."

Nathan's jaw went slack. Debbie stared at her son, unbelieving.

"That's not possible," Debbie said, incredulous. "You've never seen one of those in your life. They stopped printing those before you were born, honey."

"I dunno," Martin said and shrugged his shoulders. "But I dreamed about it." He took another big bite of pancake.

"What kind of toys did you see in the catalog in your dream?" Nathan remained incredulous, though a bit concerned.

Martin gulped the food down.

"Well, there were these big robot toys. Two of them were called Shogun Warriors. Another one was all silver and called ROM. They also had a big Godzilla that could shoot off his fist!" Martin was very impressed with that. "Then there were these dolls for boys that stretch! One was just a big muscular white guy, but they also had a green monster man. He looked really cool. There was another one that looked like an alien, and you could see all his insides through the skin, even his brain."

Nathan gawked in disbelief as Martin rattled off more toy descriptions.

"Those toys are very old," Nathan said.

"Really?" Martin asked but didn't wait for an answer. "There was also a game with the great white shark from the movie *Jaws*. You put a bunch of stuff in his mouth and then take them out one by one. When it gets too light, it snaps shut!"

Martin clapped his hands together like they were the shark's mouth snapping shut in an instant.

"But the two I liked the most were a huge *Millennium Falcon* ship from *Star Wars* and a toy called Mighty Men and Monster Maker. You can create your own heroes and monsters, then color them! I want that one bad, Dad."

Martin grabbed the syrup, poured more on his pancakes, and proceeded to finish eating them in silence.

Debbie finally found her tongue. She started to speak, but Nathan motioned to her to leave it be and follow him outside.

"That's pretty wild, sport," he said to Martin. "Very cool stuff, but I've got to go to work. We'll check into it more later. Let me know if you dream anymore about those toys. Okay?"

"Sure thing, Dad."

Nathan stood, kissed Martin on the top of his head and scrubbed his hair, grabbed his jacket and briefcase, and walked out the door. Debbie followed. Once outside, Debbie was unable to keep quiet any longer.

"What the hell just happened, Nathan?" she spat out in a hushed tone, her eyes wide and head trembling. Worry creased her furrowed brow.

Nathan clutched Debbie's shoulder with his free hand. Bending down to look her in the eye, he stuttered for the first time since high school.

"I-I don't know, honey." Nathan squeezed his eyes shut and took a deep breath. He was rattled and not sure why. He told his brain to knock this shit off and get with the program. He didn't believe in weird or supernatural shit, which lacked an explanation grounded in material reality.

"I have no clue how he could know about those toys…much less describe them. Those were toys popular in the late seventies. I remember my older brother passing some of those toys down to me. But there *has* to be a rational explanation for it. He must have seen pictures somewhere. Something we showed him. Something he saw on the internet or at a friend's house. *Something logical.* There's no way he just dreamed up real objects from forty years ago."

Nathan paused and looked off in the distance, his mind searching the recesses of his memory.

"What is it?" Debbie asked him.

"Um…um…" Nathan snapped his fingers and looked at her. "I wonder if there are any pictures in the photo albums that show me playing with any of those toys? Maybe he saw them there? That's probably what it is." He knew he was reaching, but it was better than the disturbing alternative that made zero sense to him.

"Okay," Debbie said, latching hold of the possibility, "I'll look through them today and see what I can find. And I'll contact his teacher to see if they have done any projects that might have involved them."

"All right, baby," Nathan said, touching her shoulder with one hand. "Don't get worried needlessly, though. I'm sure it's nothing to worry about, but text me if you find anything. I've got to get going." He bent down and kissed her on the lips and then on her forehead. "It'll be okay," he reassured her. "I love you."

Debbie kissed him back, and they parted ways.

DEBBIE DECIDED TO DRIVE MARTIN TO SCHOOL. SHE was going to check her bases and not let this catalog silliness get under her skin.

Martin wasn't happy about her walking him to class, but that was just too bad. She informed him she needed to ask his teacher a question. Martin pulled away from her and walked ahead when they got close to his classroom. By the time Debbie came to the doorway, he was already in his seat. She waved at his teacher, Mrs. Etchinson, who was seated at her desk, and motioned for her to come out in the hallway. Mrs. Etchinson stood and walked over to meet her, a long, flowing skirt skimming just above the floor as she moved.

"Hi, Debbie," she said, remembering her face, to Debbie's surprise. "What can I do for you?"

"I'm sorry to disturb you without any warning, but I needed to ask you a quick question. I figured this would be easier than asking you to return a call."

"Oh, it's no problem at all," Mrs. Etchinson assured her, swatting her hand through the air. "What is it?"

Debbie looked at her, then looked up, down, and around. She felt uncomfortable and suddenly quite foolish. The back of her neck warmed, and her mouth dried up.

"Ummmm…" Debbie was searching for a coherent thought. Her brain finally hooked one out of the sea of distraught ideas swimming about in her head.

"I'm sorry again," she said, apologizing this time for the uncomfortable pause, "and I'm sorry for how weird this is going to sound, but I was wondering about something Martin told us this morning. It was kind of odd. Have y'all done any projects recently where the kids looked up old SEARS catalogs online or old toys, like from the seventies or eighties?"

Mrs. Etchinson's chin tucked as she pursed her lips and furrowed her brow in confusion.

"Um, no," she responded. "Not at all. May I ask exactly what he told you?"

"Well," Debbie began, talking in a hushed tone, "he described a SEARS catalog in perfect detail along with several toys inside. To my husband Nathan's recollection, they were from the mid-to-late seventies. As far as I know, he's never seen one. I don't know of any projects he ever did at his last school that would have exposed him to pictures of them. I'm going to call his old school to make sure, but I figured I'd check with you first."

"That is a bit odd," Mrs. Etchinson admitted. "I'm sorry I can't help you out, but…"

She stopped mid-sentence, her words trailing off. The teacher's face creased with concern.

"What?" Debbie asked, her stomach sinking in response to Mrs. Etchinson's expression.

"Um…" she began, "I don't want to be an alarmist, Debbie, but are there any adults that Martin has spent time with who might have shown him these pictures? You see stuff like this sometimes in abuse cases. Creating a connection, sharing things that the child will find interesting and may want. An initial lure to hook their attention and act as a jumping point for conversation and a relationship."

Debbie's stomach sank. She scrambled to search her memory for any possibilities and realized there were none. There was only one adult he spent time with during these recent months: his therapist. Martin had not even visited other children's houses since right after his sister's death. Debbie informed Mrs. Etchinson of what she knew.

"Well," the teacher replied, nodding her head, "that's a reasonable possibility. Maybe the therapist showed them to him as part of an ice breaker or something. That's far more likely." She smiled, trying to break the cloud of fear that had enveloped Debbie.

"You know," Debbie said, after taking a deep breath, "you may be right. I'll investigate that option before letting my mind go to the worst places first. Thank you for your help, Mrs. Etchinson."

"Anytime, Debbie," she said. "And call me Elizabeth." Elizabeth extended her hand.

Debbie looked at her for a moment and shook it. "Thank you," she said. "Now, let me get out of here before Martin feels even more mortified to have his mother at the new school." She laughed, and they both waved goodbye to each other.

On the road, Debbie phoned Martin's old school and left a message with the office to have his last teacher call her. Then she called his therapist and left a message as well with the front desk.

At home, Debbie pulled out their photo albums and combed through them all. It was an emotional rollercoaster seeing all the images of Bella. More torture than a pleasant trip down memory lane.

Debbie found herself pausing to stare and remember.

There were numerous birthday photos. The typical one-year-old darling with two fistfuls of yellow cake and chocolate icing, the frosting smeared across her face like tribal warpaint. A huge smile and eyes alive with a vibrant joy and determined pride as she rode a bike for the first time without training wheels. The brilliance of life gleaming in those eyes burned a hole through Debbie's heart. The album pages were awash with her daughter's giggling face. So many places and for so many different reasons. The girl had been infatuated with life and found so much of it a grand comedy.

Too young to know the truth, Debbie thought and cried.

She stood and walked upstairs to her dresser. Reaching in, she retrieved the pendant and necklace. Debbie held it tight and closed her eyes, laying down on the bed. For some time, she tried to imagine her daughter in Heaven, singing with angels. The palm of her hand grew hot, and a sense of dread seemed to creep up her arm and into her stomach. A fatigue of brutish strength seized her, cast her into darkness. The source of dread was inexplicable at first but soon became clear as her mind filled with a vision of Bella cowering in Hell before a mighty lion with blackness bleeding from the corners of its eyes. Behind it, a horde of demons followed like the train of a bride. The creatures no longer lurked in the darkness but stalked forward beneath sulfurous skies on fire. A devilish whisper on high heralded their arrival, prophesying eternal death and torment for all...but especially for Bella.

Debbie jerked awake. Tears wet her cheeks. She shook her head in an unconscious attempt to rid her brain of the dream but to little avail. Standing, she placed the pendant back in the drawer, closed it, and went back downstairs.

There, she finished going through the photo albums, then poured over them a second time, just to make sure she didn't miss anything that might include those old toys. She only found one picture that had anything possibly helpful in it. Young

Nathan played with the Mighty Men and Monster Maker toy in the picture, but the box was not in the frame, so the name wasn't visible anywhere. Debbie removed the picture from the album and set it aside. It was little comfort and did nothing to help dissolve the knot in her gut. There was a gnawing fear curled up there, and it kept telling her there was something exceedingly wrong going on.

After some consideration, she decided to call Nathan's mom and ask her if she could come over and glance through her photos. Preferring not to explain what was happening, she told her mother-in-law a lie.

"Hi, Barbara," she greeted Nathan's mom over the phone. "Can I come over and look through your photo albums? I want to see if there are any pictures of Nathan as a kid with some old toys. I'm looking for ideas to maybe buy him a collectible toy he used to have."

Barbara told Debbie it was a wonderful idea and invited her over.

Debbie decided to go online before leaving and do a search for SEARS catalogs, see if she could find one from the seventies. If she could not find one that matched what Martin described to her and Nathan, it would help allay her fears. To her distress, she located pictures with ease. She clicked on "Images" and only had to scroll down a short way before she saw the picture.

Debbie gasped, her breath catching in her throat. Her stomach withered at the sight and sunk into her bowels.

The picture revealed a 1979 SEARS Christmas Wish Book catalog, and Martin's description matched it to a T. She stared at the screen, battling the budding sense of dread blossoming inside her chest. It took great effort to suppress it sufficiently, but when she had managed to do so, Debbie saved the picture and printed out a copy.

Composing herself, she looked through numerous related photos. She saw the original *Millennium Falcon* and other *Star Wars* toys. But she also saw the ROM toy, the *Jaws* game, and the Stretch Armstrong toys. She did a search for the Mighty Men and Monster Maker and found several different pictures and full ads for it when it first came out. She saved the pictures and printed those out as well.

Debbie put them in a folder and headed for Barbara's house. The whole way over she tried to put the craziness out of her head and control her expressions so Barbara didn't pick up on her raging anxiety.

DEBBIE'S LUCK DID NOT IMPROVE AT BARBARA'S. THERE were pictures of Nathan playing with Stompers, Transformers, and He-Man toys, but none of the items Martin had seen in his dream. The more Debbie looked, the more frustrated she became. Barbara asked her more than once what was wrong, but Debbie refused to say anything more than she was feeling under the weather and a little jittery.

Which wasn't entirely a lie. She was cycling through multiple spikes in adrenaline. It was wearing her down. Debbie felt horrible. Her body trembled. She had exhausted her options at this point. Nothing was left but a desperate hope that when Martin's old teacher, Mrs. Iverson, called, she would have the answers necessary to lay it all to rest.

As if on cue, Debbie's cell phone rang. She waved goodbye to Barbara and walked out the front door toward her vehicle while answering. The conversation was short and severed her hopes of a quick resolution. They had never done anything in class at Martin's old school involving SEARS catalogs or toys.

Debbie thanked the woman and hung up, then started the vehicle. She wiped her face and ran her fingers through her hair, eyes slammed shut against this elusive mystery she possessed no answer for. She clenched two handfuls of her locks and pulled hard enough to inflict pain but not dislodge them. The frustration and familiar sense of helplessness assaulted her sanity.

Debbie saw the casket containing her daughter lowered into the ground, felt the vise-like grief crushing her chest. Beyond the assembled mourners, however, something new revealed itself. A lion, huge and mighty with blackness bleeding from the corners of its eyes. The lion from her dream. It crept along, head swaying side to side to keep her in sight as it passed behind the crowd. The instant Debbie's mind diverted attention to the beast, it disappeared, and her feelings of helplessness redoubled. She forced her eyes open and focused on the now, on the dilemma of Martin's dreams.

As she searched for an answer, any answer, one more possibility occurred to her—the local comic book shop. It was a long shot, and she drove there beneath a creeping burden of apprehension. She searched all around the store but saw nothing remotely close to the toys Martin had described.

"Can I help you, lady?" the clerk asked her when he finished pricing some inventory.

"Maybe," she responded in a hesitant tone. She proceeded to show the man the printed photos of the toys and ask him if he sold any of them or had sold any in the last few months.

He looked each of them over with careful consideration. When he finished and handed them back to her, all he provided was an emotionless, "Unh uh," accompanied by the shaking of his head.

She walked out more deflated than before. The only thing left to do was show the pictures she found online to Martin and ask him if they were what he saw in his dream.

When Martin got home from school, Debbie did just that. She hoped he would not recognize any of them. She pleaded with the universe to operate within the boundaries of sensible reason.

But the universe ignored her pleas.

Martin recognized every one of them.

Each "yes" and nod of his head was a punch in her gut, knocked the wind right out of her sails. And then it got worse. Martin pulled out his drawing book and started showing her picture after picture that he had drawn in art class and throughout the day of the toys he dreamed about.

There wasn't a bit of doubt. What he drew was a perfect imitation of the matching toy pictures she found online.

She could barely breathe.

WHEN NATHAN ARRIVED HOME FROM WORK, DEBBIE'S mouth flew a hundred miles per hour and spewed information at him like a firehouse turned wide open. He let her get it all out without interrupting. He knew she needed to, but afterward, he had to have her start from the beginning and ask questions at each step of her investigation. Once their Q&A session was complete, Nathan felt as unnerved as Debbie.

"This is totally crazy?" she asked him rhetorically. "Right?"

Nathan wanted to reassure her, comfort her, show support, and help allay her fears, but the more he considered how he might do that, the more he realized he had no means to do so.

I got nothing, he thought. *No possible explanation. This shit is nuts.*

Nathan shrugged at last and just hugged her.

"I don't know what's going on, baby," he admitted, "but I'm sure there's a rational explanation. We just have to find it, okay? We can figure this out together...and we'll get through it together."

He held her tight. She gripped his torso with a greater

strength, drawing comfort from him. For the time being, it was enough, but Nathan knew they would have to find answers soon.

THEY DECIDED NOT TO PRESS MARTIN WITH A GRAND inquisition-like witch hunt. Instead, they stuck to probing questions, enough to keep a finger on the pulse of what was transpiring and track its course without making a big deal out of it… yet.

"Dream about any other old toys last night, bud?" Nathan asked Martin as he came into the kitchen the following morning, ruffling his son's hair in the process.

Martin woofed down three bites of a whole wheat bagel with strawberry fruit spread, barely chewing before he swallowed. He washed it down with juice, then answered his father.

"Yeah, Dad, I dreamed about the same toys last night. I was playing with them on Christmas morning. It was fun."

Martin gulped down more orange juice and took another bite of his bagel. Nathan glanced at Debbie but did not hold her gaze. He saw right away she was trying to hide how much this was disturbing her. He was struggling to do the same.

"Do you remember where you saw them at yet?" Nathan asked. "Must have been on the internet, don't you think?"

"Nope," Martin said plainly after swallowing the bagel. "I've never seen them anywhere. Except in my dreams. I think it's pretty cool."

There was the sound of a horn beeping outside. Martin glanced out the window.

"Shoot!" he exclaimed. "The bus is early!"

He jumped up, shoving the last piece of bagel in his mouth,

grabbed his bookbag and lunchbox, and headed out the door, calling out, "Love y'all," with a full mouth.

Debbie watched him go with a noticeable shiver while Nathan wiped his face with both hands. Neither of them felt hungry anymore.

THAT NIGHT, MARTIN FELL ASLEEP AND WOKE INTO HIS dream. A light breeze blew across his face, but the window was closed, and the fan wasn't turned on. It tickled his flesh and pulled at his pajamas, beckoning him to get out of bed. He tossed the blanket aside, threw his legs over the edge of his bed, and slid off until his feet touched the hardwood floor. The breeze grew stronger, blowing now against his right shoulder, turning him toward his closet door, which, on cue, opened before him. A puff of wind pressed against his back, and then another when he didn't start walking right away. It nudged him off balance and forced his body to take a step forward. A draft of air emerged from the closet and reached out for him. It licked at his skin and clothes, a gentle vortex sucking him toward the open doorway, drawing him ahead until he stood at the threshold.

Martin saw the cord to the overhead light move down and click. The bulb flooded the space with illumination. He sensed an unseen presence apply pressure on his shoulders. The force of it buckled his knees, and he knelt. A glow at the back of the closet caught his eye. It was coming from behind the boxes of toys he had stacked there. There was an outline of a large square set into the wall. It grew in brightness as he watched, the incandescent aura luminous and gleaming.

Another puff of air pushed Martin, and he was sure he felt a tap against his right elbow from behind. A need swelled within him, a desire to lift the latch and open the small door that hid the compartment beyond from common observation.

He parted the clothes above his head and proceeded on all fours up to the wall. It felt as if something encircled his wrist and pulled his hand to the latch. He grabbed the metal, lifted the hook out of the eyehole, and pulled on the door. It was stubborn at first. The top corner bowed out, but the rest was stuck. Digging his fingertips behind the exposed portion, he pried the small door away from the wall with three hard jerks and opened it wide. Light spilled out from the tiny room inside.

"Hi," a young boy in pajamas said and waved. He had shoulder-length, straight black hair and appeared to be the same age as Martin. He sat surrounded by numerous toys Martin recognized from the SEARS catalog he had looked through in his previous dreams.

"Hey," Martin replied and raised his hand in greeting.

"Wanna play?" the boy asked. "I've got a lot of cool toys and nobody to share them with." The boy moved a few of the toys aside and patted the floor. "My name's Malachi. What's yours?"

"Umm, Martin. My name's Martin." He crawled over and shifted into a seated position next to Malachi. Martin looked over all the toys.

"You like them?" Malachi asked, pleased with Martin's keen interest.

"Oh yeah!" Martin replied. "These toys are so cool!"

"Which ones do you like the best?" Malachi inquired. "My favorite is the Stretch Monster." He held up the dark green-bodied figure with the green monster head made of plastic. Malachi held the toy to his chest and wrapped his hands around the monster's hands. "See what he can do?" Malachi told Martin and began pulling his arms apart, stretching the upper limbs of the toy beyond any conceivably normal range of movement. The toy kept stretching until Malachi's arms were at full extension out to each side. He held it there for a few seconds, then relaxed, bringing his hands in front of his chest again. The monster toy's arms gradually returned to their original shape and thickness.

"Neat, huh?" Malachi asked with a smile.

"Wow!" Martin exclaimed. "That's definitely cool! I like him too."

"Here's another stretch monster," Malachi said. "He's a space monster or something. They call him X-Ray because you can see his insides." He handed the toy to Martin. "You can hold on to him."

Martin took the toy and handled it with care, gauging the heft of the dense, gel-filled body. Its body was a reddish honey hue, and various colored organs showed through its translucent skin. The head was hard plastic and enlarged, a wrinkly brain clearly visible. It possessed red eyes and a small mouth lined with sharp teeth. Martin grabbed the creature's limbs and stretched them just as he had seen Malachi do.

"That does feel neat," Martin said. "And it's a little bit of a workout."

"What others do you like?" Malachi asked.

Martin examined each of the toys.

"Well, this huge robot guy is sweet! What do you call him?"

"He's a Shogun Warrior," Malachi answered.

Martin looked around the left side of the Shogun Warrior and caught a glimpse of another toy. He couldn't believe his eyes.

"NO!!!" he exclaimed, looking at Malachi. "Get out of here! You've got the original Alien toy? That sucker is eighteen inches tall! Can I hold him?"

"Sure!" Malachi leaned forward and grabbed the toy, then sat back and handed it to Martin.

He held it as if it were delicate china, admiring the sleek but ominous design.

"I've seen pictures of this but never up close. The see-through dome! You can see the white skull beneath it. Man, that is so cool!"

Martin was thoroughly impressed.

"And check this out," Malachi said, reaching a hand around the rear of the Alien's elongated skull to squeeze a trigger. The Alien's inner mouth shot out, just like in the movie.

Martin squealed with excitement. He made the mouth open a few times as well, then handed the toy back to Malachi.

"Man, that is so cool."

Malachi set it back down.

"Anything else strike your fancy?" Malachi asked.

"This *Jaws* shark game looks like fun," Martin said, "but I think my favorite is the Mighty Men and Monster Maker set. I love to draw. I'm in art class at school. My teacher says I'm pretty good for my age."

"Really?" Malachi remarked with genuine surprise. "I love to draw too, and I used to be in art class, but not anymore."

"Why not?" Martin asked. His face and tone sunk in response to Malachi's admission. Martin knew how much he, personally, loved art class. He felt a genuine disappointment for Malachi's loss, and his empathetic distress was detectable, both to the eye and ear.

"I had to leave the school I was in," Malachi explained. "They don't have art class where I'm at now."

Martin nodded in understanding. "Bummer. Sorry to hear that."

"It's okay," Malachi acknowledged. He grabbed the Mighty Men and Monster Maker and slid it over to Martin.

"Here you go. You can play with this for a while, and then maybe we can try the *Jaws* game. Sound good?" Malachi put on a big smile, and his eyes seemed to brighten on command.

"Gee, thanks," Martin said and began picking out the parts he wanted to use to make his first monster. Malachi brought out several pieces of paper with the creatures he made using the toy and showed them to Martin. Martin ooed and aahhed at the display of monsters Malachi had created. There were no good guys in his pile of papers.

Martin decided to use the reptilian head and lower body. It possessed sturdy legs with talons and a long tail. For the upper body, he chose a muscular torso with one hand holding a laser pistol.

"That's a good combination," Malachi noted with an approving nod of his head.

Martin looked up and smiled, then picked up the purple crayon and bent over to start the shading process that would bring the outline onto the page. After that, he would have to choose which colors he would use to fill the image in.

Malachi opened a blue soft plastic case and began taking Matchbox and Hot Wheels cars out of it to play with while Martin worked on his picture. In time, they played with the cars together before setting up the *Jaws* game. Malachi pulled the jaw down and held it open so the rubber band didn't cause it to clamp shut. He took the various game pieces and filled the mouth, more than enough to weigh it down. Malachi then produced a skinny piece of plastic with a hook on the end.

"So, the object of the game," Malachi explained, "is for us to take turns retrieving pieces of stuff out of Jaws' mouth, and whoever the mouth shuts on loses. Easy enough, right?"

A mischievous grin spread across Malachi's face.

"You first," he said to Martin and extended the plastic hook to him.

Martin took the hook and eyed the various items in Jaws' mouth. There was a large white bone on top of everything else. It had a hole in one end to hook it by, like all of the solid game pieces. Fortunately for Martin, the hole was closest to the teeth and not on the end reaching down the shark's throat. He turned the hook sideways, eased it under the end of the bone, and slid it upward through the hole. Martin eased the piece out of the beast's mouth without disturbing anything else.

"Nice!" Malachi congratulated him. "You must of played Operation before. You've got some steady hands."

"What's Operation?" Martin asked.

"Oh, it's just another game," Malachi responded. "We can play that too, later, if you want."

"Sure thing." Martin beamed. "If it's as fun as this one, I'm in."

"Neat."

They took turns. Malachi pulled out a broken wagon wheel. Martin retrieved a large jug. Along with the bone, that was three of the largest pieces removed. Most of the rest were small, except for a tire, which happened to be on top now. Malachi went for the smallest piece, a pistol, snagging it and slipping it out the side of the open jaws. Martin hooked a small axe-like item and managed to drag it out from under the tire without disturbing it too much.

Malachi assessed the positioning of the other pieces. He would have to disturb the tire to get at any of them. He decided on a flipper. Slipping the hook through the flipper strap, he gently tugged on it, turning it until the flipper part itself was the only portion under the tire. He eased it out while tilting the flipper up on an angle, causing the tire to slide over on top of the skull, covering access to the other smaller items.

"Ha!" Malachi cackled. "I think I just made it hard for you."

"I think you did," Martin admitted. "Well played."

Malachi stared intently at the mouth of Jaws, watching for any movement as Martin made his move.

Martin was competitive when it came to games. He was a good sport, but he didn't like losing. He tried nudging the skull and tire out of the way, but he saw the jaw lift up slightly, then lower back down when he ceased his efforts. He wasn't getting a small item out. It was either the tire or the skull, but if he went for the skull, which looked a bit lighter, he would have to move the tire, and that might be the final straw. However, if he tried going for the tire, it most likely would be enough to make the jaw snap shut. Martin decided to try and risk hooking the skull.

It took a steady hand to slip the hook underneath the tire and thread the end first into an eye socket and then out through the hole where a nose would have once been. He tugged on it and jiggled it, subtly twisting the hook back and forth in between his fingers. The skull began to squeeze loose from beneath the tire. The mouth bobbed minutely. Martin paused, holding dead still.

"Ooooohhhh," Malachi hooted. "The pressure! The pressure!"

Martin ignored Malachi's taunting and focused on the task at hand. He tugged with exaggerated care and slowly managed to free the skull from beneath the tire. Martin tried to relax and prepared his hand to give the final pull that would clear the creature's mouth. He took a deep breath, held it, then started drawing the skull out. He realized too late an axe had caught itself on the inside of the skull and began exiting the mouth as well.

SNAP!

Martin jumped, shoulders spasming upward nearly to his ears, as the bottom jaw slammed shut against the top, clamping down on the axe handle and sending the skull flying through the air.

"Oh man! So close!" Malachi shouted. "You're really good. I'd never have gotten that far. We definitely have to play Operation at some point. I bet you'll kill me in that."

Martin smiled at Malachi.

"One more time?" he asked.

"Sure!" Malachi responded, excitement tinging his voice.

They reset the game and played again. This time Martin won.

"Well, Malachi," Martin said, "I'm tired. I need to get back to bed and sleep before school in the morning. Can we have a tie breaker tomorrow night, maybe?"

"You bet," Malachi replied and extended his hand.

Martin shook it vigorously, and they both smiled. Martin noticed the boy's palm glowed and it felt quite warm to the touch. It made his own hand seem warm, his arm too, as if something slithered inside him and disappeared into his body just past his shoulder.

A visible shiver passed through Martin's torso. He stood and waved goodbye to Malachi, paying the temporary sensation no heed. Once back in bed, he fell asleep almost as soon as his head touched the pillow.

He dreamed he played with the toys in that room until morning.

DECEMBER 17

Martin finished his class assignments early, leaving him with time to spare. He pulled out his sketchbook and pencils and doodled pictures of the toys from his dreams. Mrs. Etchinson noticed Martin hard at work drawing. She stood and walked around the outer edge of the classroom, circling around to come up behind Martin and get a peek at what he was working on. She glanced over his shoulder. After observing him for a short time, she spoke.

"You mind if I take a look?" she asked Martin.

He startled a bit, surprised by her presence.

"Ummm, sure, I guess," he replied and pushed the sketchbook closer to the edge of his desk so she could inspect it. He seemed his normal congenial self at first, but while Mrs. Etchinson looked over the drawings, Martin's brow furrowed, his eyes narrowed, and his lips pursed together.

"You know, Mrs. Etchinson," Martin stated with blunt dislike, "it's not polite to sneak up on people and look over their shoulders. Is it?"

He turned his head and looked up at her, his eyes darker somehow and possessing a grave seriousness.

Mrs. Etchinson shrunk away from his gaze, feeling like a child caught with their hand in the cookie jar. She knew she was wrong and decided it was best to just admit it and apologize. She folded her hands together over her stomach as she spoke.

"Yes, Martin. You're right," she confessed. "I shouldn't have looked over your shoulder. I'm sorry for prying."

"Well, okay," he responded. "I forgive you. But don't do it again." He looked at her severely for a second, as if emphasizing that this would be her only warning, the only instance of mercy allotted, and then he looked down. "Do you like them?" he asked, his voice casual once more and sounding like the usually happy Martin she had grown fond of.

It took Mrs. Etchinson a couple of seconds to mentally shift gears and catch up.

"Well, yes, I do," she said. "They look like cool toys, and your lines and shading are nice."

She paused for a second, remembering what the boy's mother had told her about his dreams and old toys.

"Are these toys something you already have or something you have on your wishlist?"

"They're on my wishlist," Martin answered as he began drawing again while they talked.

"Where did you see them at?" Mrs. Etchinson inquired. "I know some other young boys who would like to have toys like these."

"I only share my toys with Malachi because he shares his toys with me. Nobody else here wants to play with me or share their toys."

"Well, you haven't been here long," she tried to console Martin. "I'm sure you'll make friends before the end of the year."

Martin turned the page and started sketching the outline of a bipedal figure.

"What do you like better, Mrs. Etchinson?" Martin asked her without looking up. "Heroes or monsters?"

The question was a simple one, but it pricked something inside Mrs. Etchinson. Something primal. Instinctive. Something that made her heart flutter and her pulse quicken.

"Well, I'd say I like heroes," she admitted, fidgeting in place, uncomfortable with the air surrounding her. It had become oppressive. "Unless it's a nice monster, I suppose."

"No such thing as nice monsters," Martin said matter of fact. "By definition, monsters are mean, wicked. Monsters hurt people. Kill people. If they're nice, they aren't really a monster at all. They're just…different. If they do what's right, they can be a hero. That's what I think."

Mrs. Etchinson shifted in place, wringing her hands in the pleats of her skirt.

"Well, I can see your point, Martin." She paused and watched him drawing. The figure was taking shape. Thick thighs ending in clawed feet, arms that divided into two tentacles on each side, and a head like a shark with jagged teeth scrawled within the open jaws.

"Which do you like best, Martin?' Mrs. Etchinson managed to bring herself to ask. "Monsters or heroes?"

"Monsters," he said without hesitation. "They always look cooler. Heroes always look the same. Act the same. Monsters look however they want. Do whatever they want."

His words plunged through her bowels in a way she couldn't explain. She'd never seen the boy appear so menacing. Never seen him act like this. This boy before her was totally different than the Martin she knew.

"See?" Martin exclaimed before she got a chance to formulate a response. His face beamed. "How cool looking is that?" he asked her, pointing at his drawing.

"Oh yeah," she agreed with him. "Very cool." The last thing she wanted to do at that moment was disagree with Martin. She was horrified at the possible explanations and justifications that might come out of his mouth. She shuffled away leaving him to return to his drawing. A drop of sweat rolled down the center of her spine and plopped onto the skin at the small of her back. It sent a shiver through her whole body, which she tried unsuccessfully to play off.

Mrs. Etchinson watched the clock on the wall intently, begging it to hurry. When the bell finally rang for the end of the day, she was relieved to see Martin walk out of her classroom.

MARTIN AWOKE TO A BREEZE ON HIS FACE AND moonlight in his eyes. He stretched, arms extending above his head with a yawn, and slipped out of bed. His head turned as if moved by the will of another. He didn't think about doing it. It just happened.

The closet door was open, and the smaller door inside was open as well. The light was on in that tiny room. Malachi wasn't there, but several toys were sitting on the floor, spread out as if on display.

A display for me, Martin thought, then shuffled over to the closet, got down on his hands and knees, and crawled to the toys.

The first thing that caught his eye was the *Millennium Falcon* parked in front of all the other toys. It lassoed his eyes and wrangled them to the ground like a young steer. He stared at it in awe for several seconds before allowing his eyes to be dragged elsewhere. There were *Star Wars* action figures of Han Solo, Chewbacca, Luke Skywalker, and Princess Leia. Next to it was Darth Vader's Tie Fighter with a Darth Vader figure seated inside. Vader and his ship drew Martin's attention more so than the *Falcon*.

Next to those toys stood an AT-AT Walker and the Alien toy,

looming over the smaller figures. They appeared eager to crush and devour them.

Excited, Martin scanned the other toys. A Shogun Warrior stood tall above them all. It had a missile launcher for a left hand, three red and white missiles locked and loaded. Martin tested it out. Aiming the hand at the AT-AT Walker, he pressed the red button down that corresponded with each projectile, launching the missiles one at a time. Each one struck its target.

"Boom!" Martin said. "Woo-hoo-hoo! Man, that's sweet!"

The Shogun Warrior wielded a large red sword in its oversized right hand, and its arm could be moved up and down to create a swinging motion. What really caught Martin's eye was the face. It was menacing, a vertical grill of gray bars stretching across its black void of a mouth. In the catalog, it had radiant yellow eyes that made it seem potentially friendly. They brightened its countenance, giving it the appearance of goodness. But this one had fiery red eyes.

It looked terrifyingly cool to Martin.

In front of it sat a case full of Matchbox cars, and on top of it was the Mighty Men and Monster Maker box. The *Jaws* game sat off to one side, preloaded with the pieces in its mouth and hooks lying beneath it. The boardgame Operation lay next to it.

There were also others he had seen in the catalogue.

Two little wind-up Rascal Robots tottered around on the hardwood floor. The evil leader of the Micronauts, Baron Karza, and his nightmare steed, Andromeda, stood in the forefront. Both were made of diecast metal parts with magnets in the joints holding the pieces together and allowing for different ones to be swapped out, mixed, and matched. Many more were stacked among the other toys. A View Master, a Rock 'Em Sock 'Em Robots game, Hungry Hungry Hippos, a pair of orange Clackers, and an Etch-A-Sketch.

Martin touched each one of them, caressing the cold metal and smooth plastic and admiring the textured details, the beautiful craftmanship. This was better than any Christmas morning he'd ever had. He tried most of them, forgoing the ones he thought might make too much noise and wake his parents. He played for a couple of hours before his adrenaline came down enough for him to get tired again. He cast a longing gaze at the toys before turning off the light, crawling out, and shutting the door. He slid the boxes back in place and shut his closet door.

Crawling back into bed, he pulled the covers up and turned on his side, staring out his window at the moon. He fell back asleep with ease once he closed his eyes and imagined himself playing with his new toys. Before he knew it, he was dreaming. In his dream, he was in that room with the toys.

He played and played and played but morning never seemed to come.

DECEMBER 18

"So, WHAT DID YOU DREAM ABOUT LAST NIGHT, Martin?" Debbie asked at the breakfast table. She fiddled with her eggs and tried to act nonchalant despite the gnawing anxiousness in her gut.

"Oh, just more cool toys," he answered. "That's all."

"Different ones? Or the same as before?" Debbie pressed.

"Both." Martin kept his reply succinct, then took the last big bite of his eggs, chewed twice, and gulped it down.

"Hey, Hoover," Debbie said. "Slow down."

Martin ignored her, picked up his glass of orange juice, and began guzzling it.

"Where did you see the new toys? In the catalog again?" Debbie had a bone in her mouth and didn't want to let go until she cracked it open and got to the marrow of the matter. Something useful that might allay her fears.

Martin kept drinking the orange juice until it was gone. He sat the glass down and belched loudly on purpose.

"Martin Loch," Debbie scolded him. "Where are your manners?"

"Umm…sorry, Mom," he offered and shrugged his shoulders. He stood and grabbed his backpack. "Gotta catch the bus. Have a nice day, Mom." Martin kissed her on the cheek and hurried out the door calling over his shoulder, "Love you!"

"Martin!" The sharp change in tone stopped him in his tracks, hand lingering on the door to hold it open, eyes wincing in anticipation of her grabbing him again. He turned around slowly.

"Yes, ma'am?" he said and gulped with much trepidation.

"I was asking you a question," she informed him, "and you didn't answer me. In fact, I think you're avoiding answering me, Martin. Now, tell me, where did you see the toys you dreamed about last night?"

Debbie stared at him. Her eyes almost smoldered. She didn't like this newfound evasiveness one lick.

"Well, there were several others I saw in the catalog, but last night, I dreamed I played with them…with a friend."

Debbie's eyebrows rose with a pronounced twitch.

"What friend?" she interrogated him. "I thought you hadn't made any friends here yet." It was a statement. Not a question.

"Umm…well, I hadn't," Martin confessed, the pitch of his voice rising just enough to add some levity to the moment and insinuate his coming revelation of good tidings and great joy. "Until yesterday." He forced a smile onto his face.

"Who is it?" Debbie crossed her arms and fixed him with a mother's skeptical stare, her face rigid as flint. It was the kind of look that would give mafia thugs torturing a mark for information a run for their money.

"A boy at school," Martin tried to say with a bit of cheer.

"And what's his name?" Debbie immediately followed up, not giving Martin time to think.

"Malachi," he said, realizing if he paused to create a name, she would suspect he was lying and push further.

The honk of the school bus horn reached them.

"That's the bus, Mom. I gotta go. Love you."

Martin let the door shut and hurried down their driveway to climb aboard the bus.

Debbie watched him go through the screen door with a nagging sense of mistrust. She continued gazing out until she saw the bus pull away.

She decided right then she was going to have a look around his room.

Debbie entered Martin's room and scanned it, looking for anything unusual or odd. Dirty socks and underwear lay on the floor next to his clothes hamper where he missed the Hamper Hoop. His bed was made but disheveled, a rush job. Two toys sat on top of the covers, a Stomp Rocket he had just recently gotten and tried out in the front yard and a remote control 4x4 truck. His drawing desk had a planetarium on one end and his pencils, crayons, and sketchpads on the opposite side. On the windowsill behind the desk, multiple Transformer toys stood on display.

ON ANOTHER WALL, HIS BOOKCASE HELD A VARIETY OF books. Classics like *White Fang* and *Call of the Wild*, *The Hobbit*, *Lord of the Rings*, *Bridge to Terabithia*, *Gentle Ben*, and *Beowulf*. In addition, there were Goosebumps, Rick Riordian books, and numerous other science fiction and fantasy titles. Posters of dragons, robots, and warriors covered the ceiling above his bed.

She walked over and opened his closet door. Glancing inside, she saw multiple boxes with other toys and board games piled up in them. Multiple pairs of tennis shoes and boots surrounded them.

Nothing unusual.

Debbie closed the door and proceeded to his dresser. She pulled out each drawer and searched inside, moving undergarments around, pajamas, socks, balled-up T-shirts, and shorts.

Nothing.

She looked under his bed and only saw the beginning of dust bunnies and some board games she recognized.

"Hmph," she grunted and turned to inspect his nightstand. It was empty except for an alarm clock and a coaster with an empty glass. Debbie pulled the drawer open. Inside were pieces of hard candy, quarters, dimes, nickels, and numerous pennies scattered about. Martin also had several prepackaged cookies stashed away for when he felt snacky. Debbie moved the cookies aside and noticed a folded piece of paper. She pounced on this potential piece of evidence and unfolded it. Reading every word, she scrutinized the content as well as the handwriting.

It was a list of the toys Martin said he saw in the SEARS catalog, but to Debbie's surprise, each toy also had a corresponding page number.

How in the hell could he know the page numbers? flew through her mind, but then something else caught her eye.

The handwriting was wrong. It was cursive. Martin struggled with cursive and did not enjoy it at all. He never wrote in cursive unless he was made to. And the letters weren't quite right either. They were similar to his handwriting but not quite the same. She was unable to place what was different, though.

Debbie turned the paper side to side and canted it up and down, trying to figure out what was off about it. Frustrated, she bent her head to one side and then the other, and finally, she saw it. She saw what was wrong with the letters.

They were slanted in the wrong direction. Martin was right-handed. The letters were slanted like a left-handed person had written the list.

It made no sense. Unless this new friend of his had written

the list. This Malachi he mentioned. Even then, it was oddly similar to Martin's handwriting, just slanted the wrong way.

And what are the chances that some kid at school has access to a SEARS catalog from 1979? she asked herself. Debbie shook her head in astonishment and wiped her face.

This is just too fucking weird.

She carried the list downstairs, used her printer to make a copy of it, and returned it to Martin's nightstand drawer. Afterward, she went online and hunted up a copy of the 1979 SEARS Christmas Wishbook catalog. She found it on a used book website for $200 but did not blink at the price one bit. She clicked "Buy Now," selected "Expedited Shipping," and gladly paid the exorbitant price. The need to see if the page numbers were right was paramount, whatever the cost. She *had* to hold it in her hands, show it to Martin and see what he said. A burning impatience consumed her. She wanted the catalog now, not later, and certainly not three days from now. But she would have to wait.

In the meantime, she intended to find out who this Malachi kid was from Mrs. Etchinson.

Debbie called and left a message for Mrs. Etchinson. It was shortly after noon when her phone rang. She had been distracting herself with cleaning house in between pacing like a caged animal.

"Hello."

"Hi, Debbie. This is Mrs. Etchinson, returning your call."

The teacher's voice was a pleasant surprise.

"Yes! Thank you so much for calling me back. I really need to ask you a question."

"Sure. What can I help you with?"

"Well, we're still trying to sort out this catalog dream stuff with Martin. I think I may have located the source, but I need you to confirm. Martin says he made a new friend. A Malachi. He said the boy is the same age. Are you familiar with this Malachi?"

There was silence on the other end of the line. When Mrs. Etchinson spoke, it was with more than a little hesitancy.

"Debbie, I'm sorry, but there is no student here named Malachi. Not in Martin's grade or any other that I'm aware of."

Debbie's stomach convulsed, forming a tight knot in the center of her abdomen. It pressed against her diaphragm, stealing her breath for a few seconds.

"Did you hear me, Debbie?" Mrs. Etchinson asked with a hint of concern.

"Uh. Yes. Yes, I heard you. I'm just…confused. There is no way Martin made friends with a boy his age anywhere else but school. It's the only place he goes right now. Are you sure?"

Debbie's tone begged for a different answer.

"Quite sure." Mrs. Etchinson paused for a moment before offering another possibility. "Martin hasn't really made any friends here yet. I was encouraging him about that the other day. Have you considered the possibility that he has made up an imaginary friend? It might be his way of coping."

"An imaginary friend?" Debbie asked. Her brain didn't want to believe her son might do such a thing. Years ago, it was not highly suspect behavior. Kids would just grow out of it or become writers or something. But nowadays, a kid would need a therapist to sort out such behavior.

"Yes, Debbie. If you can't think of any other way Martin met a child named Malachi, and I know there isn't one here at the school, then an imaginary friend seems the only rational possibility. Maybe we should get him to talk with the school counselor?"

Mrs. Etchinson paused to see if Debbie might be open to the

idea. It took a bit for Debbie to answer, but when she did, it was with a tone of reservation.

"Yeah. I guess that might be a good place to start. Can you help set it up?"

"Yes. Absolutely," Mrs. Etchinson said. "I'll let you know when it will be so you can be here when Martin gets done."

"Thank you," Debbie said. "Bye."

She hung up the phone and collapsed into the chair.

An imaginary friend, she thought. *What the hell?*

WHEN MRS. ETCHINSON RETURNED TO CLASS, MS. Harbough was halfway through the art lesson and walking around looking at each student's work. The children sat in the back around the lab tables, their sketchpads laid out on the black marble countertops.

Mrs. Etchinson walked over to her desk and sat down to go over her lesson and write notes on the board for the next class. She stood, picked up a piece of chalk in one hand while holding her notes in the other, and began writing.

The click and tap of chalk on the board produced a smooth rhythm in her hands. She easily lost herself in it. But today something yanked her out of that happy place no sooner than she had arrived.

"I said...leave me alone!"

It began as a growl and ended in a shout. Everyone turned to look. It was Martin, still seated but turned, looking at another student, a boy named Kyle standing next to him. Kyle was pointing a finger at Martin's sketchpad and laughing.

"Stop it!" Martin commanded, but the boy continued to laugh, looking around at his friends, encouraging them to join in and laugh too, which they did.

"Stop it!" Martin yelled again. "Stop it! Stop it!" His voice rose in a crescendo. Now Mrs. Harbough was moving toward them, getting ready to speak. But not in time.

Martin gripped the biology book sitting next to him with both hands. Thick, dense, heavy. He swung it, his body exploding into action as if trying to hit a baseball. He struck Kyle square in the nose, mashing the soft tissue. The cartilage made a distinct crunching sound that caused Mrs. Etchinson to cringe. A concerted gasp sprang from the lips of every other child looking on.

Kyle was bigger than Martin, but it didn't matter. He hit the ground, hands already cupping his nose, blood flowing. He rolled onto his side and groaned. The world was spinning while his face blazed with pain, a supernova of agonizing sensations pulsing straight into his brain. Tears poured down the side of his face and fell to the linoleum floor.

Martin glared at Kyle, his face a blank slate except for his eyes, which were both cold and burning with hate.

"I *told* you to stop," he said to Kyle, menace in his tone.

Martin turned around and set the book down, ignoring the blood splatter on its cover. He picked up the pencil with his left hand and went back to drawing.

Ms. Harbough scrambled to help Kyle stand up and stop the bleeding. She glanced down at Martin's drawing in passing but stopped in her tracks. Her eyes hung on the image for a few seconds while she held a handful of paper towels to Kyle's nose, then it released her, and she kept moving toward the door. The other children oscillated between gawking at Kyle's misshapen nose and bloody face and staring at Martin ignoring the chaos he created, calmly shading his work.

"Holy crap!" a kid blurted out. "Did you see Kyle's nose? It's crooked!"

The other children erupted in an uproar of cacophonous exclamations. Mrs. Etchinson shook off her shock and disbelief and attempted to bring order back to her class.

"Children!" she said and raised her voice, her tone and pitch growing sharp with the repetition of the word. "Children!"

The sound of their teacher's voice cut through the noise. They all shut up and looked at Mrs. Etchinson.

"Return to your seats now. Take out your biology books and begin reading at page three twenty-eight. Except for you, Martin. You're coming with me to the principal's office."

Mrs. Etchinson stood waiting at the front of the classroom. Martin just kept on shading in his drawing.

"Martin Loch." Mrs. Etchinson stomped one foot as she said the words, her wooden heel creating a resounding clack as it struck the hard linoleum. "Come here this instant."

All the children turned to observe Martin, infatuated by his sudden rebellion. He apparently was not the shy teacher's pet they all assumed him to be.

Martin's hand stopped moving but did not lift from the page. He raised his head and cut his eyes at Mrs. Etchinson.

"Why?" he asked.

Mrs. Etchinson's face flushed with anger at the boy's disrespect.

"Because we're going to the principal's office." Her body was rigid, her face hardened.

"Why?" Martin asked the question with a distinct indifference.

"Why?" Mrs. Etchinson's voice turned shrill. "Because you crushed Kyle's nose with a book! That's why!"

"He deserved it," Martin said. Smiling, he looked back down at his sketchpad and started shading again.

Ms. Harbough looked between Martin and Mrs. Etchinson, then began walking Kyle toward the door. As she passed Mrs. Etchinson, she whispered to her.

"I'll send Principal Beatty down here right away."

Mrs. Etchinson nodded and continued to stare at Martin, who was quite content to continue ignoring her. A silent stand-off took place over the next five minutes. Mrs. Etchinson glared at Martin with both anger and a growing unease. Martin never looked up, just smiled and continued drawing. She scrutinized Martin during their little taciturn intermission. His aberrant behavior confounded her, but as she assessed him, one detail stood out. Martin was drawing with his left hand. Mrs. Etchinson had never seen him use his left hand for writing or drawing, only his right. It was a simple thing, but the realization made her stomach knot for reasons unknown to her.

Principal Beatty appeared at the door and motioned for Mrs. Etchinson to step outside and speak with him. The children all remained quiet, trying to make out the whispers between the two adults. After a couple of minutes, Principal Beatty came in, walked straight back to Martin, and stood beside him, his authoritative presence looming above the boy.

"Martin, come with me."

Martin stopped his work and looked up at Principal Beatty. He knew he would have to obey now. Without a word, he picked up his books and sketchpad and stood.

Principal Beatty extended a hand and said, "After you, son."

Martin glared at him but started walking. As he passed by Mrs. Etchinson, he met her condemning stare with his own unflinching disdain, turning his head to hold her gaze until he exited into the hallway.

DEBBIE'S PHONE RANG. SHE PICKED IT UP AND

glanced at the number. She recognized it and thumbed the answer button.

"Hi, Mrs. Etchinson, I didn't expect to hear back from you so soon."

"Excuse me. This is Principal Beatty. Is this Deborah Loch? Martin Loch's mother?"

The surprise threw Debbie for a loop.

"Um…yes, sir. This is she. What's wrong?"

"Mrs. Loch, I'm afraid Martin has gotten into significant trouble. I need you to come down and speak with myself and Mrs. Etchinson. And you'll need to take Martin home as well when we're done."

"Oh my," Debbie said. "Well, I'll be right there. I'm so sorry for the inconvenience."

She hung up.

What the hell has he done? she asked herself.

DEBBIE WALKED INTO PRINCIPAL BEATTY'S OFFICE. HE stood from behind his desk. Mrs. Etchinson and Ms. Harbough sat in chairs next to the man. They stood as well. Mrs. Etchinson's expression was a mix of regret and sheepishness. After greeting each other and shaking hands, they all sat down. Debbie took the chair next to Martin. She looked at him, but he did not look up at her. He just continued drawing in his sketchbook. It was the start of a new monster of sorts, Debbie noted.

"Mrs. Loch," Principal Beatty began, but Debbie cut him off.

"Debbie, please," she insisted with a smile.

"Debbie, then," he corrected himself, "there's no easy way to say this. Martin injured a student today. Broke the boy's nose with his biology book. Home-run swing, I'm told."

He indicated Ms. Harbough next to him, who nodded and spoke.

"A fellow student, Kyle Brighton, was making fun of Martin's drawing. Martin got loud and told Kyle to stop, but Kyle kept pointing and laughing. Martin yelled for him to stop a few more times and then surprised everyone present when he picked up his biology book, drew back, and swung for the trees. He hit Kyle square in the nose. Blood spattered against the child sitting next to Kyle, and then I saw the boy's nose start to bleed profusely. It took some effort to get the bleeding to stop. We couldn't apply much pressure at all. The impact bent the bridge of his nose out of shape and mashed it in. Kyle's parents took him to the ER, and they just informed me a few minutes ago he may need cosmetic surgery to repair the damage. They're waiting to hear the doctor's final prognosis, now. Either way, his parents are furious."

Debbie's jaw dropped open wider and wider the longer Mrs. Harbough talked. By the end, she was covering her open mouth with one hand. She glanced sideways at Martin and back at Mrs. Harbough. All she could do was shake her head and stutter.

"I-I-I'm so sorry," she managed to spit out at last. "I can only imagine how angry they are. I assure you all, my husband and I will pay the doctor bills."

"That's good to know, Debbie," Principal Beatty cut back in. "There's absolutely no dispute as to whether Martin meant to do it or not. As a matter of fact, he showed no remorse or concern for Kyle after injuring him."

"None?" she asked after gasping and glancing at Martin again.

"None," Mrs. Etchinson said. "In fact, he said to Kyle right afterward, 'I told you to stop,' and then returned to drawing."

Both of Debbie's hands flew to her mouth. She was flabbergasted.

"And when I told him he needed to come with me to Principal

Beatty's office, he asked me why. I told Martin it was for hurting Kyle, and he just said, 'He deserved it.' Then he started drawing again and ignored me until Principal Beatty arrived."

Debbie looked down, her hands moving from her mouth to her forehead. She shook her head back and forth in bewilderment. When she lifted her eyes back up to meet theirs once more, she gulped at the air, searching for words.

"I'm…I don't know…I'm… Where do we go from here?"

"Well, Debbie," Principal Beatty spoke. "There's five school days left before Christmas break starts. I'm giving Martin out-of-school suspension for those five days. Before he leaves today, I want him to speak with our counselor. Get a feel for what brought on this violent episode. Mrs. Etchinson tells me this is completely out of character for him. Perhaps that can direct how you handle this over the holiday. Are you okay with that?"

Debbie answered without hesitation.

"Yes, sir. I understand. That is fine with me, and I'd very much like to learn what the counselor finds out speaking with Martin." She paused, looked down, then cut her eyes at Martin and watched him. He was oblivious, uncaring. "I'm at a total loss right now," Debbie confessed.

Principal Beatty nodded, then pulled his phone closer and keyed in the extension to Mrs. Copeland, the counselor.

"Yes?" Mrs. Copeland answered.

"Are you ready to see Martin Loch?" he asked.

"Yes, sir. Send him over."

"Yes, ma'am. We'll be right there."

Principal Beatty stood and slipped around the teachers.

"Come on, Martin," he said. "Let's go talk with Mrs. Copeland."

He stood and waited. Martin ignored him at first. Debbie felt the heat of both embarrassment and anger rising on her neck. She wanted to jerk Martin out of the seat by his arm and shake him. Instead, she only gripped his arm and spoke.

"Martin," she said, "Principal Beatty said it's time to go with him. Now go."

Martin looked her in the eye. She saw the glint of rebellion there, but he glanced around and decided now wasn't the time to push it. He stood, set his things down in his seat, and walked past her and Principal Beatty without a word. Principal Beatty pushed open the door, and they filed out together.

Debbie watched Martin go, her stomach sinking. She looked up at Mrs. Etchinson, her face etched with utter confusion, her eyes pleading for a rational explanation.

"Where is this coming from?" she asked, shaking her head. Tears sprung forth, and she tried to wipe them away with her hand.

Mrs. Etchinson grabbed a tissue and handed it to her.

"I wish I had an answer for you, Debbie, but I don't. I was taken aback by the whole incident."

"Me too," said Ms. Harbough, joining the conversation. "Martin's been a quiet, kind boy since he arrived. Never a problem. It was jolting."

They stood around nodding in agreement like a bunch of hens pecking at corn on the ground.

"Oh," Debbie broke in, addressing Mrs. Etchinson. "While they're at it, is it possible for the counselor to talk to Martin about the imaginary friend issue we spoke of earlier today?"

Mrs. Etchinson smiled. "Already done."

"Oh, good." It was a small comfort, but Debbie calmed down a bit knowing that both problems would get dug into by someone who knew what they were doing.

Ms. Harbough looked at them both.

"Imaginary friend?" she asked. "What am I missing out on here?"

Debbie gathered her composure and explained to Ms. Harbough everything she had told Mrs. Etchinson on the phone earlier in the day.

While Debbie brought Ms. Harbough up to speed, Mrs. Etchinson scribbled a note and tucked it in her pocket.

It read: *Tell Ms. H. about Martin's behavior the other day when he spoke about monsters.*

When there was a lull in the conversation, Mrs. Etchinson interjected to ask about something else on her mind.

"I've got a question for you, Debbie," Mrs. Etchinson said. "I'm just curious. Is Martin ambidextrous?"

Debbie looked at her as if she wasn't making sense.

"I mean, does he write and draw with both hands?" Mrs. Etchinson elaborated.

Debbie shook her head as she spoke.

"No. No, he's right-handed. He's never written or drawn with his left hand. Ever. Or thrown a ball or anything. Are you sure you saw that right?"

"Positive." There was no doubt in Mrs. Etchinson's mind.

"And you?" Ms. Etchinson asked Mrs. Harbough.

"I've never seen Martin use anything but his right hand before today," the art teacher answered. "But right after he hit Kyle, he started drawing left-handed."

"What does that mean?" Debbie pleaded with them for an answer that might make sense of the spiraling chaos her son had become.

"I don't know," Mrs. Etchinson said. She shrugged her shoulders, then touched Debbie's and gave it a squeeze.

Ms. Harbough nodded her head in agreement.

"Maybe Mrs. Copeland can provide some insight when she's done," Mrs. Etchinson offered.

It was a slim hope, and even smaller comfort for Debbie.

"There's one other thing," Ms. Harbough said. "Open his sketchbook and look at what he was working on. It's...disturbing." A shiver ran through her.

"I saw it when I first sat down," Debbie said. "It looked like the beginning of a monster."

Ms. Harbough's face scrunched, and she squinted at Debbie.

"That's not what I saw in the classroom."

Debbie blinked in confusion.

"Hmmph."

Without another word, Debbie looked down in the seat next to her and pulled out Martin's sketchbook. She opened it, flipped to the picture she saw, then backed up one page.

She dropped the sketchbook as if it might possess the plague or some other deadly disease.

"Did you see it?" Ms. Harbough asked.

Debbie stared down at the drawing for a moment, then looked away. She dared not say what came to mind. Instead, she simply said, "That's horrifying."

"What is it?" Mrs. Etchinson asked, leery to find out.

Ms. Harbough picked up the sketchbook and handed it to the teacher. Mrs. Etchinson scrutinized the work of art. The depiction of a huge lion stalking forward with demons dancing behind him was menacing enough, but the portrayal of the little girl crouched in a corner, crying, face terribly affright, was far worse. It was indeed a horrifying sight.

"This is...not like Martin's normal work," Mrs. Etchinson said, then looked at Debbie. "Do you have any idea what inspired this?"

Debbie gasped in shock at the wretched image her son had conjured. She scrutinized it and quickly determined two things. First, the lion was the same one in her dream and the one she imagined. This realization made her skin crawl. But the second observation was far worse. The little girl in the picture bore an undeniable resemblance to Bella. A cold sweat sprung forth upon her brow, and she found it difficult to breathe.

Mrs. Etchinson and Ms. Harbough watched Debbie's reaction with more than a little concern, but Debbie managed to swallow at last and rein her emotions in. She straightened her shoulders and sat up in the chair. Pulling her eyes away from the drawing, she looked back up at Mrs. Etchinson.

"Well, Debbie?" the teacher asked again. "Any idea what inspired this?"

Debbie forced her shoulders to shrug and shook her head.

Mrs. Etchinson looked dubious at Debbie's response, but instead of challenging the lady, she considered how best to voice her thoughts.

"Who do you think the little girl is supposed to be?" she asked Debbie.

Debbie dreaded the thought of saying what she knew to be true but could also offer no sane reason for the truth she knew. So, instead, she framed her answer as pure speculation.

"I hate to say it, but the girl does resemble his sister Bella."

"Your daughter that died?" Mrs. Etchinson confirmed.

Debbie nodded.

"Are you religious?" she asked Debbie. "Is there anything that might have given Martin the idea his sister is in Hell? Anything at all? That would be highly disturbing to anyone, but especially a child his age."

Debbie wondered the same thing but had no explanation at all. She shook her head in response.

"Hi, Martin," Mrs. Copland greeted him from where she was seated behind her desk. "Please have a seat." She indicated one of the two available chairs. Martin sat down in one and placed his books in the other before leaning back and crossing his little arms.

"Well, Martin," she said, "I've been told why you're here, but why don't *you* tell me in your own words what you did?"

"I creamed Kyle in the nose with my biology book. Broke it good, they said."

Martin gave a slight smirk and made it vanish before there was time for Mrs. Copeland to study it.

"And why did you do that to Kyle?" she asked.

"Because he wouldn't stop making fun of my drawing. He's always picking at me."

"What does Kyle pick at you about?"

"My size. My clothes. My hair. My house. My backpack. My lunchbox. My drawings. Everything."

Martin listed them off rapid fire.

"Is he the only one?" Mrs. Copeland asked.

"No. He's just the worst one. And the leader most of the time. If he laughs, the other kids laugh too."

"I see. And what made you snap today?"

"I don't know," Martin said. "I guess I just decided I wasn't going to take his insults anymore. He's a bully. Sometimes you just have to punch a bully in the nose to make them stop."

"Who told you that?"

"I don't know. I think I saw it in an old movie or something. That's how they handled bullies, years ago."

"Martin, you can't solve problems with violence."

"Really?" he asked, his tone unmistakably sarcastic. "It sure made him stop today. Shut his fat mouth up real quick. And I bet he won't do it again."

Martin stared at Mrs. Copeland and didn't look away.

"It may temporarily solve things, but it only gets you in bigger trouble. Like suspension from school. Or jail."

"Sometimes it's worth it...I think."

"Martin." She chided his attitude.

"I believe," Martin continued to argue, "it's better to suffer a little while for your actions than to live your life knowing you were a coward who did nothing to stand up for yourself. You can't let people walk all over you. It kills the soul and breaks the spirit." He looked down when he was done.

Mrs. Copeland was speechless.

Who is this boy? she wondered. *He isn't talking like an eight-year-old. Hell, I've met grownups who couldn't formulate thoughts like that, much less communicate them that well.*

"Who told you those things?" she finally managed to ask.

"A friend," he said.

Mrs. Copeland's eyes squinted. Her chin dipped, and her brow furrowed. She watched Martin like a hawk to see his reaction to her next question.

"You mean your friend, Malachi?"

Martin's head snapped up, eyes wide with astonishment.

"Surprised I know about your buddy Malachi, huh?" she asked. "Well, your mom spoke with Mrs. Etchinson, and she told your mom there isn't a Malachi here at our school. Which is correct. Your mom swears up and down there's no way you met a new friend anywhere else. So, that really only leaves us with one option."

Martin watched her but didn't speak.

"Malachi is your imaginary friend," she said.

"He is not imaginary!" Martin blurted out.

"It's okay, Martin." Mrs. Copeland took on a consoling tone. "Plenty of kids throughout the history of mankind have had imaginary friends when they didn't have access to real ones. I'm sure you miss your old friends and you haven't made any good ones here yet. You live at a secluded location. It's understandable. But you can't act out and say you're doing it because of your imaginary friend. *You're* responsible for your behavior. No one else."

Martin waited for her to finish before speaking again.

"Malachi is *not* imaginary," he said with conviction and a rising hostility. "I've met him."

"Where?" Mrs. Copeland challenged him.

"At my house. He stopped by my house."

"And how did your mother not see him then? Or your father?"

"My parents don't see everything."

"I can't imagine you've had a boy over to your house while your parents are home and they didn't see him or hear him."

Martin paused to consider his response before speaking further.

"I saw him in the woods behind our house. We meet there to play."

Martin lied, but it was a lie that would shut Mrs. Copeland up. Or so Martin believed.

"So, let me get this right," Mrs. Copeland said. "There's an eight-year-old boy wandering the woods behind your house who's not in the school system here, and he's having a bad influence on you. Is that about right?"

"I guess so," Martin said and zipped his lips.

"Hmph. Well, Martin, I suppose we're at an impasse of sorts for right now. Guess I'll have to let the sheriff know we got us a wild child wandering our woods. See if we can locate this bad egg and get things under control. In the meantime, you will be out on suspension until after the beginning of the year when we come back from Christmas break. I'm going to take you back to the principal's office and have you wait there while I talk to your mother."

Mrs. Copeland led Martin back to the principal's office, then returned to her office with Debbie in tow. Once inside, she closed the door, and they both took a seat.

"Mrs. Loch, I'm afraid your son is exhibiting some very disturbing behavior, and he's told us things that have raised serious concerns."

Debbie wrung her hands but looked Mrs. Copeland in the eye, eager but afraid to hear her professional insight.

"Martin made a conscious choice to use violence against Kyle today. He decided that violence would get him the result he wanted."

"And what result was he looking for?" Debbie asked, bewildered at her son's motives.

"Pretty simple, actually. He wanted Kyle to stop picking on him. According to Martin, Kyle picks on him all the time for all kinds of different reasons."

Mrs. Copeland picked up her notepad and read from it as she quoted Martin.

"*My size. My clothes. My hair. My house. My backpack. My lunchbox. My drawings. Everything.*"

She set the pad down and continued.

"Today Kyle was making fun of his drawing during art class and getting other kids to laugh at it with him. Martin basically told me he decided he wasn't going to take it anymore. He was going to make Kyle stop...with a book to the face. I told him he can't solve problems with violence, and he seemed highly doubtful I was telling him the truth. He seems to think that using violence to stand up for oneself was not only a perfectly acceptable option, but a good one."

"Say what?" The words tumbled out of Debbie's mouth as her eyes nearly crossed, her entire face contorting in consternation. One side of her nose rose up in contempt while the opposite corner of her mouth hung loose in utter disbelief. She was incapable of comprehending why her son was acting and talking this way. She shook her head.

"Where in the hell is he getting this from?" Debbie wondered aloud.

"Well, that's the other thing I find quite concerning."

Debbie refocused on Mrs. Copeland and listened.

"This supposed imaginary friend of his, Malachi. I'm not so sure he's imaginary after all."

"Huh?" Debbie was caught off guard. "But Mrs. Etchinson said there weren't any kids here named Malachi."

"There aren't any children named Malachi here, Mrs. Loch. But Martin insists that Malachi has been in your house and that he meets him in the woods behind your house."

Debbie gasped, hand flying to her heart.

"But," Mrs. Copeland said and paused, despising the bomb she was about to drop on Debbie's world, "I don't believe this Malachi is a boy, Mrs. Loch. I think Malachi is a man."

Both Debbie's hands covered her mouth as she bent at the waist and tried unsuccessfully to moan aloud. Her vocal cords constricted, sealing her lungs. Thoughts of her son being molested by some man sprung to life, full grown in her mind.

"Oh my God," Debbie finally managed to get out. "Oh my God. Oh my God. Oh my God. No. No. No, no, no, no, no, no, no, no, no…"

Mrs. Copeland grabbed a box of tissues and handed it to Debbie just in time. The tears poured and the snot ran. Debbie grabbed a handful of them, blew her nose, and threw them away before pulling out more to wipe her eyes. When she thought Debbie was ready to process what she had to say, Mrs. Copeland started to explain her opinion.

"Mrs. Loch, when I questioned Martin, he spoke of Malachi as if he were a young boy. However, when pressed, some of the things Martin said were far too complicated to have come directly from an eight-year-old. It's likely Malachi is older. Maybe a young man, college age but still young in appearance."

Debbie's hand shot out across the table and gripped Mrs. Copeland's hand. Her forearm muscles stood up off the bone and her knuckles turned white.

"No. Please, no," Debbie begged. "Please, please tell me… Oh God, are you sure?"

Mrs. Copeland looked Debbie in the eye and saw the dread, the anguish. It was clearly gnawing a hole through Debbie fast.

"Debbie, I can't really imagine what you're feeling right now, but I can empathize with you. This isn't the first time in my career I've had to tell a parent their child was possibly being molested. I've seen the heartache and fear. I'm sorry to put you through this when I can't say with any level of absolute certainty it's happening, but considering what we do know, I think it would be wise to inform the police and have them investigate. They can search behind your house and knock and talk at the nearest houses to you and see who is living there and what they've seen. And most importantly, they can have Martin checked for any signs of abuse."

"Oh God," Debbie groaned, not wanting to accept what was happening. It was too much. Too much to bear alone. She wished with all her heart Nathan was there with her, but he was knee deep in that big meeting. It might yield a huge bonus, and they could certainly use it right now. Besides, even if she decided to call him, she'd be lucky to get ahold of him at all. She decided to cowboy up and do it alone. She was a big girl, she told herself. She could handle it…she hoped.

DEBBIE'S DAY ELONGATED FROM THAT MOMENT ON, stretching beyond measure. It was as if time was laid upon a torture rack and its limbs pulled in tiny increments until the joints and ligaments bulged, ready to break with each second that ticked by. And yet they never broke. They refused. There was no relief as she waited for the police to interview Martin, for the ER doctor to check Martin out, for him to speak with a children's psychiatrist, and eventually speak with the police again. They asked more questions and took an official statement.

She wanted to scream. Take a deep breath, open wide, and let loose a blood-curdling scream capable of peeling paint, shattering glass, and making eardrums bleed.

The only thing that saved her sanity was hearing the doctor say he did *not* find any physical signs of sexual abuse.

When she finally walked to their vehicle with Martin and tried to hug him, he stood stick straight, wooden, emotionless. She squeezed him tighter, but he shrugged his shoulders and twisted away from her embrace. Her heart ached.

What the hell is happening to my boy? she wondered.

Once inside the minivan and buckled, she started the vehicle, but she did not drive away. She looked at Martin and finally asked what had been nestled in her gut like a burning stone for hours now.

"Martin," she began. "Ms. Harbough showed me what you were drawing in class."

He cut his eyes at her but said nothing.

"Was…was the little girl supposed to be Bella?"

Debbie threw the question out there while she had the courage to ask.

"Yes," he responded, then remained silent.

Debbie felt sick and full of disbelief. It didn't make sense to her. Martin loved Bella.

"Do you think your sister is in Hell?"

"I can't say for sure," he answered her, "but I think she might be."

Debbie's head rattled side to side, unable to process such a thought coming out of her son's mouth so clearly and with absolutely no emotion.

"What in God's green Earth would make you think that?" she exclaimed.

Martin shrugged his shoulders.

"I don't know. Just a gut feeling, I suppose."

Debbie's world tilted on its axis and spun faster and faster like some carnival ride operated by a drunk man. She dared not ask anything further for fear of losing her grip on sanity. She waited for her head to settle, then put the vehicle in gear and drove away.

NATHAN ARRIVED HOME AND FOUND THE DRIVEWAY empty. He went inside and called Debbie and Martin's names a few times. There was no answer. He dialed Debbie's cellphone. It rang twice, and she picked up.

"Nate," she said but couldn't go any further.

"Yeah, Deb," he said, "I'm home. Where are y'all at? The store?"

"No," Debbie managed to say, trying not to cry. "It's been a very bad day. We're on our way home now. Can you please cook dinner? We have a lot to talk about."

"Uh...yeah, honey," Nathan answered, feeling his stomach twist at the notification of this unknown threat looming before him. "I'll start on it now," he told her.

"Thank you," she said. "We'll be home soon. Okay? Bye."

With that, Debbie hit end and focused on the road.

When they arrived home, Debbie informed Martin he was grounded to his room for the rest of the night. She would bring dinner up to him. Martin didn't acknowledge his mother, but he obeyed, turning right and heading up the stairs as soon as they entered the house.

Debbie dropped her purse beside the couch on her way to the kitchen. Nathan was browning hamburger while spaghetti noodles boiled on another stove eye when she walked into the room. Her countenance was beaten and bruised, reflecting her emotional and mental state, as well as the condition of her spirit, which was profoundly despondent and confused, questioning this new reality without ceasing.

Nathan turned, and she marched into his chest. He stepped away from the stove and wrapped his arms around her. Debbie already held his midsection in a death clench.

"What's wrong?" he asked her, turning them so he could lean on the island and let her rest against his body.

"God, Nathan," she said, "I haven't been gut punched like this since Bella…" Her voice trailed off.

Nathan felt gut punched with uncertainty himself by her words but waited to see if she would pick back up without prodding. She did.

"I mean, so many fucked-up things happened today. It's ludicrous. I don't know how I'm not a puddle of melted wax or something. Hell, I'm damn lucky I didn't just say fuck it and go find the nearest looney bin and check myself in for a holiday vacation."

Nathan chuckled a little and squeezed her tighter.

"I don't even know where to start," Debbie said, burying her face in his chest. She wept, too tired to bawl, too emotionally spent to muster more than quiet tears.

Nathan let her cry, let her get it out of her system for the most part, and when she settled, he spoke.

"How 'bout just start at the beginning?" he said. "What's the first thing that happened today? I need to know it all."

Debbie lifted her head, took a long breath, and began laying out the significant events of the day. Martin's admission that a new friend from school named Malachi showed him the SEARS catalog and then finding out no such kid was registered anywhere in the school system, so it might be an imaginary friend. Locating the note which had both toy names and page numbers listed on it in Martin's nightstand drawer. Getting the call notifying her that Martin had attacked a classmate, intentionally, and done serious injury to the boy's nose, which might require surgery, which they would be responsible for. Martin's utter disrespect for Mrs. Etchinson. His candid admission of what he did plus a total *I don't give a fuck* attitude. His justification of using violence against the boy and not only saying it was the right thing to do but that the boy deserved what he got. And then, to top it all off, finding out that Malachi probably wasn't an imaginary friend, but real, and probably a young man, not a little boy, because their son swore Malachi had been to their house and played with him in the woods behind their house. And that meant their son might have been sexually abused by this man Malachi. Having to talk to the police, go to the ER and have a doctor check their son for signs of sexual abuse—which, thank God, none were found—then talking to a counselor and to the police again. But the icing on the cake was the drawing depicting his sister in Hell, stalked by a huge lion and demons. Though she refused to tell Nathan she had dreamed the same thing.

Nathan's jaw went slack early on and stayed that way, his head shaking in disbelief at every new piece of information she recounted to him. Debbie concluded by saying, "And that's how fucked up today was. Bet you can't top that."

"Holy fucking shit," Nathan muttered. "What in the hell is going on? What has gotten into Martin? This is not like him. It's not like him at all."

Nathan could no longer chalk anything up to coincidence and label what was happening as insignificant and just assume all would be gumdrops and sweet dreams.

Something is wrong. Seriously fucking wrong, he thought.

"Oh God," Debbie said, suddenly stiffening.

"What is it?" Nathan asked, reeling from the idea there might be something worse than everything she just told him.

"The note and something both Mrs. Etchinson and Ms. Harbough, the art teacher, said during our meeting. The note, I didn't mention an important detail. It was written in cursive, and the letters were slanted to the left, like a left-handed person wrote them."

"So, the note could have been written by this Malachi guy or boy or whatever?" Nathan asked.

"Well," Debbie said, "it's possible. But here's the disturbingly crazy part. Right after Martin drilled that kid in the face with the book, both his teachers said he picked his pencil back up and started shading his drawing…with his left hand, not his right."

"Say what?" Nathan said, his face incredulous in its expression. He found it impossible to believe.

"I know, I know," Debbie said, "I felt the same way, but they were adamant. They even asked me if he was ambidextrous. He was using his left hand as if he was just as proficient with it as his right."

Debbie paused and gazed into Nathan's eyes.

"How?" she asked, demanding Nathan provide her with a sane, rational explanation. "How in the hell could he do that? And that note, it looked very similar to his cursive writing, but it was slanted the other way. What if he wrote the note? How did he do that? Or maybe, what is enabling him to do that, is a better question. Just what the hell is going on inside that head of his? Is he sick? I've heard of brain tumors causing drastic personality changes."

Nathan spoke up fast, denying deadly suppositions outright. "He doesn't have a brain tumor. Let's not jump to conclusions."

Debbie fired back, though.

"Well, that's a logical explanation, isn't it? Would you rather I voiced some irrational ones? I mean, he's acting like a textbook case of possession in the early stages. Every damn possession horror movie I've ever watched starts out like this. Or it turns out to be a multiple personality disorder."

Debbie was ready to cry again. She shook her head.

"For fuck's sake, Nate, I'm not sure which one would be worse. Brain tumor, possession, or just plain crazy!"

Nathan held his tongue for a moment and took stock of his emotions before speaking.

"Debbie, I think you're jumping the gun here...on both fronts. Let's not be hasty to assume the worst, with brain tumors or personality disorders...or to assume the outrageous with things like possession. It's too soon in this game to start making assumptions. We don't have enough information. Let's take it one step at a time," he said in an attempt to console her. "Let's see what the police find out. Let's be informed in our analysis of the situation. Okay?"

Debbie was too tired to argue, even though she knew in her heart, in her bones, something was deathly wrong, whether natural or supernatural she could not say.

Nathan held her and held the insanity at bay, rationalizing everything into neat, uniform compartments and excluding anything that might not fit in his limited categories.

DECEMBER 19

The following day was not better. In fact, it was worse. The breakfast table freaked Debbie out. Nathan too.

When Martin came down to eat, Debbie's world was consumed. It was as if an alternate reality had creeped in during the night, integrating itself with her own, infiltrating, merging, and transforming life as she knew it.

Martin turned his nose up at the food and refused to eat one of his favorite dishes—cheesy scrambled eggs with a blueberry bagel and strawberry spread. Instead, he asked for fried eggs with runny yolks, something Martin hated. He demanded white bread with grape jelly and told her, not asked her, to cut the crusts off. He even wanted grape juice instead of orange juice.

It was madness, utter madness to Debbie.

This Martin was a totally different person. His demeanor was unlike her son's as well. He didn't ask politely for the food he wanted. No. He shoved the plate away and told Debbie, "I'm not eating this crap," before informing her what he expected her to make.

Nathan sat dumbfounded, struggling to find words to speak, unable to do anything beyond watch this little stranger seated at his table, in his house, in his son's skin, eating their food. There was an ominous force of dread contained within that small, fragile frame. A foreigner in their midst—alien, even. As Nathan observed Martin eat, he noticed the boy held the fork in his left hand, just like Debbie had said Martin held the pencil the day before. It defied eight years of history. Martin had always lacked the coordination with his left hand that his right possessed. What Nathan was witnessing at their breakfast table was unnatural...sinister. There was *no* rational explanation. He was at a loss, and it unsettled him at his core.

Even the boy's body language was different. His shoulders slumped. His eyes were dark and foreboding, not Martin's typical bright and cheerful eyes, which always shined with excitement, ready to tackle a new day and new things. No. This other Martin looked at everything around him with contempt, including Nathan and Debbie. There was no respect for his parents in his gaze, and he ignored them when they spoke.

Nathan had merely heard of it from Debbie the night before, but he had not seen it himself. Martin had gone to bed as soon as he and Debbie arrived home, and Nathan didn't go up to speak with him. Debbie carried the boy his dinner, and Martin went to sleep after eating.

But now Nathan saw what was transpiring firsthand; saw it with his own two eyes, and yet still found it nigh impossible to comprehend. Fear clamped its icy fingers about his throat. After much observation and struggling with an overwhelming sense of consternation, he found his courage at last and spoke, although the words fell out of his mouth more than they were actually formed into speech.

"Martin, buddy...how are you doing this morning?"

Nathan diddled with his cheesy eggs, not hungry at all. Adrenaline coursed through his body, pulling blood from his brain, stomach, and skin, then forcing it into his skeletal muscles. His body was preparing for action. Fight or flight. It was the body's natural response to fear. Nathan didn't consciously want to fight his son or run away, but something in him was afraid he might need to.

Martin's head snapped up and locked his father with a cold gaze that challenged him to say another word.

Flee. That's what Nathan's body told him to do right then. In fact, there was nothing else Nathan wanted to do more in the whole wide world at that moment. Run and not look back.

Nathan gulped, and sweat sprung forth onto his brow like the morning dew.

"We didn't talk last night, buddy..."

Nathan's mouth dried up like the Sahara in an instant. He tried to swallow and could not. He grabbed the jug of orange juice and chugged it in a desperate attempt to rehydrate his throat and tongue.

Debbie watched Nathan, a puzzled uneasiness spreading across her face.

Nathan set the jug down and wiped his mouth as he met Martin's eyes again.

"Woo! I needed that all of a sudden." Nathan adjusted his tie. It helped relieve a portion of the pressure in his throat and allowed him to gather his thoughts before continuing to speak.

"So, where was I?" he asked. "Yes. Last night. Yesterday. School. Tell me what happened."

"I smashed a guy's nose with my biology textbook," Martin said. His tone was matter of fact and annoyed at being asked about the incident again.

"And why did you do that?"

"He wouldn't stop picking on me. I told him to stop. Several times. And not just yesterday."

"So, you just got tired of taking this kid's crap and creamed him, huh?"

"Yep."

"And what made you think that was okay?" Nathan asked. "Did your mom or I ever tell you that was acceptable behavior?"

"That's how they deal with bullies in the movies. Stand up to them. I've seen both of you clap at scenes like that." Martin smirked. "I'm sorry, Daddy. Is that *not* a display of approval? Perhaps I received conflicting signals from my parents."

Nathan felt an icicle stab his guts. This level of rational introspection was beyond his son's age.

"Um, well...I could support standing up to a bully if you've exhausted other avenues of dealing with the problem, but this is the first we've heard of it. First your teachers heard of it too."

"The teachers are oblivious, and kids like Kyle are smart. They know when the teachers are paying attention and when they're not. When they're close enough to hear something said and when it's safe. Besides, all they'd do is sit us down and make us 'talk.'" Martin made quotation marks with his fingers when he said the word talk. "It doesn't change the bully. Talking never fixes anything with people who want to control others. Especially if they're stronger. You have to take action."

"Did Malachi tell you that?" Debbie interjected.

Martin's head snapped sideways to glare at his mother, but he didn't answer her.

"Well, did he?" Debbie wasn't backing down.

"Maybe," Martin said, head shaking back and forth, the movement almost imperceptible, but Debbie and Nathan noticed it. They saw one side of his upper lip raising in disdain as well.

"Who is Malachi?" Nathan asked.

Martin turned back to his father.

"He's my new friend."

"Is he imaginary or real?"

"*Real.*" Martin was emphatic. His eyes narrowed. His brow furrowed. It appeared this question above all others irritated him most.

"Where did you first meet Malachi?" Nathan was regaining

confidence the longer their Q&A session sped along uninterrupted. His need to flee was subsiding.

"I dreamed about him."

Nathan and Debbie exchanged glances.

"How is he real if all you did was dream about him?"

"He's real enough to bring me toys," Martin asserted.

"What toys?" Debbie asked.

"The toys from the catalog. He brought them to me."

"Show me," Debbie said, standing up and slapping both hands on the tabletop. Her eyes challenged Martin to make good and prove it. Put his money where his mouth was.

"Sure." Martin stood as well, holding her gaze, then turned and walked toward the stairs. "You too, Dad," he called out. "Seeing is believing," he said in a sing-song voice reminiscent of a cartoon kids' show where they tell kids an important life lesson.

Nathan got up and followed Debbie, who was already walking fast to keep up with Martin as he hurried up the stairs.

When Debbie and Nathan walked into Martin's bedroom, he was standing in front of his closet, the door held open, the light inside turned on.

"So," he began, "I didn't tell you about this because I really wanted my own secret space. A place to be alone, where Mom wouldn't be checking in on me all the time while she's still struggling with this overprotective phase of hers."

Debbie looked at Martin in shock and then at Nathan, but her husband refused to meet her gaze on this one.

Martin ignored her look and got down on his knees and crawled into the closet. Once inside, he pushed the boxes aside and opened the small door to his hiding spot. The light was already on inside.

"But it doesn't matter now," Martin explained. "You're *going* to give me some breathing space, Mom. I know you will."

Martin moved aside, holding the tiny door open and giving them a clear line of sight to see into his secret room.

"Come on down here, guys," he invited them. "Take a look."

Martin smiled for the first time all morning.

"Told you Malachi was real."

Debbie and Nathan both knelt and moved forward, though with significant apprehension. They poked their heads inside the main closet and peered inside the smaller space beyond. And there they were: numerous toys laid out in a semi-circle, each one recognizable from the catalog pictures Debbie had seen online. She crawled forward in awe and entered the little storage room first.

She was a doubting Thomas. Debbie had to touch them. She wouldn't trust her eyes. She scrutinized each one, noting they were not brand new. The toys were lightly used, and it was clear time had left its mark. Some colors were faded. Some boxes worn. But all the pieces appeared to be present.

Martin crawled in behind her and moved around to one side. He grabbed Stretch Monster and held him tight to his chest.

"I'm actually glad this happened," Martin said. "Now I can play with these all day and not just at night when y'all are asleep."

He grabbed the Mighty Men and Monster Maker box as well and crawled back out, then stood and squeezed past Nathan.

"Go on in there, Dad," he chided his father and walked over to his desk, where he laid the box down, then returned to the closet still hugging Stretch Monster.

Debbie sat speechless. Nathan crawled forward and laid down on his stomach, half inside the small room, legs hanging out.

"What the fuck is going on?" he whispered to Debbie, not wanting Martin to hear him. "How did he get all these toys into the house without us knowing? And who the hell could possibly have all these toys and manage to bring them to Martin?"

Nathan shook his head. He was at a loss and unable to hide it. Debbie had no better insight and appeared unnerved along with him.

"Martin," Nathan raised his voice.

"Yes, Dad?"

Nathan was sure the boy had a smug look on his face by the sound of Martin's voice.

"Did you meet Malachi in the woods?"

There was a long pause before Martin answered.

"No."

"So you lied to the guidance counselor and the police?"

"Yeah. I knew they wouldn't understand. I'd end up in a funny farm. But you guys see it's true. The toys are real. Malachi is real. There's no denying it."

"And he's not an adult?" Nathan asked.

"Nope," Martin answered. "He's my age."

Nathan paused for a few seconds to figure out his next question.

"Where is Malachi from?" Nathan asked.

Martin was silent.

"Do you know where he's from, Martin?" Nathan asked.

"No," Martin said. "He hasn't told me."

"Can you ask him when you see him again?"

Martin was quiet for several seconds, then answered.

"He doesn't want to tell me. Not yet."

Nathan and Debbie stared at each other.

"What the fuck?" she mouthed to Nathan.

"Are you talking to Malachi now?"

"Yes," he said.

"Can we talk to Malachi now?" Nathan asked.

"You already are," Martin said, glancing at them with a sinister grin.

The words were like an icy dagger slipped surreptitiously into their guts and twisted. It turned their stomachs and filled their throats with a cottony dread which ballooned, filling the space and forcing them to struggle to take in each breath.

BEING STUCK AT HOME WITH MARTIN NOT ACTING LIKE himself was torturous. Waiting for the police to speak to neighbors and get back to her only exacerbated the nagging panic trying to overwhelm Debbie. Her heart was untethered. Her reality unmoored from any sense of normalcy. A storm had struck their lives without warning, *again*, and its winds were decimating what little order she had regained in the last few months.

Martin wasn't drawing. He wasn't asking to play outside. He wasn't interested in his normal foods. In fact, all he wanted to do was surf the internet and look at toys. He was writing down a wish list for Christmas. After watching him stare at the screen for a long time, Debbie spoke up.

"Martin, don't you want to do something different? You've been looking at toys for two hours now."

He ignored her for several seconds before answering.

"Don't you think if I really *wanted* to do something else, I'd have gotten up and done it by now?"

He didn't even turn around to look at Debbie. His response was casual, callous, dismissive. Debbie's ego bristled, and she stood to walk toward him. Martin spun around before she was able to take a single step.

"I *said*, I don't *want* to do anything else right now." Martin glared at her, his eyes darker than she recalled ever seeing them. Beneath his unflinching gaze of disapproval, she suffered a sudden piercing pain inside her chest. It seared her lungs and took her breath. Debbie sat back down and tried to breathe. Martin turned back to the computer screen without saying another word and continued his hunt in silence.

Debbie clutched her torso with both hands, pressing against each side of her ribcage as if working a bellows. Force air out, draw it back in. With great effort, she coaxed her body into properly functioning once more. She left the room, choosing to avoid his presence and hide away in the kitchen.

It was an hour later when Martin stood and approached Debbie, piece of paper in hand. He held it out to her, his eyes and body language demanding she take it.

"These are the toys I *expect* to get for Christmas. *Don't* disappoint me."

Martin pivoted one hundred eighty degrees on the ball of his foot and walked back to the computer and sat down. Debbie looked after him, her face slack, her expression dumb with disbelief.

This is not my son, she told herself. *This is not my son. It can't be.*

After much denial, she looked down at the list Martin had given her. The page was full of items. A bike. A PS4 and numerous games for the console. A remote-control drone with Go Pro. An iPad. An iPhone. Board games. DVDs. Collectible figures and more.

Debbie's mouth hung open. Before she could think better of it, words of disbelief were already flying forth.

"Have you lost your mind, Martin? We can't afford all this!"

Martin didn't look at her as he spoke, an angry growl edging its way into his voice.

"I think you can…and I think you better."

A shiver ran through Debbie's spine, but she didn't back down. Her dander was up now and ready to rage at Martin's insolence and disrespect if it continued.

"Martin," she said, "go to your room." The command was delivered without animosity. It was a simple display of authority as his mother. An authority Martin was not inclined to recognize and obey any longer. He spun around in the chair and glared at her.

"*No!*" he yelled, locking eyes and refusing to break contact.

"Yes, you will." Debbie asserted her parental might and stepped toward him to back it up further.

"*No!*" Martin yelled again, standing to face her and flipping over the chair. His face was indignant, neck stiff, hips squared off. He planted his feet as if his legs were little trees refusing to be uprooted by Debbie's blustering storm.

Debbie snapped.

In an instant, she crossed the distance, grabbed Martin by the nape of his neck, fingers clamping into muscles and nerves. She jerked him sideways and drove him toward the stairs.

"*I told you to go to your room!*" Debbie roared.

Martin shrieked unintelligible gibberish and dropped his weight, flailing his arms and kicking his feet the whole way down. Once on the floor, he turned in a circle, wresting his neck from Debbie's grip and continuing to spin and kick until he was able to strike her in the shins.

"*God dammit!*"

Debbie grabbed her shin. The fury inside her overcame any shock at Martin's behavior. She was determined to win this battle of the wills. He would submit. She would make him.

Martin continued his breakdance tantrum with full surround-sound screaming. Debbie timed his spinning and moved in. Her fingers clasped around the back of his neck again and pinned him to the floor face down. He struggled to move, but he was stuck like a dead bug on a display board at a science fair. Once she had control, Debbie grabbed an arm with her free hand and dragged Martin to his feet. He flopped to the ground, his weight dragging against her strength. But as soon as his butt hit the floor, Debbie scooped her whole arm under him, lifted him up in the air, pulled him to her chest, and began walking for the stairs.

His feet kicked out, striking knickknacks and sending them flying off a table to crash and break on the hardwood floors. One hand reached out and grabbed a curtain, pulling the rod loose from the wall and dragging it behind them. Debbie stepped up onto the stairs and plodded ahead, her determination and granite resolve unwavering. A heel struck her in the upper thigh, then another glanced her groin. She winced and groaned but ignored the pain and kept climbing upward. Martin drove his heels into his mother's hips over and over. Debbie bowed over near the top of the staircase after a heel landed square against her pubic bone. She collapsed to her knees, but leaned forward, intentionally using her body to press Martin against the stairs. He squalled and tried to thrash, but he was immobilized beneath her weight.

I'll smother your little ingrate ass if I have to, she thought, anger consuming her mind in the midst of the searing pain in her groin.

Deep breaths. One after another, Debbie sucked air in and blew it out, gathered her strength, and pushed the burning sensation out of her mind. She lifted Martin and surged up the last three steps, dropping him on the floor. She hurried to snatch hold of a wrist and began dragging him. Four long strides and she cleared his doorway. Two more and she pulled Martin to his feet and shoved him onto his bed, curtain still gripped in his hand. He pulled it up over his head.

She stood before him, feet planted wide, breathing ragged, a rage-filled countenance challenging him to move. Both hands ran through her hair, pulling it away from her face and partially correcting her disheveled appearance.

"I told you," she said, chest heaving, unable to speak but a few words at a time, her index finger fixing Martin like a firing squad. "I told you...go to your room... You disobeyed...threw a fit...*hurt* me!" Her eyes were like diamonds splintered by those last two words, hard yet vulnerable. She paused, heart beating against the inside of her chest wall with the fury of a gorilla. Debbie struggled to breathe, to remain sane, to contain the bitterness coursing through her body and mind. With much effort, she finally managed to clench her teeth, swallow her wrath, and speak again.

"Now...you will stay here until morning...and not another word. You understand?"

Martin eased the curtain down and glared at her from where he lay on his side upon the bed. Silent disdain was his only answer.

"Do you understand me?" Debbie yelled and took a step forward, muscles standing out from her neck and arms, sweat beading along her collarbone.

"You're going to regret this," Martin told her. "You're going to regret this so, so much."

That was Martin's only response. He tucked his face into the bedspread and pulled the curtain back over his head.

He mumbled under the curtain. Debbie thought she understood him.

"Mothers are supposed to love their children, give them what they want. Bad things can happen when they don't. Isn't that right, Mother?"

Debbie watched him for a minute, a battle waging inside her, one side saying enough was enough, let it go, and back off. The other side demanded she make him comply. Like her mother did with her and her siblings when they were kids. The boy was lucky she didn't grab him by the hair and smash his head into a wall repeatedly. Which was exactly what her mother would have done.

But I've never done anything like this before, much less treated my children the same as my mother did me, she thought.

With much effort, she managed to back out of the room and shut the door without saying another word. She eased back down the stairs and into the kitchen, ignoring the carnage left behind from their struggle for now. Opening the freezer door, she withdrew an icepack, then reached inside the refrigerator and grabbed an open bottle of wine. With those two items, she made her way to the living room, her steps tentative and short, stiffness setting in already.

The recliner received her like an old friend as she eased it back and lifted the footrest. She walked her fingers over the area where Martin kicked her, fingers pressing in, testing for pain. There were several tender spots, but she found a knot on her pubic bone. It hurt to touch and ached a great amount. *A bruised bone?* she wondered, rubbing it briefly before applying the icepack. She turned on the TV, found an episode of *Seinfeld,* and tried not to think about what had just happened.

"That isn't my son," she assured herself aloud, "and that wasn't me either."

She sipped the wine. As she began to relax, the adrenaline dumping out of her system was followed by a heavy fatigue, which overtook her body like a robber erupting out of an alley on a fog-covered night. Without warning, she nodded off, but not before realizing somewhere in the recesses of her brain that when Martin asked, "Isn't that right, Mother?" he was *not* speaking to her.

However, she wouldn't recall said revelation when she woke up.

DEBBIE AWOKE AN HOUR LATER, DRAGGED HERSELF out of the chair, and cleaned up. When Nathan arrived home at six o'clock that evening, the police still hadn't come back by or called. She figured they were either being lazy or very thorough. She couldn't decide which one it might be, but she hoped it was thorough.

If Nathan had failed to notice the missing décor items their son destroyed, Debbie might not have uttered a word about what had occurred with Martin earlier that day.

But Nathan did notice, and he asked as well.

Debbie looked at him, her eyes downcast, heavy with fear, shame, and misery.

"What happened?" he asked and moved to hug her.

Debbie melted into Nathan's body, burying her face in his chest. The tears came first, then the sobs. Her torso heaved and shuddered. Her limbs grew weak, and Nathan tightened his hold on his wife to prevent her from sliding to the floor. He reached down and scooped her legs up, then carried her to the couch where he sat back and cradled Debbie.

"It's okay," he said. "Everything will be all right," he added, even though he had no clue what exactly had happened. He simply comforted her through the cathartic expulsion of grief.

When her sorrow had bled itself mostly dry, she managed to speak. Telling Nathan what Martin had done was painful but nowhere near the anguish she experienced while confessing to him how she responded and what Martin said to her in the end.

Nathan withheld any words expressing his shock at both Martin and Debbie's actions. It was insane. Unfathomable. Inexplicable. He started to open his mouth and speak multiple times, but the words simply refused to form and address the madness invading his life, his family, his house.

It was like a *Twilight Zone* episode. Another dimension. Another reality, not his own. The glaring differences were grotesque, alarming. They perplexed him beyond words. The revelation they proclaimed threatened the foundations of understanding. The rock beneath his feet was now a sea of angry waters, the constant undulation beneath him a sickening force eroding his beliefs, his judgment. At this rate, the center would not hold, and he would not hold on to the world as he believed it to be, as it must be.

After sitting in silence for several minutes, he shifted Debbie off his lap, stood, and kicked off his shoes.

"I'm going to go speak to Martin."

"Be careful," was all Debbie said.

Nathan ascended the stairs, each step filling him with a bit more dread than the one before.

HE MADE SURE HIS APPROACH WAS SILENT, EACH footfall slow and precise as he moved toward Martin's room, partly because he wished to remain unheard until the last second. However, if he were honest with himself, it was more due to the gnawing fear of an unidentifiable threat nibbling at his spine. A threat that, if acknowledged, posed tremendous danger to his mental stability. He strained mightily to deny it, but the prickly heat tickling the back of his neck and the waves of ill portent making his stomach squeamish at the very prospect of confronting his son revealed the truth that refused to die.

Nathan eased up to the doorway, listening for any sounds that might tell him what Martin was doing or what kind of mood he might be in. It wasn't until he peeked his head around the doorjamb that he heard something—mumbling sounds. He scanned the room. The missing living room curtain was bunched up on Martin's bed, but he was nowhere in sight.

The closet door was open. There was an ambient glow of light creeping out, low to the ground. It wasn't the main bulb. The light wasn't bright enough. It was coming from Martin's secret room. Nathan shifted his feet, sliding them across the hardwood floor and sticking to the wall out of Martin's sight as he moved closer to the closet.

After several feet, Martin's words finally became discernible.

"I don't care if I hurt her. She shouldn't have ordered me around like that. And she *never* should have touched me. We're gonna make her pay."

We're? Nathan was puzzled.

"I don't care if you love her!"

What in the fucking hell? Nathan thought. *Who the fuck is he talking to?*

Nathan squatted and stretched himself out flat across the floor.

"I'm in charge! You understand? Me!"

Nathan hardly recognized his son's voice as he pulled his body forward until Martin and his secret room came into view. There he was, sitting cross-legged in front of his toys.

"I make the decisions now," his son said to no one apparent.

The *Jaws* game sat on the floor directly before him, its mouth opened wide and leering with hunger. Martin held a Princess Leia action figure in his hands.

"And I want to see her suffer."

Martin laid the figure inside the mouth of Jaws and smiled.

"Nope." He shook his head. "There's nothing you can do to stop me."

Martin sat still, body stiffening with what appeared to Nathan to be anger.

"Stop asking me! I said no. You can come out when I let you out."

Nathan pushed himself back out of sight.

What the fuck? What the fuck? What. In. The. Fuck?

There was no way he was going to talk to Martin now. He did not want the boy to have even an inkling that he might have witnessed him talking to himself in there. Nathan slid back into a squatting position, silent as possible, stood, then creeped out of the room and down the stairs.

When he walked into the living room, Debbie looked up, and immediately her face dropped.

"What's wrong, honey?" she whispered.

Nathan's face was pale, his eyes almost sunken, as if fighting not to be devoured by a dreadful Charybdis full of alien knowledge.

"We're taking him to see a psychiatrist tomorrow." His voice was a whisper as well.

Debbie gasped and covered her mouth.

That was all Nathan said. All he was willing to say despite the seeming multitude of questions Debbie asked. It wasn't until they were in bed that he dared to whisper more and answer her primary concern: "Why? Why do we have to take him to a psychiatrist?" Which meant he had to explain to her exactly what he heard Martin say. And despite many efforts to come up with an easy way to tell his wife that her eight-year-old son wanted to make her suffer, in the end, it was a hopeless cause. There was no getting around the inevitable. His words would break his wife's heart. He had no doubts.

DECEMBER 20

When Debbie and Nathan awoke the next morning, a blanket of dread smothered them and drained their vigor. It was a struggle just to rise from their slumber and get ready. Debbie cooked breakfast, and Nathan woke Martin after he was dressed and ready.

They ate their food in silence. Once done, Nathan told Martin to brush his teeth, comb his hair, and get dressed.

"Why?" A single word loaded with disdain.

"Because we're going somewhere." Nathan's voice cut through the space between them without a moment's delay. His tone was sharp and authoritative.

"But I don't *want* to go anywhere." Martin stared Nathan in the eye. "I want to play with my toys and search online to finish my Christmas wish list."

Nathan took a deep breath and sighed. He wanted to shrink away, but he had to show a shred of dominance, stand his ground while making a slight concession.

"You can bring one toy with you, and I'll let you use my iPad to look for toys online. That's as good as it's going to get."

Nathan sat upright, shoulders back, hands folded on the table.

He tilted his head downward and looked down his nose at Martin.

"Deal?"

Neither looked away from the other at first, but after a tense silence, Martin turned from the table.

"Okay." The two syllables fell like bricks from his mouth. Unhappy but unwilling to push Nathan on the matter, Martin gave in. The bitter resolve in his father's gaze was plain as day.

Without another word, Martin went upstairs and got ready.

THEY WERE NOT ABLE TO GET A WALK-IN APPOINTMENT with any psychiatrist in the area, so instead, they took Martin to the ER. The nurse manning the front desk paged the on-call doctor in the psych ward. When he arrived, he spoke with Nathan and Debbie first, one at a time.

Debbie described what her son was normally like in loving detail. She struggled, unsuccessfully, to hold back tears of loss at his sudden transformation. After painting the picture of a near-perfect child, she then relayed his recent unusual behavior and finished by recounting Martin's violent outburst the day before.

Nathan followed up by telling the doctor what Martin said while talking to himself last night.

The doctor agreed the boy's behavior was unusual and said Martin's actions and words did indeed rise to the level of being a threat to others, namely his mother.

The doctor walked out into the waiting room with Nathan and told Martin to follow him. Martin looked uneasy and was tentative to stand, but when the doctor called him a second time, he complied. Debbie gripped Nathan's hand in hers as soon as he sat down, then watched her son disappear. She simultaneously experienced both a sense of relief and shame at the relief she felt.

"Well?" she asked, on edge.

"I think he's going to commit Martin," Nathan informed her. "He said Martin's actions and words rise to the level of being a danger to others. Meaning you, mainly."

The realization that her son was going to be committed broke Debbie's heart and left a lump in her throat no amount of swallowing would fix.

DRIVING AWAY FROM THE JUVENILE MENTAL FACILITY without Martin felt wrong to Debbie, dreadfully wrong, as if she were the one committing a crime. Debbie knew it was for the best, but the act of leaving her son felt unnatural, reprehensible even. Guilt gnawed at her the whole way home, and she felt as if she had marked herself with some social stigma—the letter A branded on her bosom, not for adultery, but for Abandoned, because she was sure that's what she had done.

Debbie bore her shame in silence, not wanting to infect Nathan with her sense of transgression if he was not feeling it as well.

When they arrived home, a package was waiting on the front porch, leaned against the door. Debbie picked it up and took it in the house. Nathan made a beeline for the kitchen and began preparing lunch for them both. Debbie grabbed a pair of scissors, made her way into the living room, and plopped down on the couch.

She cut the top of the package off, looked inside, and pulled out the contents. It was the 1979 SEARS Christmas Wishlist catalog she had ordered. Despite having seen a picture of the cover online, the sight of it drew a gasp from her. There it was, in the flesh, in her hands. Undeniable. It looked exactly like Martin had described.

She stood and retrieved the list of toys and page numbers for comparison. Everything was correct. Not one of them was mixed up or wrong. Her stomach churned, a warm sensation emanating throughout her upper torso and lower abdomen. Her chest tightened. It was difficult to breathe. The phone rang, but she ignored it, didn't even care about it. Gripping the catalog to her body with both hands, she ran up the stairs. She felt dizzy, her breathing rapid and shallow.

Debbie stumbled into Martin's bedroom and went straight to the closet. Throwing the door open, she dropped down on both knees and one hand, clutching the catalog with the other. She swiped at shoes and slid boxes out of the way in a rush, then opened the door to the small room.

The toys were still there, arrayed in a semi-circle against the far left corner. Like soldiers ready to report for duty. Debbie crawled inside and sat down, then opened the catalog to the toy section and began searching for them. One after another, she matched the toys in front of her with their counterpart inside the catalog. With each one, her anxiety increased, and her ability to breathe grew more restricted, required more effort. One hand shot up and gripped her shirt above her sternum, fingers clawing at the material, curling into a twisted ball of fabric and flesh.

"Oh God," she said, each breath knocking in her chest, unsure whether to go all the way in or come back out right away.

"Oh God, how? How?"

Tears burst from Debbie's eyes while sobs racked her torso. She hugged the catalog close and rocked back and forth, lungs laboring in a staccato rhythm, jolting her shoulders up and down, neck waving like a flamingo as her body tried to get more oxygen.

"Debbie!"

Nathan entered low, sliding under the hanging clothes and scrambling to move behind Debbie. He pulled her back against his chest and hugged her gently.

"It's okay, baby. It's okay. Breathe. Just breathe."

He tried to rub her shoulders, to relax her, but it was useless. She had lost control, and now her body was ready to reset.

When she slumped against him and her head dangled, chin resting against her collar bone, a jolt of terror pierced Nathan's heart. For a moment, he felt the panic try to overtake him, to consume him, but he fought back.

She's just hyperventilating, he told himself. *You can only do that for so long before you black out. It's normal. Check for breathing.*

Nathan leaned her back, supporting her head, then put his ear to her chest and listened for a heartbeat. It was strong and fast. He brought his ear close to her mouth and waited. Her breath was warm against his flesh. It had already slowed and become deeper, not short and shallow. He lifted his head and watched her chest rise and fall. Scooping her up with both arms, he drew Debbie into his lap and cradled her body to his own, holding her close until she regained consciousness.

Debbie's eyes fluttered open a couple minutes later. She snuggled her face into Nathan's chest, unaware of how she arrived there.

"Did I fall asleep?"

"No," Nathan answered her softly. "You blacked out. You were hyperventilating."

Debbie looked at him in obvious confusion.

"You don't remember why?" he asked.

Debbie's eyes glazed over as she searched her memory. It didn't take long to locate the traumatic precursor to her loss of consciousness. A pained expression shot across her face, causing her skin to wrinkle and her eyes to flinch closed for a moment.

Looking around, Debbie pointed at the catalog now dropped on the floor.

"The catalog I ordered came. Everything is just like Martin described it. *Everything*." She grabbed Nathan's shirt and stared into his eyes, the intensity of her desperation and fear palpable and gripping. "This isn't a coincidence, Nathan," she continued. "I don't know what the hell it is, but whatever is happening, it's real and it's snatching our son right out of our hands." Debbie balled her fist, still holding his shirt, and pulled hard. "You understand me, Nathan? *We don't have control anymore.* We don't have control." Her voice faded, its power spent. "We don't even know enough to try and control."

With that, Debbie buried her face in his shirt and cried. Nathan didn't know what else to do, so he just held her. He knew better than to tell her it would all be okay. He had no idea. So instead, he just told her what he knew he could promise.

"I'm here, baby. I'm here, and I'm going to do everything in my power to help figure out what's going on with Martin and get our son back. I won't give up on him."

It was enough for Debbie to not be alone. To know Nathan was facing this unknown darkness with her—this evil crouching not at their door, but in every room of their house and in the heart of their son, waiting to devour them.

Nathan held Debbie until she recovered enough to handle the news he had to share.

"The police called earlier. Right when you came upstairs." He let it hang in the air. Waited for her to engage.

Debbie didn't know if she was up to finding out what they said, but she knew she desperately needed to.

"What did they say?" she asked, cringing as she did so.

"The officer gave me a run down on their investigation. They canvased every nearby neighbor. Searched the woods behind our house and even took some dogs back there to try and pick up on the scent of anything unusual. They got nothing. No unfamiliar people. No young men of any kind living nearby. No evidence of activity behind our house—not in our yard or in the woods. Nothing. They suggested we take him to a psychiatrist to see if they can get to the bottom of things. For now, they're going to close the case unless further leads pop up."

"So, they can't tell us anything, huh?"

"Well…" Nathan kind of hemmed and hawed for a couple of seconds. "It does tell us two things."

"And what are they?" Debbie asked, frustration plowing furrows in her brow.

"There's no grown man involved, and there's no kid named Malachi around here."

"And how does that help us?" She glared at him, her frustration targeting Nathan in that moment. "Without either of them, how the fuck do we explain the toys? Real, physical fucking toys? Huh? How?"

Debbie's voice grew louder as she demanded answers Nathan was not able to give her.

"I'm sorry," he said. "I don't have a fucking clue."

Debbie closed her eyes and shook her head.

"None of this makes any sense. Not one ounce of fucking sense."

LATER IN THE DAY, AFTER DEBBIE TOOK A NAP AND recharged, she went into Martin's room and entered the secret room where the toys were and turned on the overhead light. She sat in the middle looking around for anything out of place. Any clue that might provide her additional information. Anything.

Debbie pressed along the walls looking for any hidden compartment or additional hiding place of sorts. She continued searching around the floor, but nothing gave, until she started digging her fingers into the edge of the carpet. She reached a corner where the carpet lifted. Peeling it back, she found a thin leather portfolio. Debbie retrieved the item and opened it. Inside were several pieces of art rendered by a child. Most of them appeared to be produced by the Mighty Men and Monster Maker game, but there were three original works as well.

The first one she saw depicted a plain full of golden grass with a lion walking through it. A chill ran through Debbie as she noticed the lion's eyes bled black from the corners. She stared at it, and the lion's eyes seemed to stare back, stare into her. She remembered Martin's drawing, and a shiver shook the length of her spine.

But she had little time to consider the similarities. Debbie perceived an odd rumble, or at least what she thought was a rumbling sound at first. She glanced around and listened intently. She nearly threw the drawings into the air when the noise came again along with a tremor that passed through her hand at the same time. Something clicked in her brain, and she identified the sound. It was the purring of a cat, perhaps even a large cat. The throaty rumble was quite distinct once she realized what it was. She looked down at the drawing. The lion was lying down in the grass, eating a freshly killed gazelle. Blood covered its mouth, facial fur, and the sides of its mane, where the beast had buried its jaws into the belly of its prey. Debbie dropped the portfolio, blinked, and rubbed her eyes. When she looked back down, the picture had reverted to the lion walking in the grass. Its eyes still bled blackness, and they seemed to smile at her, a greedy, wicked gleam in them. Debbie shuffled the page to the bottom of the stack.

What appeared on top next was worse by far, except it did not play with her perceptions. Its horror was plain to see and did not fluctuate in the least.

It was quite artistic. A fine piece of pencil work. It depicted a bedroom at night. The only light was that of the moon shining through a window. A bed contained three figures—a man, a boy, and a woman, all tucked in under the covers. The boy was nestled in between his mother and father, a content smile upon his cherubic face, eyes closed. But the parents, their eyes were wide open and empty, their faces full of terror. Red crayon had been applied to their necks and showed where blood soaked into the blanket pulled up to the top of their chests. Red crayon also adorned the blade of a knife lying at the foot of the bed.

Debbie felt ill at the sight of this drawing. She shuffled it to the bottom as well.

The last original piece of art showed the lion again. It was seated on an altar of some kind, and a naked man and woman bowed before it, their foreheads pressed to the floor. She found this one more confusing than disturbing. It didn't make sense to her. But her lack of understanding left her uneasy.

After significant consideration, Debbie decided to put the artwork back. She did not want Martin, or this supposed Malachi, to know what she had found. To know that she knew. Not yet. She pulled the carpet out of the way to put the portfolio back and gasped.

There, on the floor underneath, was a symbol carved into a board. It was the exact same image as the one on the back of Bella's pendant. A triangle of lines with multiple trumpets or partial iron crosses branching off each side and the letters *S M A R B A* encircling the symbol.

"What in the fuck is going on?" she asked out loud. She reached out to touch it, confirm it was real, but withdrew her hand as one who realized they were reaching for a serpent. She blinked, rubbed her eyes, shook her head, then looked again. It was still there.

"I suppose you're real then," she muttered. "I can't make sense of it, but I know it's not a coincidence. No way in hell."

Debbie returned the portfolio to its hiding spot, turned off the light, and crawled out of the tiny room, shutting the door behind her. She had no idea who hid these pictures or how long ago, but she did not like it. Not at all.

WHEN DEBBIE WENT DOWNSTAIRS, NATHAN WAS asleep on the couch. She lifted his feet gently and slid in underneath, laying them across her lap. She turned on the TV and put something on she had seen a dozen times or more. Something to help her zone out.

Later, Nathan stirred and woke. Eventually, he sat up next to her, propped his feet up, and held her hand as he watched the TV show with her. A comfortable silence lingered between them for some time before Debbie broke it.

"Nathan?"

"Debbie?" he answered, looking at her with a warm smile and touching her leg with his hand.

"I want to talk."

"Okay. Shoot."

"I want to talk about what's happening. But I don't think you're going to like it."

"All right. Why do you think that?"

"Because I honestly don't believe we're dealing with something that has a rational explanation. And I know how you feel about that type of stuff."

Nathan cocked an eyebrow and dipped his chin to look at her.

"What you talkin' 'bout, Willis?"

Debbie almost laughed at the old sitcom reference but shrugged the humor off and stayed on point.

"The more I think about everything happening, the more I'm convinced we can't find a rational explanation because there isn't one. The answer is not scientific. Not logical in the normal sense. It's not in the box at all. At least not inside the 'atoms and matter all the way down' box."

"You think it's supernatural?" Nathan asked, cutting in, his voice rigid, bristling. "You think we have a ghost or something? Our son is possessed?"

"Nathan," Debbie began, doing her best to not sound patronizing, "just consider what we know. It all started when we moved into this damned house. Martin's dreams were the beginning, and from there, it progressed to behavioral changes. You know he's not acting like himself. Not one bit. Even his tastes in food have changed, for god's sake!" She struggled to rein in her emotions, control her voice, and continue. "He's talking to someone who isn't there. Someone he says is in this house. Like an imaginary friend but one who's actually changing him, taking him from us. It's got to have something to do with this house. I can't think of anything else that fits the bill. Can you, honestly?"

Nathan's posture stiffened. He answered her question with his own question.

"What about the toys, Debbie? How the hell do we explain the toys? A ghost made them materialize? This house fashioned them out of the void? Is that what we're going with? Is it?" Nathan's voice dripped with a sarcasm he tried to keep out, but it crept in anyway. He was at his wits' end. No matter how much he desperately wanted to, there was no way to flat-out deny the possibility of a supernatural explanation, but he just couldn't swallow it either. It was stuck in his throat, choking him.

Debbie bristled at the offense in his tone but looked in his eyes, her own pleading that he remain open to the possibility. When she saw the likelihood was slim, she decided to bring out the big guns she had hidden away. She stood in haste and grabbed Nathan's hand.

"Dammit, Nathan!" she almost yelled. "Come with me."

She dragged him off the couch and up the stairs to their room. When they stood in front of her dresser, she released his hand, opened the top drawer, and reached inside. The pendant gripped in her hand out of sight, she spoke.

"I'm going to show you something. Something I've had for a couple of months now. You and the police both thought I was going nuts and hallucinating when I kept seeing the old pickup truck driving around."

Nathan's face dropped, his skepticism turning to fear, fear his wife was losing it again.

"But you remember the night I followed it to the cul-de-sac and the police came and searched the area and when they didn't find an old truck they left? You remember that, don't you?"

Debbie's eyes were defiant now, challenging him to admit he recalled that night. Nathan nodded but didn't dare speak at that moment.

"Well," she continued, face grim and determined to prove her case, "as I was about to leave, guess what, *of all things*, I found lying on the pavement in front of my vehicle? Just lying there!"

Nathan's face was a terrified but blank slate. He had no idea what to expect, what might come out of his wife's mouth next. The fact he was so fully in the dark concerning her intentions scared him. Debbie lifted her hand from the dresser drawer and held it out, allowing the pendant to dangle from the necklace gripped in her fingers.

"This!" she nearly spat. "This is what I found on the asphalt where that pickup truck had just driven and disappeared. So, I'm not convinced shit doesn't sometimes appear out of a void or some other crazy-ass options we can't explain. But, regardless, there it was and here it is."

It spun and twisted back and forth in front of Nathan's face, but when it slowed enough for him to focus on it, he saw the pegasus, and his eyes grew wide, his face slack.

Months of being doubted and feeling her ideas suppressed bubbled out with a fury in Debbie's eyes and an edge to her voice.

"You recognize it, don't you?" she demanded.

Nathan's face seemed to skip like a scratched record as he struggled to find expression for what was going through his brain. He tried to speak and nod, but his mind stuttered before his mouth could even try.

"Don't you?" Debbie raised her voice.

"Yes," Nathan finally managed to say, fingers pressing against his temples.

"Touch it!" Debbie commanded.

Nathan looked at her and then back at the pendant. He was a doubting Thomas still, and Debbie knew it.

"Touch it, dammit!" she ordered again, louder this time.

Nathan took the pendant in his hand, rubbed it with his thumb, and scrutinized the design.

"Is this your daughter's pendant?" Debbie asked. "The one *we* bought for her?"

Nathan nodded in admission but still struggled to believe despite his hand being fully thrust into the wound he and Debbie shared.

"How?" he mumbled.

"I don't know," Debbie admitted, "but right now I don't care about the how. I just want us to be on the same page and agree that it *is*." She paused for a second to let her words sink in, then dropped the hammer on him again.

"And there's more."

Nathan looked her in the eye in disbelief.

"Turn it over," she said.

Nathan squinted, his head twitching to eye her sidelong.

"Turn it over," she repeated.

He obeyed. When he saw the symbol, his face contorted in confusion.

"What the hell is this?" he asked.

"I don't know," Debbie said, "but follow me."

She released the necklace and let Nathan hold onto it. Grabbing his other hand, she led him down the hallway into Martin's room, then guided him into the secret room with her. She turned on the light.

"I found something disturbing in here earlier today while you were napping."

Debbie sat down and pulled the carpet back from the corner of the room. She retrieved the portfolio and set it on the floor.

"I'll show you what's in here in a minute. It's disturbing on its own, but you have to see what's under the carpet. Pull it back and look at the floor, underneath where this portfolio lay."

Debbie scooched over out of his way. Nathan eased forward, not sure whether he wanted to look or close his eyes, cover his ears, and shout, "La la la la la!" As much as he desired to do the latter, he knew there was no choice. Debbie would hold his eyes open and shove it in his face if need be. He pulled back the carpet with his free hand and bent down to look.

Nathan stared, head shaking back and forth. The sight of the same symbol that was on the back of his dead daughter's pendant being carved into the floor of a secret room in their new house and hidden out of sight was almost too much to accept.

"What is this symbol, Deb?" he asked. "And who the fuck is Smarba?"

"I don't know, Nate. I don't have a friggin' clue. But whatever it is, it's real. It's real, and that's what matters most right now."

"This is nuts," he said, more thinking aloud than expressing himself to Debbie. He looked down at the portfolio, wanting this chain of revelations to end and dreading the knowledge still to come.

"For fuck's sake, what's in there?" he asked.

"Drawings," Debbie answered. "A few were made using that Mighty Men and Monster Maker game, but there's three that someone drew. And it wasn't Martin. They look too old. Look for yourself."

Debbie opened the portfolio, pulled out the stack of papers, and handed them to Nathan. He perused them, taking his time to assess the original works of art. Disgust filled his face, as well as confusion and fear. At last, he stuck the papers back into the portfolio and closed it. Before he could speak, Debbie hit him with one last revelation.

"And that lion in those two pictures," Debbie said, "I dreamed about it recently. Woke up scared as hell. And it wasn't just any lion, it was *that* one. In my dream, it had the same blackness bleeding from the corners of its eyes."

Debbie's gaze dared Nathan to question the validity of her experience at his own peril. He just shook his head.

"How?" he asked again. "How in the hell is this happening to us? And why? Why the fuck is it happening to us?"

"I don't know," she confessed. "I'm not sure of anything at this point, but so far, rational explanations aren't giving us any fucking answers. If we don't start looking elsewhere, now, by the time we find out what is behind Martin's changes, it may be too late to get him back. I've got to be willing to explore this angle. And you've got to let me, even if it bangs up against your militant atheism and hate for the church. If I don't, I won't be convinced I'm doing everything in my power to fix this."

Nathan's lips pressed together tight enough to form a sharp line and squeeze the color out of them. His eyes closed in pain, and his head shook ever so slightly, then stopped. He opened his eyes and spoke.

"Deb, I get it. I do. I can't figure this shit out either. I have no idea how to explain the crazy things we've seen. No fucking idea. But if I open the door to the possibility of ghosts and spirits and possession, and all kinds of other weird-ass shit, there's a tidal wave of adjacent reality coming with it that I just *can't* accept. I *won't* accept."

Nathan's lips pursed tightly again and trembled.

Debbie fixed him with a scornful gaze.

"Not even to save your son?" she challenged him.

The air left Nathan's lungs with an audible whistle.

"Goddammit, Deb. Goddammit."

That's all he said. It was all he could say. And the irony of his words was not lost on him either.

DECEMBER 21

After Nathan left for work the next morning, Debbie called the children's psych ward to get an update on Martin.

"How has he been behaving, Doctor?" she asked.

"Pleasant as can be thus far. A little too pleasant possibly. Makes me wonder if he's behaving well just to get out of here. Happens often."

"Did you ask him about Malachi?"

"Oh yes. He swears Malachi's just an imaginary friend and nothing more."

"That's not what he told us. He said the boy was real. He was quite adamant about it and got angry when we challenged the notion."

"Yes, I asked him about that. He said he lied to you on purpose. To get back at you, he said."

"Get back at me?" she asked, confused. "For what?"

"He says you have been smothering him since the death of his sister. He can't do anything without you jumping in and exercising control over every little thing he does. He clearly resents your efforts at control. It's likely the source of his acting out."

"You think this is all *my* fault?" Debbie was incredulous. A combination of angst and rage boiled in her gut.

"Well, I understand how much stress you've been under, Mrs. Loch. It can be quite difficult to deal with. But the loss of his sister combined with the subsequent tightening of the metaphorical reins in his life can certainly create a backlash of animosity toward the parent responsible."

Debbie cut in.

"What about the toys? What about the toys, Doc?" In her mind, it was *the goddamned toys*, but she managed to exercise a shred of control and choose her words with care. "Did you ask about them?"

"Oh yes. Martin was quite candid about them. Said he found them in a secret little storage room on the other side of his closet. He had to pry the door open. It was probably shut up for years and no one realized it was there or the trove of goodies it contained."

Debbie blinked, dumbfounded by the slew of lies she was hearing and by the accusation that she was now, somehow, the source of all Martin's problems.

"I'm going to go ahead and keep Martin here another day. I'll spend time talking with him about his own stressors and how to deal with his problems in a healthy manner and open up to you about his concerns. But you will have to be willing to listen to his concerns and do your best not to suffocate him with your fear for his well-being. A child needs room to breathe and grow."

Debbie held the phone out in front of her, ready to spit fire in the receiver if only she possessed the capacity. Her face contorted with dismay and disdain for the doctor. She was flabbergasted. And pissed beyond description.

"Are you there, Mrs. Loch?"

Debbie practically bit her tongue to keep from cussing the man out.

"Yes, I'm here. I appreciate your help, Doctor. And I'll do my best when he comes home tomorrow."

"Good. Good. That's what I want to hear. Let's plan on you and your husband being here tomorrow morning at, say, nine a.m.? Sound good?"

"Yes, sir. That'll be fine."

"Good. Well, I'll see you then. Goodbye."

"Bye." The word was nearly a croak. Debbie thumbed the end call button and slammed the phone into the cradle before screaming like an enraged banshee into her empty house. It took a few times before the cathartic release finally took effect.

ONCE DEBBIE RECOVERED FROM THE PHONE CALL AND composed herself, she left the house and drove into town to the local public library. She planned on researching her house. She figured searching for any old news articles related to her address would be a good starting point and might bear quick fruit.

She wasn't wrong. As soon as she pulled up the archived articles from the local paper and put her address in the search bar, she quickly found several entries. She filtered them by date and began skimming. There were a few bylines before 1979, but nothing of note. But then there it was, December of 1979.

The first byline read, "Tragic slaughter claims family days before Christmas."

"A family was killed in my fucking house?" Debbie whispered to herself. "You've got to be fucking kidding me." She immediately thought of the drawing and felt an oppressive dread bearing down on her, a truth she did not want to know but had to discover.

She raced to read the article. It was tragic indeed. Police

responded after reports from the mailman that no one was picking up the mail or answering the door despite all the vehicles being home for the past three days. When they conducted a welfare check and entered the house, the stench was overwhelming. What they found was even worse. Both the mother and father, Natalie and Richard Barber, were found dead. Cause of death appeared to be stab wounds to the neck. A pocketknife was found at the scene. Gruesome for sure. But their eight-year-old son, Malachi...

Debbie froze when she saw the name, unable to move past it. A massive shiver ran through her spine. Her stomach fell away, then rebounded into her throat.

She failed to stifle a loud gasp. Looking around with a clear appearance of guilt, she met the gaze of the young librarian and mouthed an apology before returning her attention to the screen and continuing to read.

The most shocking detail of the murders belonged to how Malachi died. The killer had pummeled his face severely before choking him to death with their bare hands. The boy's larynx was crushed. Debbie finished the article and was disappointed to learn there were no suspects at the time of the first article.

The second byline stated, "Police try to find motive for mysterious murders." The article recapped some of the details from the first report and indicated police were checking for prints on the murder weapon and the boy's body. They still had no motive for the murders after significant investigation. Any kind of match to the prints recovered might provide the insight and clues necessary to figure out who murdered them. It was obvious to Debbie from the tone of the articles that everyone in town was shook up over the murders and feared for their own families during the holiday.

Debbie came to the final article. "The shocking truth of the Barber family murders." The fingerprints on the pocketknife had come back a perfect match to the boy, Malachi. There were no other prints on it. Malachi had killed both his parents. But the prints on Malachi's throat belonged to his father, Richard.

Holy mother of God, no, Debbie thought. *That boy drew a picture of what he intended to do to his parents.*

"Little fucker got a surprise, though," she whispered under her breath. "Daddy put him down on his way out."

Debbie paused as the reality dug barbed hooks into her mind and demanded she consider the horror at further length and sound its shadowy depths.

How could the father have murdered his own son? Was it in anger? Revenge? A last, dying act, attempting to save future innocents from his child's murderous desires? And what would it take to do such a heinous, unnatural thing? To carry through to the very end, fingers strangling the tender throat of evil dressed in familial flesh, even as his own life bled inexorably away? What kind of fortitude and resolve would a parent have to possess to snuff out the life of their own child? Surely it would have to be substantial, even if they knew their child's spirit was twisted to the point of committing violence?

Debbie wondered if the mother and father were privy to any clues foretelling what exactly was to become of them. Did they suspect what their son might do? Were they tormented with dreadful possibilities ahead of time, or did their end pounce upon them out of the blue? Debbie believed she would prefer the latter. If she believed Martin truly meant to kill her, how would she behave? Would she sleep at night? At all? Could she will herself to prepare for the day the violence in his heart blossomed into action? If he attacked her with the intent to do serious harm or even kill her, would she barricade her bedroom door with a chair or similar item to ensure the boy did not come for her life in the night? Would she hide a weapon beneath her pillow? A knife? A gun? A hammer? And, most troubling of all to consider, could she bring herself to use a weapon if the emissary of death appeared at the foot of her bed with disheveled hair and wearing

Spiderman pajamas? Could she smite her son in self-defense? And if so, what would be the cost to her soul? Would it be worth the life she preserved? Could the person she became, to save her past self, live with what they did? She didn't know. She didn't want to know. She didn't want to even consider this line of thought any longer. Her heart trembled and swooned beneath the burden of such a reality.

Debbie closed the door on such possibilities and after wiping the tears from her eyes continued reading the article.

Upon further investigation, reassessing the scene and recreating events based on the evidence gathered, the police were confident they knew what transpired. According to their report, it began with the boy, Malachi, crawling up on the bed between his parents and stabbing his father in the throat first and then his mother. The father must have attacked Malachi after the mother was injured and tried to stop him. The bruising covering Malachi's face certainly was a result of punches. In addition, there were right hand bruises and prints covering the boy's throat and left handprints and bruises on his right wrist. This indicated the knife hand had been restrained during the struggle. The father lasted long enough to choke his son to death before succumbing to his injuries.

It took tips from the public, however, to help figure out the motive behind Malachi's deadly attack on his parents. The detective in charge spoke with the boy's schoolteacher. She informed him that Malachi had grown increasingly selfish and self-absorbed. He routinely placed his own wants before the well-being of other students.

But it was the manager of the local Toys R Us who provided the key puzzle piece after seeing the police were looking for any leads that might help their investigation. Malachi stole several toys before the murders occurred. His parents refused to buy him the toys he asked for, and he snuck back in each day over the course of a week, stealing some each day. Malachi's parents disciplined him. The manager said the father called him back to assure him he had spanked the boy, grounded him, and took the toys away. He stated he would bring the items back within the next couple of days, as work allowed.

Debbie had rabidly devoured the text of each article, but her eyes came to a jarring halt at the next piece of information. The police never located the toys, and according to the Toys R Us store manager, the father did not return them either.

"Where the fuck did they go?" she muttered under her breath, but a little voice inside her head told her.

You know exactly where they went…and where they are now.

She scrolled down to the next page, and her heart skipped a beat at what she saw. One hand flew to the crushing pain in her chest and the other covered her mouth. The impossible reality she witnessed in a picture forty years old punched her in the gut with the force of a semi-truck, and the impact sent a wave of nausea spreading throughout her whole body.

Debbie lurched out of her seat and ran for the restroom, struggling not to vomit before she got there. Crashing through the door, she skidded in front of a stall, shoved the door open, and dropped to her knees. She managed to pull her hair back a second before she retched violently into the toilet. Her stomach twisted and heaved over and over, expelling all its contents, then giving it the old college try several more times to ensure it was empty.

Debbie released her hair when the dry heaves died down and posted out on the stall walls with both hands, panting, the need to throw up finally over. She grabbed some toilet paper and wiped her mouth.

"Are you okay, ma'am?" a meek female voice called out to her.

"Yes," Debbie said, her voice hoarse and weak.

"Can I get you anything?"

"Thank you," Debbie said, managing to pull herself up to a standing position. She exited the stall, first seeing her pale face in the mirror, then the young librarian who was nice enough to check on her. "I'll be okay. Must be something I ate."

The girl winced, not sure how to answer.

"But you can help me," Debbie told her, then bent over the sink and rinsed her mouth out a few times.

"With what?" the young lady asked.

"I need to print out a few articles I was looking at. They're old ones from the local paper. Can you help me do that?"

"Sure. Absolutely. When you're ready, we'll walk back to your computer. You tell me which ones, and I'll take care of it for you."

"I'm good, darling. Let's go."

Debbie led the way, and the librarian followed. As she approached the computer screen, Debbie braced herself to see the picture there, still on the screen. It was a picture of Malachi and his father standing next to their pickup truck. It was *the* vehicle Debbie had witnessed run over her daughter six months ago. And the father was the spitting image of the man she had seen driving the vehicle.

How? The question shot through her mind and ricocheted around. Reality was determined to unravel beneath her feet, but Debbie grabbed hold of the loose thread and gripped it with what sanity she had left.

"Looking into the Barber debacle, huh?" the librarian asked her, her cheeks pink with cheer.

"Um...yes," Debbie answered with some trepidation.

"What piqued your interest in it?" the woman asked, politely curious.

Debbie debated on what information she wanted to reveal.

"Well...to be honest," she confessed, "we moved into their house. I had no idea of the history until just recently. I was hoping to learn more."

"Oh my God!" the librarian exclaimed. "*You're* the one who bought the house, huh?"

Debbie nodded her head.

"Wow," the woman continued. "I'd have it out with the realtor for not revealing that information before closing. Geez. Do you have kids? No one with kids stays there for long."

Debbie put her hand over her mouth and nodded again. "Why do they leave?" she mumbled from behind her hand.

"Well, there's a horde of rumors surrounding that house. For starters, everyone with kids who have ever lived there swore it was haunted and moved out in a hurry. There have been five couples with children who lived in your house. The little girls have always complained of a creepy presence in the room groping them, the sound of footsteps, and a light in the Barber boy's old bedroom closet coming on at odd times of the night accompanied by a voice inviting the children to play."

Debbie's hand clenched her mouth tighter, but she managed to ask, "The spirit only took an interest in girls? No boys?" She felt a bit confused.

"Yeah, just girls, so far," the lady answered. "No little boys have ever lived there since the Barber family."

"What?" Debbie spat in surprise. "But what about the couple we bought the house from? They had a son."

The girl cocked her head, looking at Debbie almost out of the corner of her eye.

"Um…I'm sorry, but you're mistaken," the librarian informed her. "I know Marcus and Blair. They have a little girl named Angela. They don't have a son."

The world spun beneath Debbie.

What the hell does that mean? streaked through her mind. *Did Martin just mistake the girl for a boy?* Debbie searched her memories. *But then why did the parents tell us their son was sick and running a fever? Oh my god.* The truth hit her. *They knew and didn't want to tell us. And they didn't tell us when they sold us the place either. No wonder they were in such a damn rush to close.*

Debbie's face shifted from confusion to anger and then to fear as realization dawned.

Malachi took to Martin right then.

The thought horrified Debbie.

The librarian scrutinized Debbie's facial expressions as they cycled between fear, consternation, and horror.

"You have a boy, don't you?" she interrupted Debbie's thoughts.

Debbie choked up, eyes squinting, tears squeezing out to roll down her cheeks and pool against her thumb and index finger. She nodded, unable to speak at the moment.

"Have you experienced anything strange?"

Debbie pursed her lips behind her hand, restraining a cry of panic, and nodded.

"Oh my god," the librarian said, trying to console Debbie, but also looking quite curious. Little did Debbie know, but local history was of great interest to this librarian and she prized any opportunity to discuss such matters, especially with someone who might have firsthand knowledge. "I'm so sorry you're going through this," the girl sympathized with her, then pried for further information. "Do you want to talk about it?"

Debbie shook her head violently.

"No!" she blurted. "No. Not at all. No. I can't."

The librarian took a step back, giving Debbie space.

"Okay," she said. "But can I ask you one question?" She didn't wait for a reply but pressed on. "Have you seen Mr. Barber and his old truck?"

Debbie thought she might retch again.

"What do you mean?" she managed to croak.

The woman brightened at the opportunity to speak further and spelled out all she knew without waiting for an invitation.

"Oh, Barber and his truck are a bit of an urban legend around here. Particularly amongst the younger crowd. There have been numerous reported sightings of Barber driving his truck around town ever since the murders all those years ago. There's plenty of theories as to why too."

The librarian sat down next to Debbie and continued.

"Some people say he's looking for a child to replace Malachi. A good son instead of the rotten one he got in that boy. Others say Barber and his wife were involved in a form of Satanic worship, and that Malachi's innocence was powering an ongoing ritual of sorts, but during the repeated performance of the ritual, a demon or spirit bled through into the boy's soul, corrupting Malachi's spirit and mind, changing his personality. They think it's the best explanation for the radical change in his behavior in the months leading up to the murders. Also, they believe that Malachi killing the parents prevented them from completing this complex ritual. Between that and all the negative energy surrounding the massacre, it's left them all in limbo, angry, resentful, longing to live and breathe again, and if you believe the satanic stuff, the parents are driven to finish their ritual by whatever forces they served before they died. So Mr. Barber rides around searching for the perfect child, a perfect son, and maybe the perfect boy to complete the ritual with and a playmate that meets with Malachi's approval."

Debbie looked visibly sickened by the librarian's account. The lady noticed and tried to deflate Debbie's concerns.

"But nobody knows anything for sure. It's all just speculation about a bunch of silly superstitious mumbo jumbo. It's okay."

Debbie wasn't comforted in the least bit. Her stomach wrestled with her will, demanding to vomit again, despite being emptied of all contents. She scurried back to the bathroom, kneeled, and dry-heaved above the toilet, her stomach managing to eject a small amount of bile after great effort. She strained to calm her mind.

This can't be true, she told herself. *My God, my God, my God, this can't be true.*

She wiped her mouth with toilet paper for the second time in less than an hour and squeezed her eyes against this new reality she refused to accept. Minutes passed before she stopped the mental mantra and opened her eyes once more. She stood, walked to a sink, and rinsed her mouth. Glancing at herself in the mirror, she was horrified at how disheveled and haggard she appeared. She washed her face and rubbed her skin roughly before drying her hands and running a brush through her hair. Feeling more human, she exited the restroom and returned to the computer. The librarian saw Debbie and met her at the computer once more.

"Is this the only article you needed printed?" the librarian asked her, trying to be as helpful as possible and hoping she didn't end up getting a complaint.

"Um…no," Debbie said. "There's a couple others."

Debbie backed out of the last article and showed the girl which ones she needed. While the young lady took care of printing out all the articles, Debbie built up her courage. When the librarian returned, she asked the woman what was burning in her brain.

"Miss," she said, "can I ask you one question about those urban legends?"

The librarian's head canted to one side and withdrew in surprise, obviously not expecting to get any further inquiries from Debbie on the subject.

"Um…yes, ma'am," she replied. "Certainly. What would you like to know?"

"What's the farthest away from my house that people have reported seeing Mr. Barber in his truck?"

The librarian had to pause and consider for several seconds. Her lips pressed together, then curled inward as she searched her memory for the information requested. At last, she answered.

"Well, don't quote me on this, but I want to say that all the sightings have been either on the backroads near your place or here in the downtown area. I can't recall any other locations where people have reported sightings."

Debbie was not sure whether that was reassuring or not. She thought of one other avenue of questioning and decided to explore it.

"One other thing," she said.

"Sure," the librarian answered, game for any discussion on the topic. "Shoot."

"Were the police reports ever released to the public? Was there any real evidence discovered at the house to indicate satanic rituals were happening there?"

The librarian's eyes lit up.

"You know," she began with excitement, "I don't think they were, and I don't think anyone ever petitioned for their release through the Freedom of Information Act. Man, you are one smart cookie. That is a great question!"

The librarian was excited at the prospect of finding out more information on the subject and had to check the volume of her voice.

"What about the officer who worked the case?" Debbie asked. "Is he still alive?"

"Oh, I'm sorry," the librarian said. "That I do know, and no, he passed some years ago. My father knew him. Knew him well, in fact. I remember my parents attending his funeral when I was in high school."

Debbie's countenance dropped in disappointment but then brightened at a possibility. "Was your father close to the officer? Do you think he might have told your dad details that weren't released to the public?"

The librarian looked up and to the left for a few seconds, considering the possibility.

"Hmm. I don't know," she said. "I can ask my dad, but as much as we've talked about the subject over the years, I'd think he would have told me if the officer had revealed anything about satanic rituals to him in confidence."

Debbie's face turned downcast again.

"Either way, it's okay," she reassured Debbie. "We can still go petition for the release of any reports related to the case. In fact," the girl continued, "I'd be glad to do that and get back with you on what I find."

"Really?" Debbie said.

"Absolutely!" the librarian said. "I've always found the case fascinating. I dig reading about real crime and supernatural stuff, so the two together is a win-win for me. I'd love to get copies of those reports!"

Debbie noted the librarian's keen excitement and agreed to her proposal.

"That sounds great. I already have so much on my plate right now. If you can get the reports and let me know what you find out, I would be so thankful."

The librarian pulled out her cell phone and smiled.

"What number should I call when I get the reports?"

"Oh, yeah, duh," Debbie said, demeaning herself. "I guess that would help, wouldn't it?" She laughed nervously, then gave the librarian her number.

The girl punched the number in and hit send. A moment later Debbie's cell phone rang. The girl hit end.

"All right. I guess we're good... Oh, I didn't get your name."

"Debbie. Debbie Loch."

The girl entered Debbie's name into the contact field and saved it.

"Okay, Debbie," she said, "I've gotcha in my contacts now. I'll go file the request later today." She leaned in closer to Debbie, looked around, and lowered her voice. "I know the secretaries, personally, so perhaps they can expedite things for me. Oh, and I'm Rachael, by the way. Rachael Hill."

They shook hands. Rachael moved back and smiled a helpful

librarian smile. Debbie noticed the girl cut her eyes sideways. Following them, she saw an older librarian, probably the girl's boss, was staring at the young girl.

"I'll call you when your 'book' comes in, ma'am," Rachael told her. "Now, let me go get those papers. They should be done printing by now."

With that, Rachael turned and retrieved them. Debbie met her at the front counter, paid for them, thanked her for all the help, and left, hoping she didn't get the poor thing in trouble.

Debbie drove home, terrified to even glance at the printouts next to her for fear of getting violently ill again. When she arrived back home, she grabbed a bottle of Nathan's Scotch and started pounding shots. She didn't want to think. All she wanted to do was sleep until Nathan got home. It didn't take long for her to crash and burn on the couch.

NATHAN WALKED IN THE HOUSE AND CALLED OUT FOR Debbie. No answer. He set down his briefcase, took off his coat, and hung it up in the downstairs closet. He called out again, but still no answer. Wandering into the living room, he found her asleep on the couch. A quick glance around told him something was wrong. Debbie never drank Scotch, and there was a lot missing since the last time he drank any. He checked on her to make sure she was okay...and breathing.

Check.

He walked back into the kitchen to grab a soda and noticed a plain manila folder lying on the table. There was no writing on it. He flipped it open and looked at the top piece of paper inside.

Newspaper article? he thought. *What was she researching?*

Nathan picked up the folder, walked into the living room, and sat down in the recliner. He started with the first article on top. It didn't take him long to realize the address of the murders in question was his own. It took little more to see that the name of one of the victims was an eight-year-old boy named Malachi with a selfish streak. But when he saw that Malachi had indeed killed his parents and the toys were never found, Nathan's blood ran cold. Fortunately for him, he did not have the firsthand experience necessary to understand just how deep the rabbit hole was taking them.

Even still, what he read was more than enough to derail Nathan's supernatural doubts and make him question his beliefs.

He tossed the folder on the coffee table, grabbed the bottle of Scotch and the glass Debbie had used, and poured it just shy of the rim. He drank it down with big gulps and poured another to sip on.

"Fuck you, God," Nathan said to the silence. The need to give voice to his defiance was irresistible.

"I didn't like you or believe in you before my daughter died. Since then, I hate the very idea of you. You can't be real. This... this ludicrous shit show can't be real. I refuse to believe it. It's got to be a coincidence. It has to be."

"It's not a coincidence."

Debbie's voice jerked him out of his preoccupied thoughts. He looked up at her. She was still laying on the couch but rested on her side, facing him now. She stared at Nathan.

"What did you say?" he asked, recovering from the stabbing sense of vulnerability and exposure he was experiencing.

"I said it's not a coincidence." Debbie looked at him with tenderness, not relishing the destruction of his worldview, his precious paradigm of reality. She took no joy in it, despite their debates over the years. Her desire for the spiritual had always been as clear as his disdain for it.

"You've got to set aside your past," she told him with compassion. "Reconcile it with the present. Find a way to accept what's happening and help me rescue our son. Our family."

Tears welled up in Nathan's eyes, but he did not speak. All he could think about was the little boy he was before that day so very long ago. He'd been eager to please his youth pastor, to show himself learned and worthy of praise. He had longed for approval as a boy, and that desire was used against him. Not by his own pastor, but by one from another church at a summer camp. The young man, a pastor's son, sniffed out Nathan's need and preyed on him, twisting what was good in him to obtain sexual gratification at the boy's expense. Nathan froze during the act. Shocked and overwhelmed. He didn't resist, and he hated himself for it.

In the days after they returned home from the youth group trip, Nathan raged, lashing out at everyone around him. When finally confronted by his youth pastor and asked what was wrong, Nathan confessed what happened, what was done to him. But the man he fully expected to champion his victimization did not even rise for battle. Instead, he reported to the elders, and they huddled, circled the wagons. Afraid to offend a sister church, they didn't accept Nathan's testimony. They conspired and refused to acknowledge the truth. Even his parents joined in the betrayal, too blinded by their indiscriminate faith in mere men.

The day they called him a liar, Nathan renounced all belief in God and never looked back...until now.

"What makes you so positive it's not a coincidence, Debbie?" he asked, lips struggling to form the words without sobbing, the distant past a fresh wound once more.

Debbie sat up. She hated to see him in pain. They had spoken of his experience once, years ago, and never again since. But she knew it was there, buried deep, a huge swath of scar tissue entangled with the core of his being. And she knew this would rip it wide open.

She didn't want to speak of the photo. It was pulling on her own scars as well, threatening to tear her open and expose those nerves to raw, excruciating pain once more. But she had to. Nathan had to know. Whether the evidence convinced him or not, whether it hurt him or not, she had to tell him.

She pointed to the folder.

"Look at the last page of the last article," she said, struggling to speak the words. "There's a picture."

Nathan stared at her for a second, then leaned forward and grabbed the folder, flipped it open, and pulled the last page out. He looked at the picture of Malachi and his father standing next to the family pickup truck. Nothing stood out to him.

He looked up and met her gaze. He saw an illness in her eyes, an affliction of sorts. It was gnawing at her, and its appetite was clearly voracious.

"What's the significance of this picture, Deb?" His tone indicated a dreadful suspicion he was reluctant to vocalize. He had no idea what it was, exactly, only that it was something bad, unspeakably bad almost.

Debbie prepared herself. A deep breath, a straightening of her posture as she tensed her abdominal muscles. She closed her eyes and attempted to pretend it meant nothing to her. It was someone else, and she was like a reporter. A temporary lie told to oneself just long enough to help her do what she needed to do.

"Deborah?" Concern creeped into Nathan's voice.

"That picture," Debbie began, "that truck...that man..."

She swallowed hard, trying to push the lump in her throat back down, but it resisted. Her courage cracked, splintered. Her mouth broke ranks with her mind's original intent.

"I don't know what to make out of it myself." Debbie avoided speaking the revelation she possessed.

"Out of what?" Nathan asked, ready for her to get to the point. "C'mon. Now's not the time to spiral or beat around the bush. Shoot like an arrow and make your point."

"I...I don't want to say," she confessed. "I know you're

going to freak out, honey. I know you're going to say it's crazy… that I'm crazy. I…"

Nathan half growled in frustration.

"For fuck's sake, Debbie. Spit it out. Just tell me!"

Debbie flinched at the anger displayed across his face, looked down, and vomited the words out in a rush.

"That truck is the vehicle I saw run our daughter over. That man is the same man I saw driving it."

Nathan's head rattled back in forth in shock and recoiled as if he had been slapped. He looked at her with a combination of stark disbelief and dreadful acceptance battling it out on his face.

"No," he said. "For fuck's sake, no. No. No!" He could not look at her in that moment. He looked down, away, up, and around but not at her. A groan escaped his lips.

Still looking away, Nathan spoke.

"How sure are you?" One question, nothing else.

"Oh god, baby. I'm so sure I puked at the sight of it. It knocked me on my ass. I don't think I've ever been so sure about anything in my entire life. Down to my bones…in my marrow. Nothing could convince me otherwise."

Nathan's eyes squeezed shut, and his neck tightened. Pressing his chin into his chest, he grinded it back and forth.

"No. No. No. No." He spoke it like a mantra, in hope it would reshape the reality before him, even though he never believed in that kind of new-age bullshit.

It didn't help.

He raised his eyes to meet hers. His bottom lip curled upward in disdain, nostrils flaring, head shaking side to side in abject frustration and disgust. He struggled to open his mouth and speak to her.

"*How?*" finally exited his mouth. "How the *fuck* can that be true?"

"I don't know," she said, her words a faint whisper.

"And what the fuck does it mean?" The question popped into his head and he spit it out.

"I've been afraid to really consider what it means," Debbie admitted to Nathan. "It was six months before we moved here. It was *why* we moved here, for god's sake. So, does that mean *something* has been manipulating our lives to lead us here? To *bring* Martin here?"

The mere concept pierced her heart with a terror she could not fully comprehend or give voice to, a terror that refused to find true expression in any form but pure, primal panic. It seized her like a lion biting down on the throat of the gazelle. The image flashed before her eyes. But the lion's eyes bled black and the tender flesh looked more like a child than a gazelle. Debbie snatched up the bottle of Scotch and gulped the burning liquid. Four quick mouthfuls down the hatch.

She paced around the living room, unable to remain still. She ran her hands through her hair as if the fear were dripping from her pores and she might wipe off the excess, then cast it off.

"And I haven't even told you the crazy-ass urban legends surrounding what happened that I learned today!"

Debbie blurted it out before she had time to think about Nathan's response and reconsider.

Nathan rose and rushed to her, wrapped his arms around her, and hugged her tight to his chest.

"What urban legends?" he asked, not so much because he really wanted to hear them or might believe them, but because he knew his wife needed someone to share the burden of knowledge with. She needed him, her husband, to bear the load with her.

Debbie recounted everything she could recall the librarian said. Nathan held her and swayed back and forth. The information, in light of everything else, was shocking, even if his anti-supernatural sensibilities butted up against the story. It nagged at his subconscious and chanted, "What If?" to him repeatedly. The same fear plaguing Debbie burrowed through his mind too, but he felt stronger while touching her. Comforting her helped him as well.

"We're going to figure this out, okay? We'll figure it out. We'll figure it out."

He had no faith in his own words, however. He found no hope in them. But it took courage for him to speak them because if God was real, He certainly knew Nathan did *not* want to figure this spiritual mystery out, not wholeheartedly anyway. The philosophical and spiritual ramifications would crush the worldview he clung to and crush him as well by a long-repressed proxy.

The rest of the night passed in relative silence and with much Scotch. Debbie informed Nathan that they would be picking up Martin the next morning, but she wasn't up to broaching the subject of her conversation with the doctor. Not yet. She decided to save it for first thing in the morning.

When they went to bed, they both slept the sleep of the dead.

DECEMBER 22

Debbie told Nathan what the doctor said over breakfast the following morning. He just stared at her, and for a second, she could not tell whether he was going to agree with the doc or back her.

"You gotta be fucking kidding me!" he exclaimed. "That fat bastard is blaming you?"

Nathan was incredulous. Debbie was beyond relieved.

"So, he just accepted whatever Martin told him as true, did he?"

"Pretty much," Debbie said. "I didn't even argue with him. I knew if I said too much about what I suspected, I'd sound crazy."

Nathan shook his head.

"Moth-er-fucker."

An intense loathing for the doctor oozed from Nathan's voice.

"When we pick up Martin, I am going to tell that mother-fucker where to stick his bullshit diagnosis," Nathan declared.

"No," Debbie cut in. "Do not stand up for me. Just let me take my lumps. I want this doc talkative, not defending himself. We need to get as much info out of him about Martin's behavior and what he told the doctor as possible."

Nathan didn't like it, but he knew she was right.

"Okay," he begrudgingly agreed.

DEBBIE WAS BOTH THANKFUL AND ANXIOUS WHEN THEY left the doctor's office, thankful to be away from that condescending bastard telling her everything was her fault and anxious to have her son around her again. She did not trust him. She could not feel comfortable around him. It was like having a predator in the house and wondering exactly when it would get hungry and pounce. Or knowing you had a sleeper terrorist in your house planning his attack but there was no one who believed you and you possessed no means to get rid of him.

It was a terrible position of powerlessness. And not just a subjective sensation. This was her objective reality.

She had no choice but to let her son back in the house, even though she was convinced the boy was a stranger now. She saw no trace of her Martin, only this Malachi child. He was a foreigner. She tried to feign sorrow at her actions and appear to agree with the doctor. She treated the Martin imposter with kindness and made the food he wanted, the way he wanted it; however, the hate never left his eyes. In fact, it was joined by a look of satisfaction at her subservient demeanor, at the admission of her wrong. But she knew beyond a doubt there was no forgiveness in those eyes. None at all.

During the day, Martin spent much of his time in his room. He dragged all the toys from the inner closet out into his bedroom and found a place for each of them to sit on display when he wasn't playing with them. One time, he came downstairs to use the laptop and refine his Christmas wishlist further, but afterward, he went up to his room to play there.

Debbie could not stop thinking about how they arrived in this nightmare. All the contributing factors. And one factor was gnawing at her more than any other.

How in the fuck did no one tell us about this house's past before we signed the papers?

The more Debbie considered how Marcus and Blair Gentry, her home's prior owners, obviously knew something about the Barber murders and the ongoing paranormal troubles but said nothing to her about it, the more infuriated she became.

"Ggrrrrrr," Debbie growled as she looked through their mortgage paperwork, hoping to find a phone number.

After much searching, the only thing she could find was the landline number, which was now her own. Debbie dialed information and crossed her fingers as she read off their name and the nearby city she remembered them moving to. A few seconds later, the computer voice read her the number. She copied it down, keyed it in, and stepped outside to make sure her conversation would be out of Martin's earshot. On the third ring, she heard someone pick up on the other end.

"Hello," a female voice said.

"Hello," Debbie began. "Is this Blair Gentry I'm speaking to?"

"Umm...who's asking?" The lady sounded instinctively evasive.

"It's Debbie Loch, Blair," she said, blunt as a hammer and with a hint of malice. "We need to talk. Particularly, we need to talk about the first day we met. How when my son said your son asked him to play and you said he was sick, and it would be best if we waited in our minivan. Kind of odd, in retrospect, since I found out you don't even have a son. You know something about the spirit in this house, don't you, Blair? You knew about it that day."

Debbie was on a roll and didn't give Blair a chance to interrupt.

"How could you sell us that damned house when you knew we had children?"

Debbie had to pause to prevent herself from crying. Silence reigned on both ends.

"Dammit, Blair," Debbie demanded at last. "Say something!"

"I can't," the woman said, stoic and indifferent to Debbie's pain. "Talk to the real estate agent all you like, but I have nothing to say."

"You bitch!" Debbie said, trying not to yell. "You knew about the murdered family, the rumors, and the ghost of their son. Didn't you? You had to know your house was haunted! Otherwise, you wouldn't have led us to believe you had a son when Martin said a boy asked him to play."

"I have no comment," Blair insisted. "Now, do not call me again. Goodbye."

A click resounded in Debbie's ear as the line disconnected. She cussed and redialed, but it only went to voicemail. Debbie left a scathing message telling Blair just how much of a piece of shit human being she was. The message timed out and turned off on her mid-sentence, which frustrated her further. Debbie hit end on her phone and leaned against the door while she breathed in deep and blew out the air forcefully multiple times, trying to relax before going back inside.

DEBBIE LET MARTIN BE UNTIL IT WAS TIME TO CALL him to the dinner table. They ate without talking. Martin returned to his room. Debbie and Nathan put a movie on they had seen before to try and present an appearance of normality.

They had no idea of the nightmare lurking in wait for them, crouching right at their bedroom door.

DEBBIE AND NATHAN MADE SURE MARTIN BRUSHED HIS teeth and got in bed. They told him they loved him even though both felt the child in their house was not really their son, couldn't really be trusted or loved. When they said they loved him, it was more a statement to the hidden son within who was secluded somewhere, held captive perhaps by the callous-eyed little bastard smirking at them.

The look, the sardonic grin, they sent a shiver through Debbie she was unable to shake as she and Nathan walked down the hall to their bedroom. Nathan slipped into his boxers while Debbie pulled a white lace nightie over her head. Once in bed, all they wanted to do was curl up and hold each other, to create a stronghold against the storm hammering their lives.

Nathan fell asleep first. Debbie was almost asleep when their door creaked open a few inches, a shaft of light from the hallway piercing the darkness of their room. She roused and looked toward the entrance. She expected to see Martin there, asking for a glass of water, like he would at times, but there was nothing.

She squinted at the light, searching for Martin's shadow or a silhouette to appear at the door.

Nothing.

"Martin?" Debbie called out, her voice faltering, quivering

with trepidation. A chill nagged at the primordial part of her brain, something instinctive, urging her to flee.

When the silhouette finally appeared, it wasn't at the door. It was climbing up on the foot of the bed. And it was too small to be Martin.

Debbie lunged for her bedside lamp, twisting the switch to cast light throughout the room and causing Nathan to jerk awake.

What Debbie saw froze her in disbelief. It was surreal, dream-like, made her question her own senses.

Clambering up onto their bed was the green Stretch Monster and the Stretch X-Ray Monster with its honey-colored body and see-through skin revealing the organs within. She gaped at the sight; their movements were reminiscent of old Ray Harryhausen stop-motion films. Not quite stilted but not perfectly smooth either. Their faces seemed to sneer at her as they approached, and the eyes were full of murderous intent.

"What in the fuck?" Nathan muttered, not accepting what his own eyes testified to.

There was a loud crash as the door flew open all the way and the overhead light buzzed to life, the bulbs glowing brighter than normal. An electrical energy of sorts charged the air with a current that tickled their flesh and made their bodies tingle.

Martin stood in the doorway. Toys swarmed around him and flowed into the room, followed by a mass of papers fluttering like a horde of bats fleeing their den. Each page carried the image of a monster made with the toy Martin loved so much. Both Debbie and Nathan gawked at the insane spectacle unfolding before them but were not allowed the opportunity to inspect their son.

Stretch Monster lunged forward and leaped, diving head-long at Debbie. Its bony skull slammed into her forehead, knocking her back against the headboard. Little hands swelled in size and began pummeling Debbie's face with a bestial rage, snarls and barks emanating from the creature as it attacked.

Nathan reached for the Stretch Monster, but a honey-colored limb encircled his wrist and jerked. His eyes spotted the Stretch X-Ray figure, both arms elongated far beyond their normal stature. One held Nathan fast while the other anchored itself to a footboard post, pulling him farther away from Debbie. Its organs and brain were glowing in various colors, pulsing bright then fading and pulsing again.

Nathan saw the *Jaws* game swimming through the air above them. It circled above his head, then turned and darted for Debbie. He strained with all his might, but the Stretch X-Ray figure did not budge. Its job was clear: keep Nathan out of the way. He glanced back at Debbie.

She was on her knees now, the Stretch Monster riding her back. Both its arms wrapped around her throat and squeezed. It gnawed at her skull, head turning side to side, grunting and growling as it attempted to find a way to break through, its mouth too tiny to exert sufficient force.

Debbie hacked and gagged, struggling to breathe. The arms constricted ever tighter, cutting her wind and blood flow off. She bowed forward, hands clawing at the toy's arms, searching for any purchase she might find. Jaws missed her on its first pass as her head dropped. It swam off through the air to circle back for another attack. Debbie dug her fingers in, jamming them in between the creature's skin and her own, buying herself seconds more before she started to black out. She wheezed, sucking air in with a jagged inhalation.

Her mind scrambled for a way to fight back. She turned around, putting her back toward the headboard, and fell back, flailing her head into the wood. The impact rattled her skull and spine, but the Stretch Monster took the brunt of force. She leaned forward and did it again and again and again. Stars sparkled in her fading vision, but she saw Jaws come zipping at her. Mouth opened wide, it rolled on its side and darted in, chomping down on her face. Plastic teeth dug into both her cheeks, its gaping maw covering her mouth. Its tail fin thrashed as it attempted to maul Debbie and further inhibit her breathing.

Nathan watched in helpless terror as his wife fought for her life. In a desperate move, he planted his feet on the footboard and threw all his weight backward, arching his back and heaving against it with one explosive motion. He felt it stretch as he extended his body. He grabbed his bound wrist and, leaning forward, curled it toward his mouth.

He bit down on the arm binding his. A bitter-tasting gel filled his mouth and oozed around his lips. He gnawed at it like a starving man biting through meat on a bone. Except there was no bone. Nathan managed to chew through the toy's flesh, severing it.

Flying back, he landed on the bed next to Debbie and scrambled to claw and tug at the Stretch Monster choking his wife. Both hands found a purchase at last, wrapping around the hard-plastic head. He peeled it back and away from Debbie. One of Nathan's thumbs slid inside the monster's mouth by accident. It chomped down. Hard. Nathan screamed but refused to let go.

Gritting his teeth, he continued to pull. A flurry of tiny hits pelted both sides of his head. He ducked and bobbed to one side, trying to see what struck him while not letting go of the monster.

What in the hell? his brain cried out at the sight. The bizarre world he'd been thrust into was only getting stranger. A floating blue robot man was attacking him from the left and a red robot man from the right. He recognized them from his early childhood —Rock 'Em Sock 'Em Robots. They ran at him on the air, fists punching straight ahead. One of them struck him directly in the eye, causing him to wince and cry out.

It hurt. It hurt a lot, but he focused on saving Debbie and pulled with all his might, twisting the monster's head back and forth. Without warning, it popped off, and Nathan fell away.

The head hissed and snarled at him. He tossed it across the

room and crawled back toward Debbie. The beast's body was not giving up its efforts to kill his wife, despite the loss of its head. Something wrapped around one ankle, and Nathan knew it was the Stretch X-Ray monster trying to hold him back again. He clawed his way forward enough to grab the Stretch Monster's headless body and pull Debbie to him.

She struggled to breathe, choking sounds barely escaping her throat. Nathan was desperate and did what he had to. He dug the fingers of his right hand around the creature's upper arm and gripped the neck stump with his other. He pulled it to his face and bit down where the upper arm inserted into the shoulder. Nathan took bite after bite until he chomped his way through the limb, severing it, then he changed sides and began chewing through the other arm.

Three tiny points of skin on his back flared with a searing pain as the Shogun Warrior's missiles struck him all at once and lodged in his flesh. Matchbox cars zipped all about the room, slamming into his back and head. A Tie Fighter helmed by a Darth Vader action figure buzzed by his right ear, making shooting noises. Miniature lasers stung his skin and burned.

Nathan ignored it all, knowing he was close to freeing Debbie. He mauled the limb with his teeth, spitting out chunks of rubberized flesh and gel, then biting again. A thin and long object struck his leg, his back, his head. It split his flesh.

The second arm gave way and tore loose from the joint. Nathan ripped the Stretch Monster's body away from Debbie and spun around to see what was hurting him. He came face to face with the Shogun Warrior, its metal grill of a face grinning at him as it swung its plastic sword at his face. He reflexively raised his hands, and the Stretch Monster took the sword strike square.

Nathan kicked out with his free leg, sending the warrior flying off the bed and across the room. He slung the Stretch Monster at it and returned to Debbie, pulling the arms from around her neck and throwing them aside.

Now that she was able to breathe, she shrieked at the Jaws attached to her face. Nathan gripped both sides of its mouth. Prying them apart, he pulled the plastic shark off her and slammed it against the headboard repeatedly until the body cracked and shattered. Debbie clutched at her face with both hands while he glanced over his shoulder to check on the Shogun Warrior. It was clambering to its feet, eyes focused on him.

He dug his fingers around the Stretch X-Ray's flesh and managed to pry its arm off his leg. He gripped the creature's hand and rolled off the bed, winding up and swinging the toy like a flailing weapon. It hit the Shogun Warrior square, knocking it across the room into a wall. Nathan slung the X-Ray toy toward the door, dove across the bed to his side, and retrieved the baseball bat he kept leaned in the corner against his nightstand.

Nathan picked the bat up and rushed the Shogun Warrior while it was struggling to right itself once more. He didn't give it a chance. He swung the bat with vicious force, over and over again, until the plastic splintered and broke, arms and legs snapping off, head and torso fractured and smashed inward.

When he stopped swinging at last, Nathan stood above it, breathing heavy, bat dragging the floor, his grip limp.

But it wasn't over.

The air teemed with chaos. The evil Micronaut leader, Baron Karza, and his trusted steed, Andromeda, were combined into a mechanical centaur. They flew about and shot a volley of rockets at Nathan that he barely evaded, then he countered with a swing that caught the Micronaut off guard. Magnetic parts sprayed across the room. Action figures and cars flew about in crisscrossing paths. The *Millennium Falcon* twisted and turned, banking left then right, barrel rolling and diving in between them all. Little robots buzzed and walked as they moved through the space above Nathan's head on their own.

The papers stopped flying about and dropped to the floor. The little monsters, artistically rendered, peeled themselves away from their 8.5" x 11" prisons. They transformed from two-dimensional figures into fully fleshed three-dimensional creatures about seven inches tall when they finished standing upright. They ran toward Debbie. She shrieked, but as the first ones leaped onto the bed, she kicked out, launching them against a wall. Nathan drop-kicked the closest one, then began stomping others and swinging the bat more like a golf club, splattering them on impact. Shattered corpses thudded as they impacted a wall, crashed through a window, or sailed into the bathroom.

Debbie picked up one in each hand and slung them in no particular direction. Anywhere away from her was fine. But as she watched their trajectory, she saw something else leaping and bounding from one toy to another, making its way from the shadows toward her with uncanny agility. It was black except for an elongated white skull and chrome teeth gleaming in the light. A part of her brain recognized what it was even though her conscious mind did not. She experienced a surge of terror as it closed the distance, nimbler than a cat, its body lithe and deadly. It leaped onto the *Millennium Falcon* as it made another pass and launched itself at her, hands and feet spread in front, claws and teeth bared.

Debbie stuck out a palm to fend it off. The Alien toy gripped her fingers and dug its feet into the crook of her elbow. There was a stabbing pain as its inner mouth shot out and drove through the center of her palm, then retracted, ripping flesh loose. A scream of pain erupted from Debbie, and she shook her hand while flailing at it with the other. The Alien refused to let go.

Nathan scrambled over to Debbie, dropped the bat, and gripped the Alien with both hands and yanked it off of her. It shrieked at him and hissed, twisting in his grip. It felt like flexible steel to him, unyielding. He threw it against the nearest wall, where it clung for a moment and then launched itself back into the air, moving toward Debbie again. Snatching up the bat from the floor, Nathan took a deep step and swung, the bat connecting squarely with the Alien.

Fluid sprayed on impact, striking both Nathan and Debbie. Their skin burned, the acid eating little pockmarks in their skin and dissolving holes in their clothing. The effect only lasted a few seconds, but it was enough to cause surface injuries.

The Alien landed on the floor and sizzled and popped as its blood ran onto the carpet and ate its way through to the wooden flooring beneath.

"Noooooooooooo!"

Both Nathan and Debbie looked toward the sound. Martin stood, or rather floated, inches above the floor, arms outstretched to each side, head thrown back, mouth agape. Both eyes rolled back in his head to reveal only the whites, and he continued to scream beyond the natural limits of his tiny lungs. A dark, pitch-like substance began to ooze from beneath Martin's eyelids, crawling more than running down his cheeks. It leaked out of his nose as well, gathering on his upper lip.

"If I can't hurt *you,*" he said, "then I'll hurt *him.*"

Martin opened his mouth wide and didn't stop there. His lower jaw stretched unnaturally toward his chest even as Debbie reached her hands out toward her son. Wider and wider it gaped, the oval of his mouth growing longer and longer.

Nathan and Debbie watched in abject horror as their son's body betrayed itself. There were two snapping pops, hollow clunking noises, as his jaw unhinged, dislocating from the joints. It lurched downward, crooked and dangling. The corners of his mouth split and ripped apart, their limits of elasticity exceeded. Blood flowed from the torn flesh.

And then it was over. Martin's eyes closed. His body wilted and fell to the floor in an unconscious heap.

Nathan's mind couldn't help but think that his son's collapse looked much like those little toys where you push the button and the figure goes from standing tall to a jumble of fallen limbs splayed out on a plastic base in an instant.

All Debbie could think was, *My baby boy is dead.*

DEBBIE RUSHED TO MARTIN, DROPPING TO HER KNEES and bending over his crumpled body. She checked his vitals. Head tilted sideways over his mouth, she felt for the warmth of breath. At first, cold air hissed out into her ear, but after a few seconds, it turned warm. She pressed her index and middle fingers to the boy's wrist and was relieved to detect a fast but steady pulse. One hand flew to her mouth as she tried to stifle a sob, while the other brushed Martin's hair back from his forehead.

"Is he okay?" Nathan asked, concern causing his voice to tremble.

"I think so. Can you pick him up and put him on our bed?"

Nathan nodded and did so, scooping Martin up gently, then placing him on the bed. He grabbed a pillow and tucked it beneath his boy's head.

They both stood back, staring at Martin, then about the room at the carnage. Broken toys were strewn all over—shattered, smashed, torn, dismembered. Blood and gelatinous goo of various sorts was splattered across the floors and walls. The remains of things that should not be real argued otherwise.

Nathan could not deny what just happened. It was no dream. He would not be waking up. And his worldview, his beliefs, were in no better condition than the toys. Broken, collapsed, imploded beneath the weight of a revelation both unbelievably and undeniably true.

"What the fuck are we supposed to do with this, Deb?"

Nathan was overwhelmed and in a state of rational brain-lock. The gross disparity of what he believed to be true and what he had just struggled through were so far, far apart.

Debbie touched her throat and face, confirming the injuries were indeed there and not a figment of her imagination.

Their predicament was too large to tackle all at once. Nathan tried to focus on something his brain could accept and deal with. They all had injuries, and their bedroom was a complete mess.

He voiced his thoughts aloud.

"One, how are we going to get medical treatment without raising a shit-ton of red flags? And two, we need to clean this house before anyone comes in here."

The act of speaking his concerns helped him focus.

"We've got to take Martin to the ER!" Debbie said, her voice hoarse.

Nathan looked at her. There was no doubt Debbie loved her son.

She's in mom mode, he mentally noted. *Only thinking about Martin, not the repercussions once we step outside this house.*

Debbie's body and mind persevered through the physical abuse and insanity of their circumstances by sheer will alone. Mom mode, the mama bear within her, was like an enormous shot of adrenaline, enabling her to push beyond what the normal limits of both body and mind would allow. She had to take care of her son. That was all that mattered right now.

Nathan turned to Debbie, squeezed her upper arms with tender care, and looked her in the eye. When he spoke, he knew it would come off as a bit patronizing, but he saw the wild look in her eyes and knew he had to make their circumstances abundantly clear.

"Baby, there is *no* story we can make up that will even remotely make sense of our injuries. You look like a boa constrictor wrapped around your neck and squeezed while a small shark gnawed on your face and someone spritzed you with acid. I look like I was bound by one wrist and ankle, then punched in the eye and head, hacked with a dull machete, bitten, burned with a cigarette, and spritzed with acid as well. And Martin...how in the hell do we account for him dislocating his entire jaw and tearing the corners of his mouth? If we go to the ER, we're both going to get locked up, maybe committed, and Martin will be taken from us tonight. Period. There is no version of us going to the ER that does not end like that."

He rubbed her arms as she stared at his chest, not answering.

"Deb? Did you hear me? Do you understand what I'm telling you?"

That got her. She shrugged her shoulders and turned away.

"I heard you, dammit. And I'm not daft. I understand."

Nathan absorbed the criticism. If the condescending bullshit jerked her out of her mental torpor, he was okay with her being pissed off at him.

"So, what are we going to do, then," she asked without looking at Nathan, "if we can't go to the doctor?"

Nathan did not answer right away. He was still brainstorming, but when he did come up with a course of action, he considered it a bit more because he knew how bad it sounded.

"Well?" she asked and turned around to face him, a sarcastic edge in her voice.

"You're not going to like it," he said.

"Just spit it out, for god's sake."

Debbie was not in the mood for kid gloves.

"All right," Nathan began, "first, we take care of Martin ourselves. I've dislocated my jaw before. You know that. Happens every now and then ever since that injury years ago, and I pop it back in myself. Kids' ligaments are like rubber. Should go back in a lot easier than mine. We do it right now while he's out. Won't be as painful. Then we'll disinfect the tears in his mouth, superglue them together, and put steri-strips on the outside to reinforce the glue."

Debbie's mouth made an O as she started to object, but Nathan kept talking.

"It'll work," he assured her. "They use something just like it in ERs all the time. I think it's called derma-glue. I had it used on me when I split the skin under my eye a few years back. It's basically the same chemical compound as super glue. I've read of people using that in a pinch, and I definitely think we're in a hell of a pinch right now, hon. There's super glue in the garage. I can run out there now and grab it, and we have steri-strips too."

Debbie's own jaw dropped. She looked ready to punch Nathan for merely having the idea. He saw the anger on her face.

"You got a better idea?"

He cocked an eyebrow at her in challenge. She wanted to smack it straight, but despite her frantic struggle to think of a more palatable option, she could not come up with anything. Debbie dropped her head and shook it back and forth in resigned agreement to his proposal.

"What about us?" she asked.

"Well, I'm not too bad. Most of my injuries are nothing time, triple-antibiotic ointment, and New Skin won't take care of. The small cuts can be super glued. You're more difficult than me, babe, but no worse than Martin's mouth. You've got significant cuts on your face. Deep enough to need stitches, but I can use the super glue on you too. Besides that, we've got everything else here, including hydrogen peroxide to clean the wounds first."

Nathan crossed his arms, looked at Debbie, and waited for an answer. He didn't appear to anticipate a positive response, so it surprised him when she conceded to his plan without any further debate.

"Okay," she said. "Let's do this. Martin first."

Nathan nodded once and moved toward the bed. He climbed up, sat down above Martin with one leg straddling each side of his son. He cradled the boy's head and pulled him up so his upper back rested on Nathan's lap and Martin's head jutted into his stomach.

"Okay," Nathan instructed Debbie, "grab his arms and fold them across his chest. Hold them there, just in case he wakes up and tries to grab my hands."

Nathan looked down at his son's jaw, the alien abnormality of its current position. The angles alone made his gut do belly flops. His mouth salivated. His throat contracted. He closed his eyes. It seemed insane to try and do this instead of seeking a doctor's aid.

There's no other choice, he told himself. *There is absolutely no other choice.*

His forehead broke out in a sweat, and he wiped it with the back of his wrist.

C'mon, Nathan. Suck it up and cowboy up!

It wasn't much as far as positive self-talk went, but it was enough. Nathan opened his eyes, cupped Martin's chin with his left hand, and pulled the boy's head tight to his stomach while placing his right palm on the right side of Martin's jaw joint. He pulled forcefully on Martin's chin with one hand and pressed against the ball joint with the other.

Nothing. No click. No pop. Nathan winced at his initial lack of success but refused to give up. He kept pressure against the joint and gave short jerky pulls on Martin's chin. Once, twice, three times he tried. Finally, on the fourth try, he exerted more force and both heard and felt the pop as that side of his son's jaw clicked back into place. He switched his grip, right hand at chin and left hand over Martin's left jaw joint now, and repeated the process. It only took two tries for that side to slip back into place with a loud clunking sound.

Nathan exhaled with a big sigh and wiped his brow again.

"Oh, thank god," he said without thinking. "Okay, baby, grab some hydrogen peroxide from the bathroom along with a Q-tip and put some in the corners of his mouth and let it dry. I'll run down to the garage and grab the super glue."

Debbie nodded and headed for the bathroom cabinet as Nathan headed downstairs. She caught a glimpse of her face in the mirror as she opened it. Dried blood and numerous open cuts marred her face. She didn't glance in the mirror again.

By the time she finished applying the medication to Martin's mouth and assessing his breathing and pulse once more for good measure, Nathan returned, super glue in one hand and a chair in the other. He sat down on the bed and laid Martin's head across his thigh. He clipped off the super glue tip, keeping it as long and narrow at the opening as possible. One side at a time, he spread the super glue along the tear in Martin's mouth and squeezed the tissue together. He held it in place for a couple of minutes, then repeated on the opposite side. When done, he took out the steri-strips and placed three on each side of Martin's face. Patch job complete, he laid his son's head gently on a pillow.

Nathan grabbed the chair and set it down in front of the bed before walking into the bathroom. He reached in the cabinet and under the counter, gathering cotton swabs, triple-antibiotic ointment, and the New Skin.

"All right, baby," he instructed her, "grab that hydrogen peroxide and take a seat in the chair."

She did so, and he sat down on the bed across from her, putting himself a little higher than Debbie and making it easier to treat her face.

Nathan tended to his wife with delicate care, first cleansing each wound with peroxide-soaked cotton swabs. She cringed a little at the application of the peroxide, but the pain was far less than if he had used rubbing alcohol. By the time Nathan finished with the last cut, the first one was dry. One at a time, he squeezed the glue into the cuts, pushed her skin together, and held it there for a minute before releasing. Each one held without spreading apart. He cleansed her other injuries with the peroxide as well. He coated the tiny acid pockmarks with New Skin and let them dry.

When he was done, he declared, "I think you're good. Go look in the mirror."

Debbie walked back into the bathroom, leery of what she might see, but was surprised at how good a job Nathan had done. There were several thin red lines where Nathan pushed the skin back together and glued it, but no rippled or jagged areas. Excess glue oozed over the edges in places, but that was to be expected and would peel off later.

Nathan took care of the wounds on his own body he was able to see. When Debbie returned, she helped him tend to the others.

When they were done, each one put on a shirt and pants. Nathan scooped up Martin and held him while Debbie stripped the sheets and bedspread. Nathan placed Martin back in the center of the bed, and Debbie covered him with a fresh blanket. Nathan and Debbie laid down on the bed with Martin between them. They were both far too tired to clean up the mess now, and even though the fleshy remains of certain toys were already beginning to reek, they agreed to let it all wait until morning. As she lay next to Martin, Debbie stroked his hair and whispered her love to him.

Nathan was exhausted and fell asleep, but Debbie was unable. Her brain would not stop considering what they might do next. Plus, she would not be convinced her son was okay until he woke up.

MARTIN SAT IN THE TINY SECRET ROOM BEYOND HIS closet, or at least that was what it looked like to him. He was smart enough to know Malachi had trapped him; however, he could not be sure just how it was done or where he was for sure.

He wondered if he was stuck in a version of the room in some other dimension, but he couldn't remember sleeping; and he was certain he had not eaten or drank anything, nor did he feel hungry or thirsty. This led Martin to believe he was not physically present. It was a dream of sorts, perhaps trapped in a recess in a distant corner of his mind. He had played with the toys Malachi had brought him. That was it. Nothing more, nothing less.

Until minutes before when anguish became Martin's reality.

The ball joints where his jaw inserted into both sides of his skull throbbed with incredible pain and radiated a razor-sharp agony inward. It made him feel as if metal skewers had been shoved in each ear. At the same time, the corners of his mouth burned. The torment was more than a child should be asked to bear.

The boy collapsed on one side, assuming a fetal position as both hands clutched his face. He cried out, cried for his mother, his father, for release, begged for an end to his suffering and the bitter distress he was desperate to endure no further.

But no one answered. No one brought comfort to him. No one reached down from Heaven to quench his lips and ease the pain of his affliction. Nor did a merciful guardian angel come to his rescue.

Alone. Martin was alone and helpless before Malachi's twisted power. No comfort. No release. It seemed as if he had been suddenly thrust into the bowels of Hell and a pitchfork plunged into his head.

How long it lasted, he could not tell, but it ended with a touch, when a tiny hand gently touched his cheek.

"Marty, don't cry," the little voice encouraged him. "Please don't cry."

Marty? he thought, confused. Only one person had ever called him that.

"Bella?" he mumbled in disbelief and tried to sit up. The pain had ended, but a ghost-like sensation lingered on. He opened his eyes to look upon his savior.

Bella knelt beside him, her white sundress and pale skin an ethereal vision of beauty and one he feared might vanish at any moment. Martin looked into her tiny eyes and wept for the loss of his sibling once more. Her eyes appeared full of love and empathy but also sorrow, as if she had come to learn things in this here-after little girls like her should never be schooled in.

Martin gripped the hand that touched his face while reaching out to place his other hand upon her cheek as well.

"Sis," he said, trying not to weep. "I miss you, so much." He glanced around. "How are you here? Is this a dream?"

She smiled at Martin. "Silly boy," she said to him. "It's not a dream, and it's not real. It's not Heaven, but more like Hell instead. We're caught in between," she explained. "My spirit. Your mind. The Master keeps us here."

"Master?" Martin asked. "You mean Malachi?"

Bella shook her head.

"No," she said. "Malachi is but a puppet. The Master's hand moves him, empowers him, and allows him to abuse you. Mom and Dad, too."

Martin struggled to process the meaning of her words.

"Who is this Master?"

"I cannot say," said Bella. "All I can call him is the Master. Don't ask his name again. He'll hear us and hurt me if you do."

Fear spread through her eyes like lightning splintering across the night sky.

"Okay," Martin agreed. "I won't ask who he is. Can you tell me how you got here?"

She smiled and held a finger to her lips.

"I snuck in here while he's away."

"But how did you find me?" Martin questioned further.

"Your cries of pain led me here," she said matter of fact. "As long as you were left in a room of delights, I could not find you. Suffering opened the way and called to me. I followed your tears, and here I am."

She grabbed the hand he held against her cheek.

"I've missed you so much, Marty. You and Mom and Dad. I've missed you all. I've been trapped with the Master ever since the man in the truck hit me. He stole my soul and brought me to the Master."

Bella hung her head and sniffled.

"I wept when y'all moved into this house. I knew then the Master wanted you too."

She looked back at Martin. Vaporous tears crept down her cheeks.

Martin cried for his sister and all she had suffered, but something seemed off about her. She seemed smarter than her age.

"Bella," Martin said, "is it really you? You sound so much older."

Hurt flashed across Bella's face at the sound of Martin's doubt, but then her countenance softened. She understood.

"I'm sorry to confuse you, Marty," Bella began. "Once you're dead, the mind expands, matures. I'm not limited by the number of brain cells I can access or the normal constraints of time and learning. Plus...I have seen...and experienced things beyond my years."

Martin felt sick at the implication of her last words.

"What has this Master done to you?" he asked but feared the answer.

Bella winced at the question, the answer a wilderness of terrors she did not want to relive.

"Bad things," she said. "Sometimes for rituals, sometimes in trade with other devils and beasts. I am a spirit. I'm...eternal... reusable."

Bella gulped and closed her eyes.

"But sometimes he is merciful and allows me to forget...

forget what is done to me...and what I am forced to do. For that, I am thankful."

Martin felt fury bloom in his heart along with a dreadful and helpless sense of doom. There was nothing he could do for his sister just as there was nothing he was capable of doing for himself. He wished to flail out against this Master as well as Malachi, but it all seemed so futile. So hopeless.

Martin hugged his sister and pulled her tight to his chest, relishing this opportunity while it was available.

"Bella," a female voice said. "You must hurry away. The Master will return soon. I do not want to see you punished."

Martin looked up to see a woman and man kneeling on the floor whom he did not recognize. Bella gave Martin one last squeeze and kissed his cheek, then stood, pulling away from him. She turned and walked over to the lady and took her hand.

"I'm Natalie," she informed Martin, "and I will protect Bella as much as I can."

With that, Bella waved goodbye, then she and Natalie left the room, a shimmer of light and shadow remaining behind for a moment after they passed through the walls.

The man spoke. "I must warn you. Malachi will try to make you kill your parents. You must resist."

Martin shook his head in confusion.

"I would never kill my parents," the boy professed. "I love them."

"Maybe so," the man said, "but the Master is powerful, and the torments he inflicts can weaken your resolve. You will be tempted to give in."

"Who is this Master?" Martin asked.

The man's eyes narrowed to slits, and he spoke in a hushed tone.

"He is a lion, walking to and fro, seeking whom he may devour. You have seen him...in a dream. He is there, hidden, watching. That is all I can tell you."

From a distance, a purring noise reached Martin's ears. The man looked around in a panic.

"Who are you?" Martin pressed the man.

"I'm Malachi's father," he whispered.

The purr turned to a low, guttural growl that caused the very air to rumble.

"I cannot be caught," he said and fled the room without another word.

A low growl sounded again, this time closer. Martin looked around the room, ignoring the toys. Darkness lingered at the periphery instead of walls. Except for the closet door. The outline of the door glowed as if a bright light shone through the cracks from the other side. Martin stood and crept toward the door, his feet falling as silent as a house cat.

Martin waited for the lion to approach him and enter the room. The sound of paws padding along the ground, pacing back and forth, were the sounds of dread. They pounded in his head as he extended his arm, stretched his fingers, and leaned forward, weight balanced precariously on the ball of his lead foot as he reached for the doorknob. The light grew brighter on the other side. His fingers touched the metal. It was so cold it burned, but Martin wrapped each digit around the opener and twisted.

It moved a quarter of an inch and stopped with a faint click. Locked.

The lion's roar cracked like thunder above Martin's head and reverberated throughout the room. Its rumbling aftermath surrounded him, infusing the air about him with a crackling energy. At first, it shook his chest with such violence it flung him to the ground, where he crumpled, a collapsed pile of limp flesh and bone, but soon the resounding noise vibrated his whole torso as if he were a tuning fork struck against iron.

The light snuffed out in an instant. Darkness enveloped Martin. He could hear the breathing of the beast lurking nearby. He waited, cloaked in shadow, but sure he might as well have been standing on an open plain with nowhere to hide, clearly visible to any predator, yet especially to a great lion striding head and shoulders above all other creatures.

Martin shook and shivered in terror, eyes screwed shut as he waited for the gaping maw of the lion to clamp down upon the back of his neck or about his throat and carry him off like some gazelle trapped in the teeth of a great beast. But instead, the growls subsided. The padding of feet sounded once more, but they retreated. How long he held his breath, Martin did not know, but at last he sucked in air once more.

He lay still, unable to move, and wished for his mother. But all he heard was Malachi laughing somewhere in the dark.

Not long before dawn, Martin's eyelids fluttered open, and he looked at Debbie.

"Mom?" he asked. Debbie's heart leaped and raced. She smiled and kissed his forehead. Gripping one of his hands in hers, anxiety and hope bubbled up from her guts in equal measures.

"Yes, baby," she said, her voice trembling and hushed, as if whispering might prevent Malachi from hearing what she said.

"Mom?" he asked again, his voice unsure.

"It's me," she assured her baby boy. "Is that you, Martin? Is it you?"

"Yes. It's me, Mom. Where are you at?"

Martin looked right at her with eyes wide open. Debbie's stomach sank like a cinderblock thrown over a boat.

How can he not see me? Feel me? Debbie asked herself.

"Mom?" Martin said, fear growing in his voice. "Everything is black in here. I saw the light. I tried to get to it. To you. But the door was locked. The lion roared, and the light went out."

He reached out, groping blindly to touch her face.

"I can't see you, Mom!" he cried, voice turning shrill. "I can't hear you!"

Martin's body struggled to move as if constrained, despite his panic levels visibly increasing. Short, jerky movements were all his muscles managed to perform, much like a mental patient strapped down and restrained upon a bed.

"Mom!" Martin shouted in desperation. Nathan woke with a start.

"Help me, Mom!" he cried. "Help me! Malachi won't let me out! The lion won't—"

Martin's mouth clacked shut, cutting his words off. A chip of tooth bounced off Debbie's neck. Her son's eyes came into focus, fixing Debbie with their gaze, except now, they did not appear full of fear. Instead, they glinted with a devious new presence, albeit a familiar one.

Nathan lay propped up on one elbow, eyes wild, brain trying to catch up.

"Did you really think you had your baby boy back for good, Mom?" Malachi baited her. "I won't give him up that easily." He winked at her and sat up, scooted to the end of the bed, and hopped down.

"Night, night, sleep tight," Malachi said to them and walked out of the room.

Nathan stared after his son, trying to figure out what the hell it all meant, but Debbie knew. She knew the war was nowhere near over, and she knew exactly what she was going to do next.

"WHAT THE FUCK JUST HAPPENED, DEB?" NATHAN asked, heart racing yet still trying to shrug off the grogginess enveloping his brain like a dense fog.

"It was Martin for a minute!" she declared. "Our Martin! And then that damn Malachi took over. He has our son, Nate, and he won't let go. Won't leave. He teased me and tormented me all in the same act. Let me know Martin is alive and well, just trapped and afraid…and *he wants his momma.*"

Debbie's mouth contorted and trembled with her last words. She wiped her eyes.

"I don't care what you say, Nathan. I'm going to talk to a pastor, a priest, someone who can help me rip that little ghost fucker right out of our son."

Debbie stared at the door for a long time, and Nathan just watched her. He was clueless as to what to say at this point. He had no objections left. Bring on the men of God. What did they have to lose?

Debbie finally laid back down and closed her eyes. Nathan watched over her for a minute as he called the automated number at work and advised he was going to be out sick, possibly for a few days. After he hung up, he joined Debbie. Sleep washed over them both like the high tide coming in.

DECEMBER 23

Debbie woke to the feeling of something cold poking her cheek.

Poke. Poke. Poke.

Slow at first, then, when she didn't open her eyes right away, the pace increased, and the depth of penetration deepened. Her eyes fluttered open at the mild discomfort.

Malachi stood there in her son's skin, staring at her with contempt, index finger inches from her cheek.

"I want breakfast," he said. "Now."

"Okay," she said, conceding to his demand.

Debbie didn't mind. Feeding Malachi was still feeding her son. She stood and walked into the kitchen. Malachi followed and sat at the table while Debbie cooked breakfast for him plus extra for her and Nathan. Malachi ate in silence and drank his grape juice, then returned to his room.

Debbie woke Nathan with a plate of food and a glass of orange juice in bed. While he scarfed it down, she retrieved an assortment of cleaning supplies, trash bags, and a Shop Vac. Debbie started chipping away at the mountain of mess filling their bedroom. Nathan joined in after finishing breakfast, and between the two of them, they made the place look presentable within a couple of hours. But eradicating the horrible odor of miniature monster guts and goo was going to take more drastic measures.

Debbie finally simply rolled up the bedspread and sheets along with the throw rug at the end of the bed and burned them in the brick fire pit out back. She scrubbed the walls and hardwood floors with Pine Sol. The floor cleaned up adequately, but she decided the walls might need to have the wallpaper ripped off and replaced.

When the cleaning was complete, Debbie showered and dressed, then laid on the bed and surfed the net on her phone, looking for a listing of local churches. She created a short list of the best potential options that might be willing to help her.

She told Nathan she was going out but didn't say for what.

He didn't ask because he already knew.

THE CATHOLIC CHURCH, DEBBIE'S FIRST CHOICE, WAS A big no-go. The priest advised her he would need to contact someone trained to do exorcisms and they would send someone to assess Martin and determine whether they believed an exorcism was warranted or not.

"That could take days," Debbie complained. "I need something done now. Tonight!"

The priest apologized but assured her that an exorcism was an extraordinarily dangerous ritual and couldn't be performed without making sure there were no other options. Debbie thanked the man and asked him to start the process, just in case she couldn't find someone else. Though she didn't tell the man that part.

Next, she stopped by a Unitarian church down the street from the cathedral. The reverend flat-out rejected her request after gawking at her injured face. "Just to be clear, young lady," he began, then advised her that he personally didn't believe in demons and exorcisms and the like. They were nothing but a bunch of "hubbabaloo" as far as he was concerned. Debbie stared at the man and wondered if she was in the right place.

"But you're a man of God," she objected. "How can you not believe in demons?"

"Miss, demons are just a frightful metaphor for the inherent wickedness of man's heart and the depths to which his own depravity can entice and snare him. The devil doesn't make you sin and neither do demons. If one wants to know the source of his failure in God's eyes, all he need do is look in the mirror."

"Well," Debbie began, "I can agree with that to a very large degree, but don't you think there are certain situations that *do* involve genuine demons...or ghosts?"

"Oh my," the old man exclaimed and chuckled. "First demons, now ghosts? What will it be next? Werewolves and vampires? Ma'am, it seems you may have watched too much *Ghosthunters* or similar pop culture TV drivel."

Debbie's mouth dropped a little as the hackles on her back rose up. Her jaw clacked shut. She almost bit her tongue. Almost.

"Look, buddy," she started in on the reverend, "I've seen shit in the last twenty-four hours that would curl your crotch hairs and turn them gray. You'd be scrambling to scuttle your lard ass away as fast as your diabetes-bloated feet would carry you. So, fuck off! I don't need someone like you."

The man sputtered and nearly spit but couldn't get out a word before Debbie spun on the balls of her feet and walked away.

Debbie's third choice was the Pentecostal House of Holiness. It wasn't even a real church per se. It was set into a run-down strip mall and took up three storefronts. They were the only occupants. All the others were empty. She parked on the curb in front of the building behind the only other vehicle present.

When Debbie walked through the door, a little bell chimed above her head. She looked around. The sanctuary was straight ahead. Bench seats made up the majority of seating on both sides of the aisle, but there were an additional three rows of chairs on each side in the back. She figured it was to accommodate the growth the church had obviously experienced since opening. To her left was another bench-style seat, and to her right, an office. She saw a man already on his feet and walking toward her.

He was maybe six feet tall and thin. A light-skinned Black male with kind eyes and a gentle countenance. He oozed fatherly vibes, and Debbie was drawn to him at once.

"How are you doing today, ma'am? Can I help you?" He extended his hand. She took it, and before she could form an answer, he introduced himself.

"I'm Elder Hughes. Pleasure to meet you."

He shook her hand, his grip both firm and supple, his expression amiable. His voice flowed like honey, filling her ears with comfort and warmth.

"Um, pleased to meet you too. I'm Debbie. Debbie Loch."

He released her hand and folded his together at his stomach, his waist bent slightly forward as if waiting to be charged with some lawful duty.

"Well, Debbie. I'm at your service. Would you like to sit out here and talk or come into my office?"

"Well, not to be rude, but I'm not entirely sure you're the one I'm looking for," Debbie said, blushing a bit as she did so. "I'm looking for the pastor."

"Oh!" Elder Hughes rocked his head from side to side and smiled. "I am the pastor. We just don't use that terminology around here. We prefer elders and apostles. We believe it's more biblical. I'm the head elder, you might say. Teaching and preaching are my primary callings. There are other elders here at our church. Some are blessed with gifts of hospitality, planning, worship, music, and ministering to the lost or the poor and downtrodden, amongst other things. But I handle the majority of sermons and oversee Sunday school lessons and the like."

"Oh. Okay," Debbie said, feeling a little silly.

"So, what can I do to help you, Miss Debbie?" Elder Hughes asked her, his hips and upper body swaying independently, hands still clasped at his stomach, waist still bent, waiting.

"Well, I hope I've come to the right place," she said. "I hope you can help me. I already went to the local Catholic church. They told me I'd have to wait. Then I went to the Unitarian church, and the reverend there laughed at me."

"Well, Miss Debbie, I hope I can help you, and I assure you, I will not laugh at you."

Elder Hughes continued smiling, waiting for Debbie to tell him what exactly it was she needed.

"Umm," Debbie muttered. "How 'bout we sit down in your office? Is that okay?"

"Why yes, ma'am. Of course it is."

Elder Hughes turned and vanished through his office door, then appeared behind his desk as Debbie stepped in and pulled up one of the plush leather chairs he had for guests. His own chair was much less elegant.

"Okay," Debbie said, trying to find a place to start, afraid of another rejection. More than anything, she wanted a solution to her problem. Today. "Well, I guess I should just start by asking you a couple of baseline questions."

"That's fine," Elder Hughes assured her. "Whatever makes you comfortable." The genuine congeniality of the man was disconcerting in a world full of unpleasant, two-faced snakes in the grass. The warmth in his eyes was genuine, as well as his intentional attention to her as a real person. A quiet joy emanated from his facial expressions and rolled off his lips with every word he spoke. It was uncanny. But she already felt comforted before speaking a word.

"All right, then," Debbie began. "First one. Do you believe in demons?" She looked at him, studying his features for that initial response.

"Oh, yes, ma'am," he responded, relaxing his hands on what little belly extended out as he leaned back in his chair. "I certainly do."

"Okay. Good. That's good. That's farther than I got with the Unitarian reverend." Debbie laughed a nervous laughter, but one which released her nervousness, not simply put it on display. "Do you believe in ghosts? I know a lot of Christians don't."

"Well, as a matter of fact, I do believe in them. I take my bible seriously, Miss Debbie. When God commanded the children of Israel to not speak with the dead, I think it is logical to infer that He gave them that command because it was possible to do so through some forms of witchcraft. And when the bible tells us the witch at Endor called up the spirit of Samuel and spoke with him, I believe it was indeed his spirit, his ghost, if you will. So, yes. I absolutely believe in ghosts."

Debbie breathed a sigh of relief. Her muscles released the tension knotting them together. Her arms sank into the arms of the chair as her whole body settled into the seat, conforming to it.

"What else do you believe about ghosts?" she asked.

"Well, in the Old Testament, the dead were said to sleep. But when Christ rose from the dead, he carried all those souls with him as he ascended to Heaven. That being said, there are those today who still believe the dead sleep. Righteous and unrighteous alike. I'll grant that it's possible for the unrighteous to sleep, but I believe those who believe in Christ do not."

He quoted the scripture that backed up his opinion by way of a slight paraphrase.

"'To be absent from the body is to be present with the Lord.'

That's what Paul said, 2 Corinthians 5:8. So, I consider it possible that ghosts are the souls of the damned. At times they sleep. At times, something may wake them up. They stir. It varies how active they are or how menacing they choose to be depending on their life here on earth, what kind of person they were, and what type of personal demons they carried to their death. That's what I think, anyway. The bible doesn't give any real guidance on the subject beyond the fact that they can exist."

Debbie sat captivated.

"That's an interesting take on the subject," she said. "A good one, it seems. Okay. That leads me to my next question. Do you believe people can be possessed, and if so, do you believe in exorcisms?"

"Hmm." Elder Hughes lifted his hands for the first time and made a steeple with his fingers over his chest, pressing his palms together and letting them drift apart. "My last name is Hughes. My father's name. A good Christian man born here in the north. But my mother, she was from New Orleans, and her mother came from Haiti. My grandmother was a voodoo priestess, all the way up until her death. She professed belief in the Lord. Worshipped Him too. But she never relented from engaging in the voodoo practices, which remained the focal point of her life.

"I attended some of her services as a child. My mother wanted me to see both sides of my heritage. I saw people willingly let spirts possess them. Some arguably demonic, some the spirits of their dead ancestors. I saw the change in their demeanor, the way they spoke, and the way they carried themselves. I saw times when a spirit or demon took over a person and refused to let go. Saw my grandmother forcibly remove spirits through various rituals. So, yes. I have no doubt that spirits as well as demons can possess people. And I firmly believe the Lord Jesus has authority over demons and gives that authority to us as believers to tread upon serpents and the scorpions, to trample them beneath our heels and not be harmed."

Debbie's look shifted to display skepticism. Elder Hughes picked up on it.

"Oh, dear, not literal serpents and scorpions. We're not one of those snake-handling, backwoods Christian churches. No. I mean serpents and scorpions as a metaphor for demons and principalities that we engage in spiritual warfare with, not physical."

Debbie breathed another sigh of relief but wasn't forthcoming to voice her final question. Elder Hughes detected this and broached the subject for her.

"And yes, myself and the elders here in our church have and do engage in casting out demons and spirits of various sorts that plague our parishioners."

He paused and scrutinized her before continuing. "I'm assuming that's what you're here for. You have a problem, and you believe the origin of that problem is possibly demonic. What is it?"

Debbie was both surprised at his forthcoming approach and relieved at the same time.

"It's my son," she confessed. "In the last few weeks, since we moved into a new house, our son has completely changed. He's not himself, at all. It began with odd dreams where he saw and recounted things in accurate detail that were almost forty years before his time. From there, it shifted to significant changes in behavior, even in his food preferences. He acted out at school and became violent with other kids and then with me at home. And last night things happened that made some of the scenes in the movie *Poltergeist* seem tame."

Debbie paused, pointed at her face, then pulled down her shirt collar to reveal the bruises around her neck.

"These were made by toys," she told him. "Animated toys attacking me and my husband. Animated by a ghost boy possessing my son."

Debbie stopped and looked at Elder Hughes, whose eyes had opened wide.

"And trust me, I know how outrageous this sounds. But it didn't happen overnight. It came in stages. And I struggled with trying to find a rational explanation. But last night...last night blew all hopes of rationality out of the water. My baby boy is possessed by a ghost, and it won't let him go. In fact, it physically hurt him last night before our eyes. I watched my son's mouth open so wide his jaw dislocated and it tore the corners of his mouth before he collapsed unconscious. The ghost boy, Malachi, told me if he couldn't hurt me, he'd hurt my son."

Debbie started to cry. Elder Hughes offered her a box of tissues, and she took a few. She wiped her eyes and blew her nose. Exhaustion overwhelmed her. Prey could only stay on high alert for so long, and Debbie's mind had been in lookout mode for the last couple of weeks now, even while asleep. Her body was embattled on all sides by a relentless fatigue while her mind struggled not only to maintain a vigilant watch but to keep a firm grip on her sanity.

"I need your help," she managed to articulate between sobs. "Help save my boy."

Elder Hughes looked on her with compassion, commiserated with her and her terrifying circumstances.

"Miss Debbie, I will speak with the elders, but I assure you, we will help you. How soon do you wish for us to act?"

Debbie cried more, but her sobs changed from those of dread to hope.

"Oh my God. Really? You'll help me?"

"Yes. Yes, we will."

"Tonight? Can you come to our house tonight?"

"Yes. That should be possible. Give me your phone number, address, and the name of your husband and son as well."

Debbie rattled off her number and address. "My husband's name is Nathan Loch and my son's name is Martin."

"Good," Elder Hughes said. "And the ghost boy? You said he identified himself as Malachi?"

"Yes, sir," Debbie said. "In fact, I did some research and found out that an eight-year-old boy by the name of Malachi murdered his parents in that house forty years ago. I've got a few articles I dug up at the local library if you want to see them."

Elder Hughes looked quite surprised, his eyebrows rising high before he indicated he would very much like to see those articles. Debbie retrieved them from her vehicle and brought them back. Elder Hughes read them over, shaking his head.

"My goodness. The darkness sits heavy on these pages, doesn't it?"

Debbie nodded her head in agreement.

"Do you mind if I make copies of these to show to the elders?" he asked.

"Not at all," Debbie assured him.

Elder Hughes did so, and they parted. Debbie headed for her car, and Elder Hughes picked up his phone to call the elders and gather them to do battle that night.

Debbie texted Nathan the details of what she had done. She didn't want to risk him calling before she got home. If they talked on the phone, Malachi might overhear her plans. She ran by the grocery store as a plausible explanation for her outing in case Malachi decided to ask any questions. She exited her vehicle, slipped on a hoodie, and pulled the hood up, then went inside the store. She kept her gaze down anytime someone moved toward her from the front. It wasn't until she was checking out that anyone saw her face clearly. The cashier girl gasped, then looked away, trying to play off her lack of manners, but her eyes kept coming back to Debbie's face as if drawn by a magnet.

"A cat latched hold of my face," Debbie said with blunt directness. "Never pick up a stray cat and try to kiss it. Trust me." She took a sick pleasure in concocting the story and in the look of horror that spread across the teenage girl's face.

As she loaded the groceries into the vehicle, her phone rang. She scrambled to answer it.

"Hello?" she almost shouted.

"Hi, Debbie? This is Elder Hughes."

"Oh God," she blurted out. "I'm so glad you called back this soon."

"Well, it doesn't seem like we have time to waste, now do we? I wanted to tell you, I spoke with the elders, and we'll be at your house tonight at eight o'clock. Is that okay?"

"Yes. God yes. That's perfect. Thank you so much! Oh my God, thank you!"

"You're very welcome," he said. "Okay. We'll see you tonight then. Goodbye."

Debbie said bye and thumbed the end button. She finished loading the groceries and wheeled her cart to the return corral. She climbed in her vehicle, started it up, and texted Nathan again.

It's a go. 8pm. Be ready. We won't talk about it at home.

With that, she put the car in gear and hit the road, her brain swarming with the dangers of what they would attempt tonight, both to her son and them.

"Mother?" Malachi called out from upstairs, mocking Debbie by addressing her as if there were a familial bond between them. "What have you been doing, *Mother*?"

Malachi's voice twisted into Debbie's bowels, sickening and

enraging her simultaneously as she put the groceries away. Nathan did not appear to be inside the house.

"What?" Debbie called out, feigning ignorance.

"You heard me," Malachi declared. "Now, tell me, *Mother*. What have you been doing?"

The boy's words skewered her heart with a terrible fear, a sense of exposure, the kind of dread a spy found out might experience. Her stomach coiled and twisted, sending sickening waves all the way up into the back of her throat and down through her bowels.

"I went to the grocery store," she answered him, voice catching in her throat.

She heard his steps coming down the staircase.

"What *else* have you been doing?" he asked.

Her terror was palpable. Primal. Instinctual. She wanted to flee, just drop the groceries and run out the back door. Away from Malachi. Anywhere else but there would suffice. But her brain chose silence and hiding in plain sight instead. She froze. No words. No movement. Still. She remained still, a jar of peanut butter clutched in her hand, held inches above the countertop.

"*Mo-ther.*" It was an accusation, now, not a question. "I *know* you've been naughty, Mother. Now, *tell me!* What have you done?"

Urine dribbled down the inside of Debbie's leg. The fear was unbearable. It drained her vigor. Her hands grew weak and dropped the peanut butter. She leaned forward just in time, vomit plunging into the sink and splashing off the dishes laying there.

Malachi's sock feet padded along the hardwood floor in the living room, making his way into the kitchen.

Debbie wiped her mouth and tried to remain standing. She'd never experienced such debilitating panic, such a paralyzing apprehension of dread. She was fully aware of the calamitous events descending on her, as unstoppable as an avalanche tumbling down a mountainside. Even the horror she experienced the night before during all the chaos was nowhere near this strong.

Malachi was actively doing something. She was sure of it.

But how? How is he this powerful? The thought flashed in her mind, but she had no time to consider it. The effect of his presence was too oppressive to ignore.

There was no noise, but the sensation was like the thump of bass emanating from subwoofers at a concert. The concussive energy moved throughout Debbie's entire body. Malachi cranked up the intensity, changing it from subtle pulses to jarring blows. It pounded in her chest, reverberated in her throat, stole her breath, her voice, her equilibrium.

Legs like quivering jelly failed Debbie, no longer able to support her. They gave out and collapsed. She dug her fingers into the counter and managed to lower herself to the floor. She was trapped, vulnerable, incapable of flight or fight. Worse still, she was found out and unable to hide from him. Death seemed to swoop down upon her like an owl on a mouse exposed in a field at night.

Each audible step Malachi took echoed with a frightful awe, an intuitive phobia she never knew she possessed because she'd never been confronted with anything so terrifying until now. She knew each tiny shockwave pronounced ill fortune, not just for her but for her son. A fate she dared not consider loomed large before her.

Nothing in the past was worthy of comparison with the shuddersome apprehension gripping her heart.

Not even the death of her daughter.

That tortuous injury to her soul blindsided her, like a knife ramming into her kidney from behind or being broadsided at an intersection in an automobile collision after forgetting to check both ways. It shocked her. The accident that took her daughter inflicted its wound in an instant. She never saw it coming. But this...this was a different beast. This tragedy was stalking her from the shadows within her own home, each step emitting a palpable dread as it came for her. Debbie would rather she never saw it coming than this. This was unbearable.

The only thing she had experienced in the past that might be comparable was an incident with Martin long ago.

Martin tried to do a somersault on his bed when he was only four and landed on his head, folding his chin to his chest. He stood up, eyes wide, trying to breathe but unable. Debbie's stomach dropped into an abyss. All she could think was that something had broken and his throat would not work. He would suffocate before her eyes while she waited for the ambulance to arrive. The fear was visceral and debilitating in its power, but as horrific as it was, it could not measure up to what she felt now.

She heard the light patter of his feet on the linoleum, just around the corner of the countertop and dishwasher.

"Muuuuth-ther?" Malachi called out, peeking his head around the counter as he did so. Seeing her, he stepped out into view. He held the Stretch Monster by one of its hands, letting it dangle down next to his leg. It was whole and intact, despite Nathan having ripped it apart the night before. Malachi gazed at her, and she could not help but look into his eyes, unable to glance away.

"Tell me, Mother," he commanded. *"Tell me, now!* What have you *done?"*

Debbie tried to be brave. Tried to maintain an ounce of resolve. To remain loyal to the cause and not crumble beneath the torment of interrogation and torture. And what she felt right now was most assuredly torture. It strained her sanity, threatened madness, and pushed her heart to its limits.

But there were worse things than suffering. Malachi understood this, even though he personally was not susceptible to it.

"Mother, I won't ask again. Tell me...*now!"* Malachi did not yell; he uttered the word with a growl.

Debbie shook her head, lips pressed together tight so as not to betray their confidence.

"I warned you, Mother," was all Malachi said, pointing at her with his left index finger. He stared at her as he extended all four fingers, then reached up with his right hand and grabbed the index finger firmly. A quick jerk of his hand folded the finger back, forcing the tip to touch his wrist. The popping sound caused Debbie to retch.

"Tell me," Malachi said again, not waiting for a response before grabbing the middle finger and snapping it backward as well.

He reached for the ring finger, and Debbie groaned.

SNAP!

It sounded louder than a fresh carrot broke in half.

He grabbed the pinky finger.

"This little piggy couldn't be saved because Momma wouldn't talk."

SNAP!

"*Stop!*" Debbie shouted. "Stop it! Just stop it!"

"Tell me, Mother!" Malachi commanded her, his voice controlled and full of menace. "Tell me what you've done!" He held the hand out for her to see the contorted, mangled digits, folded in ways they should never move.

Debbie bit her bottom lip.

"Very well," Malachi said and put the thumb in his mouth.

Debbie saw him open his mouth wider, his jaw muscles tense in preparation to exert a great force. She shrieked.

"*No!*"

Malachi paused, thumb still in mouth, and eyed her with a look that asked whether she would talk or not.

She did.

"I went to see a pastor. He's coming to the house tonight with their church's elders. They're going to exorcise you. Cast you out! That's all! That's everything I did."

She bowed her head and sobbed.

Malachi squinted at Debbie, then removed the thumb from his mouth.

"How exciting!" he exclaimed, eyes gleaming with anticipation. "A regular party! I'll make sure I'm ready." He grabbed one finger at a time and folded them back forward. They were contorted and out of place. When he tried to straighten and squeeze them together, they refused to lay even against one another, but it was easier for Debbie to see them like that than their prior state.

He scrutinized them, turning his hand back and forth.

"Hmph," he grunted. "I guess it'll do," he said and looked at Debbie. "Make sure not to spoil the surprise, Mother."

Malachi wiggled the crooked fingers at her, then turned around to head back upstairs.

Nathan found Debbie leaned against the kitchen counter, face in her palms, weeping without sound. Her torso heaved. He hurried to her and knelt.

"What happened?" he asked in a hushed tone, matching her attempt at remaining quiet.

He placed a hand on her shoulder and waited. It took a minute before she was able to speak. Debbie lifted her head and motioned to Nathan, curling her index finger. He moved in closer. He turned his chin and moved her lips close to his ear.

"He knows," she whispered. "He knows what we have planned for tonight."

"How?" Nathan said, more mouthing the words than speaking them.

"He asked me what I had been doing. He knew it was more than buying groceries. He made me tell him."

"How?" Nathan pulled back and looked at Debbie, inspecting her for any injuries.

Debbie stuffed a fist to her lips and sobbed.

"How, baby? What did he do to you?"

"Not me," she managed to whisper.

Nathan brought his ear to her mouth again. He was struggling to make out what she said.

"What?" he asked.

"Not me," Debbie whispered again. "Martin."

A pang of fright lanced through Nathan's gut, and he pulled his head back. He tilted Debbie's chin up so she looked him in the eye and mouthed the word, "How?"

Debbie could not bring herself to speak it. She held up one hand, fingers splayed. With her other hand, she simulated grabbing her index finger then moved her hand from the finger to her wrist in a quick motion.

Nathan flinched, sick at the idea of what his wife just communicated to him. He grabbed her and drew her close to his chest, wrapping her in his arms, as much for his own comfort as to comfort her.

"Oh, dear god," he muttered into Debbie's hair. "What kind of monster is inside our son?"

He squeezed his eyes shut and wished he would wake up from this nightmare to find his son at the breakfast table, giggling and full of sweet smiles.

THE KNOCK AT THE DOOR STARTLED DEBBIE DESPITE having just looked at the clock in anticipation of Elder Hughes's arrival. She rose and hurried to open the door and welcome him and the others inside. Her stomach was in knots. On one hand, she was experiencing an enormous amount of dread at what might unfold with Malachi fully aware of the pending encounter. On the other, she was still tenaciously holding onto hope, albeit by the tips of her fingers, praying that Elder Hughes would make good and rid her son of Malachi.

"Elder Hughes," she greeted him. "So good to see you. Please, come in. All of you, please come inside."

Debbie held the door open and stepped off to one side, arm outstretched, welcoming them all into her home. They filed by, greeting Debbie with kind words, head nods, and firm hand-shakes before continuing to where Nathan stood to do the same. There were four men total, including Elder Hughes, plus one woman.

The men were a mix of ages. Elder Hughes appeared in his forties. So did the one Elder Hughes introduced as Elder Drew. The next was an elderly white man, thin and frail looking, hair shock white through and through, but he radiated a warm vigor. What struck Debbie the most were his eyes. They blazed with an earnest benevolence. His name was Elder Bryant. Another man appeared to be in his late fifties. Hair salt and pepper, but his body was sturdy, his dark brown hands large, fingers thick from manual labor. His name was Elder Brown. The last man was younger, possibly late twenties, dark skin, short hair, fit. He stood silent at the back, out of what seemed deference toward the others, senior to him in both age and station. Elder Hughes identified him as Elder Horace. He held two brown bags, one in each hand. One was shaped like a bottle of wine, Debbie noted.

All of them wore slacks, buttoned shirts, suit jackets, and ties. Their black or burgundy dress shoes shined despite the visible scuff marks. Each of the men smiled broadly except for Horace. He chose to keep his eyes down after the initial introductions. The other men seemed to accept his shyness.

"And this is the lovely Elder Sophia," Elder Hughes introduced the lady. She wore a beautiful burgundy dress that fit at the waist, then hung loose past her knees. She carried a matching clutch purse held tucked into her side. Her light mocha skin emanated a vibrant vigor despite her age.

Malachi watched them from where he sat in the middle of the couch, Stretch Monster seated in his lap. He turned the toy's head in their direction.

After the introductions were complete, they all gathered in the living room.

"This is your young boy, Martin, yes?" Elder Hughes asked Debbie and Nathan.

"Yes," Debbie answered.

"No," Malachi said, his tone flat. He shook his head side to side as he turned Stretch Monster's head back and forth as well. "I'm Malachi. Not Martin."

"The spirit speaks so soon?" Elder Hughes asked rhetorically, then nodded his head, mouth turned down. "Very well. Let us begin."

Elder Hughes reached inside his jacket and pulled out a small vial with a light brown– colored liquid inside. It possessed a slight greenish tinge to it as well.

"This oil has been blessed and consecrated to the Lord our God," Elder Hughes said. "Whatever we anoint in the name of Christ is consecrated to our Father who art in Heaven as well."

He unscrewed the top, pressed his thumb to the opening, and tipped it upside down, then right side up. He replaced the cap and stepped forward. Reaching down, Elder Hughes placed his thumb on Malachi's forehead and wiped it to one side.

Malachi jerked back at the man's touch and pawed his forehead, trying to wipe the oil off.

"Great Jehovah, I anoint this child, Martin Loch, in the name of your son, Jesus Christ, and consecrate him, soul, mind, and body to you, oh Lord."

Malachi spat at Elder Hughes and held the Stretch Monster up like a shield.

"Yes, Lord!" the other elders uttered, then began praying under their breath. Debbie and Nathan could not make out any words, just a low hum of various syllables juxtaposed in unusual ways. Nathan stared at the toy, scrutinizing it for any signs of life. There were none.

But it's early, he thought.

Elder Hughes held his right hand up in front of Malachi's face, inches away, palm out, fingers splayed. His eyes were squeezed shut.

"Oh Lord Jesus, be with us right now as we rescue this child from the wicked one. Make war on our behalf in the realm of the spirit. Go before us. Blow a trumpet in Zion and ride forth! Save this young boy. For your glory! For your Name's sake! Show mercy, oh God!"

Elder Hughes's hand trembled and shook now. His knees buckled as if bearing a heavy burden, his torso twisted.

"*Oh unclean, foul spirit!*" he shouted, bending at the waist and rising back up. "You do not *belong* here. This child is *not your* home. He is *not* a steed that you might *ride* him and *thrash* the crop all day and night. *No!* He is a child of God. Consecrated to God Almighty! You cannot have him! Oh Lord Jesus! Eisha lakita con da lakita shon da lakita. Sita donte que lavante orronto. Oh Shonta! Shonta! Shonta lokita keenda la conte que iche."

The other men and Elder Sophia joined in the prayer with uplifted voices. Each one speaking with disjointed syllables that made no sense to Debbie or Nathan.

Nathan looked at Debbie with confusion, but her expression did not match his own. Debbie knew what they were doing. She had visited a Pentecostal church once or twice in her youth. The elders were speaking in tongues, praying with utterances only the Holy Spirit could both grant them and understand. At least, that's how she understood it way back then.

It unsettled Debbie the first time she heard someone speak in tongues, but in this moment, she had to admit, it was creating a sense of comfort. It felt like stepping down into a warm pool and feeling the waters wash over her. She closed her eyes and listened, focusing on the feelings she was experiencing and letting go of her anxiety.

Nathan remained in the dark but decided he did not care. Not if it helped. He watched Malachi. The boy squirmed on the cushion and snarled, clacking his teeth together with staccato rhythm.

"Elder Horace," Elder Hughes said. "The show bread, please."

Elder Horace set down the bag with the bottle and reached inside the other one. He pulled out a loaf of bread with a golden-baked hue. He held it out to the others. They each pulled a piece off and ate it. After Elder Hughes took and ate his piece, he pulled another portion from the loaf.

"This bread has been prayed over, blessed, and anointed with oil. It not only represents the flesh of Christ that we take in communion, but it is holy now and full of the power of the Holy Spirit. We eat the flesh of Christ. We partake of the Spirit and consume his presence. He dwells within us, and now an item filled with his might is within us as well. The boy must eat this bread."

Elder Hughes looked at Debbie and Nathan.

"Restrain him, please," he requested of them both.

This was the part they had both anticipated and dreaded. The idea of holding down her son while Elder Hughes force fed the boy made Debbie ill, but she obeyed. Debbie moved behind the couch to hold Malachi's head, leaving Nathan to deal with the feet and legs. She reached out, her movement tentative and full of trepidation. It was like stretching a hand out toward a sleeping serpent.

How long will Malachi play along with this before he attacks us all? she wondered.

Her hands touched the sides of his head. His hair was wet with sweat.

Maybe Elder Hughes is stronger than Malachi anticipated, she wondered.

The idea renewed hope in Debbie. She gripped Martin's head and pulled it back against the couch. Nathan secured Martin's feet and pinned them to the floor. The boy flailed his arms and Stretch Monster before his face.

"Grab his arms," Elder Hughes said to the men. Elder Horace and Elder Brown stepped to each side of Debbie, leaned over, and grabbed an arm each.

Malachi shrieked and snapped his teeth like an alligator, head turning left and right.

"Pull his head back and down, Debbie," Elder Hughes instructed her in a calm voice. The man oozed serenity. "So he can't bite," he explained.

Debbie moaned but did as she was told. The men lifted Martin by his arms so she could pull his head back and down over the top of the couch, causing the skin of the boy's throat to stretch taut. Nathan let Martin's feet off the floor but kept them pinned to the couch.

Elder Hughes leaned in, gripped the bony part of Malachi's chin with his fingers, and pulled down, opening the boy's jaws wide. Without hesitating, he shoved the piece of bread in Malachi's mouth and pushed his chin up. Elder Hughes held Martin's mouth closed with one hand and rubbed the boy's throat with the other, like a dog when you forced it to swallow a pill.

Malachi gagged, gurgled, and growled, spurning all attempts to make him swallow, but Elder Hughes refused to let him not. Praying in tongues again, he kept rubbing Malachi's throat, manipulating the flesh and thwarting the boy's resistance with each pinching stroke of his fingers from jaw to collarbone.

Debbie wept.

It was killing her to watch much less take part in physically assaulting her son. But she knew it was necessary.

"Anoint his head with oil again, Elder Sophia," Elder Hughes instructed, "and prepare the holy water. Bring me the wine, Elder Horace."

Elder Hughes returned to praying in tongues.

Elder Sophia removed a vial of oil from her clutch purse along with a small bottle of water with a cork stopper. She applied the oil to her thumb and swiped across Martin's forehead. Then she did it a second and third time. Father, Son, and Holy Spirit. Malachi tried to turn his head back and forth, to escape and spew the holy bread from his mouth.

The more he struggled, the faster the bread dissolved. Malachi couldn't stop it from sliding into his throat. Couldn't stop the reflex of swallowing. It burned all the way down to his stomach, where it lit a fire of agony. He screamed a muffled cry.

"The wine," Elder Hughes said. Horace took a swallow and passed the bottle around. Each of them took a swig, and Elder Horace handed it to Elder Hughes. He took a swallow and held the bottle up.

"The blood of Christ. The power of redemption. Justification. Sanctification. We drink and eat to be made whole! To partake of the power of our salvation. Drink, Martin, and be saved from this lost soul Malachi. Drink, and the power of the blood of Christ will cast him out."

Elder Hughes pulled Malachi's mouth open again and poured a liberal amount inside before pushing his jaws back together.

Malachi struggled to resist swallowing. He tried blowing out. Drops of wine sprayed from between his teeth, but not enough. He tried to breathe in after expelling all his air but inhaled wine instead and began hacking. Debbie thought he might choke but squeezed her eyes shut and held his head in place, arms straining, tears running down her cheeks into her son's hair.

Elder Hughes rubbed Malachi's throat again, forcing his body to swallow some of the liquid. A moment later, he let go of Malachi and stepped back.

"Release him," he instructed everyone. They all obeyed and took a step back. The elders continued praying in tongues.

Malachi hacked and barked and spit. Black fluid oozed from the corners of his eyes.

"You *fucking* fucks!" Malachi shouted and snarled. "You *foolish* pieces of worthless shit!"

He glared at each of them.

"You think you have power over me?" He spit at Elder Hughes. "I'm no demon. No devil. No power or principality that you can command. I was a human being. I have a fucking free will, and I can do *whatever* I will *if* my will is strong enough. And *my* will is *much* stronger than Martin's here."

A twisted smile sprung to Malachi's lips.

"He's scared!" Malachi said. "He wants his *mommy*. He's like a fawn searching for a tit to suckle, lost and mewling. *Martin is weak! But I am strong!*" Malachi shouted the last two sentences, face puffing, cheeks red.

Debbie became incensed at Malachi's words. Anger overtook her. She scrambled around the couch to face Malachi, bent over face to face almost.

"You're a despicable little prick!" she screamed, jamming her finger in his face. "You killed your parents and died. It's your own damn fault. Martin does not belong to you. Now, get out! *Get out!*" Debbie shrieked her commands.

Malachi smiled at her.

"*Get out! Get out! Get out!*" Debbie wailed with a fury.

"No!" Malachi shouted back at her.

WHAP!

Debbie's hand rocketed through the air before she thought once, much less twice, slapping her son's face.

"Oooh! Nice one, Mom!" Malachi taunted her. "Do it again.

Do it again." He giggled. "I like the way it made your tits swing back and forth afterward. I got a prime view from right here."

"*Arrrrgggghhhh!*" Debbie roared and stood upright, hand drawing back. She laid into Malachi. Slapping his face again and again and again, screaming the entire time. Elder Hughes and the others looked on in shock as Malachi took each strike, laughing, head snapping back to center every time Debbie knocked it sideways. Nathan finally grabbed Debbie in a bearhug, picked her up off her feet, and dragged her back. She kicked and howled for Nathan to release her.

"Way to go, Mom!" Malachi taunted her. "You're a bona fide child abuser for sure now!" He cackled long and loud in exaggerated fashion, mocking Debbie, then cut it short mid laugh.

"I'm done playing with all of you," he informed them. "But my toys are ready to begin."

He lifted Stretch Monster and pushed him forward. The creature's skin was pliable, scaled, and flexed like flesh as its upper lip curled in rage. Malachi threw the toy at Elder Hughes. It roared as it flew straight at the man of God, arms stretching toward the man's throat.

Elder Hughes flinched, hand extending out in from of him in response to the threat hurtling at his face. He managed to stiff arm Stretch Monster in the chest, but its arms continued reaching, elongating, beginning to wrap around the back of Elder Hughes's neck.

The other elders looked on in shock, but Nathan and Debbie reacted right away. Nathan put Debbie on her feet and let go, moving to help Elder Hughes. Debbie lunged forward for Malachi, slapping him in the face as hard as possible. Once, twice, and then she froze in mid swing as she spotted the Alien toy climb up over the back of the couch and leap at her.

Debbie dropped to the floor, ducking under the glistening projectile. It rocketed past her to land on Nathan as he pulled the Stretch Monster's arms off Elder Hughes before it could get a solid grasp on him. The Alien slammed into the side of Nathan's face and sent him spinning away, one rabid toy in his hands and another attached to his head.

A glance was exchanged between Elder Hughes and Debbie that told him this was not new to her.

"Focus on Malachi," she said to him. "We have to stop him."

Elder Sophia popped the stopper off the bottle of holy water and slung a spray of it at Malachi, making an X as she did so. The boy hissed in pain and glowered at her. His eyes squinted and another toy appeared. The X-ray Stretch Monster. It crawled out from beneath the couch and took off at Elder Sophia, arms shooting out to wrap around her ankles. It snatched her legs out and sent her falling.

Her shoulder blades struck first and then the back of her head. Her eyes wobbled about and fluttered, galaxies pinwheeling in sparkling lights against a vast expanse of darkness, but she did not pass out.

More monsters began crawling out from beneath the couch, seven-inch-tall fiends with an assortment of features. Some with saurian legs and clawed hands, others with gorilla bodies, one hand gripping a femur for a club. There were others with multiple tentacles in place of each arm and others still with a mixture of all. Heads varied—reptiles, demons, and hammerhead sharks— and colors spanned the spectrum.

Elder Hughes stomped two of the little monsters on his way to Malachi. He reached out with his right hand and gripped the boy's chin and cheeks, then shoved his head against the couch's headrest, pinning it there. With his freed hand, he poured more wine into the partially open mouth. Malachi sputtered and spit, trying to prevent the blessed liquid from passing his lips, but it was impossible for him to stop it all. As the bottle emptied into his mouth, spilling over his face and down his chest, Malachi gasped and gurgled but had to swallow some of it.

One monster struck Elder Hughes in the ankle while two

more began climbing up the backs of his legs, claws digging, piercing his clothing and skin. If he felt the injuries, Elder Hughes gave no indication of pain, only continued pouring the wine. When the bottle was empty, he dropped it on the couch and held out his hand.

"Bread!" he commanded. "Bread, Elder Horace. Now!"

Elder Horace snapped out of his frozen state, ripped off a piece of bread, and slapped it into Elder Hughes's hand, then knocked both creatures off Elder Hughes's back and kicked the one hammering at his foot.

Elder Hughes squeezed Malachi's jaws enough to part his teeth and stuffed the bread in between them.

A muffled squeal peeled out of Malachi's mouth. His legs fluttered like an Olympic swimmer having a seizure. He clawed at Elder Hughes's hands with his nails but to no avail.

Elder Hughes would not relent. He palmed Malachi's forehead and eyebrows with his free hand, fingers wrapping around the sides of his head while the other hand still clamped tight around the boy's chin and cheeks. He prayed aloud with increased zeal.

"Eecha koon de la ka lante. Kota. Kota Kota ka la kante."

His voice boomed as he continued to pray in tongues. Malachi shriveled into the couch, flailing and kicking, but Elder Hughes leaned into the boy and held his head down firm, like a bug pinned to a board. His arms strained, lean muscles bulging with effort through his suit jacket.

The monsters stopped flowing out from under the couch.

Malachi was distracted. Pressured. Not allowed to act at his leisure. Debbie punted, kicked, and stomped the little monsters, assisted by Elder Brown, who took off his jacket and flailed at the creatures, sending them sprawling across the floor before he stomped them with his size-thirteen shoes. Elder Horace fended off any other attacks on Elder Hughes.

Nathan struggled to protect his face from the Alien as it held onto him and kept biting chunks out of his flesh every time its inner mouth slammed into his skull. He started spinning in place, trying to throw it off, but it held fast, claws dug into his skin. Right shoulder shrugged to his ear and holding onto just one arm of the Stretch Monster, he swung the toy through the air. Round and round they went, until he drew close enough to slam it into its cousin climbing up Elder Sophia's chest, sending it flying across the room and into a wall.

Elder Bryant made his way to Elder Sophia to check on her.

Nathan continued spinning in circles twice more before letting go of the Stretch Monster, sending it through a window and out into the yard. Blood flowed down into his eyes as he continued to note something like a woodpecker's beak hammering his skull over and over. Nathan staggered, from both the dizziness of spinning around and around and the beating his skull was taking. He reached up, gripped the Alien's body, and lifted with all his might. He ripped it loose, its claws taking pieces of his scalp with them. Turning, he threw the creature through a different window and stumbled away, almost falling over Debbie.

"Help me!" cried Elder Hughes. The others responded. Elder Brown and Elder Horace came to his side at once and laid hands on Malachi's head. Elder Bryant helped Elder Sophia up and steadied her, then they joined the others, laying hands on Malachi's chest and shoulder. They all prayed as one, their voices rising in volume, a babble of foreign sounds overlapping and blending into a holy cacophony appealing to their God.

Nathan and Debbie eradicated the remaining monsters, and none took their place. Neither the stretch monsters nor the Alien toy returned.

Whatever they're doing is working, thought Nathan.

Black fluid poured from Martin's eyes, streaming down his cheeks onto the couch cushions.

"More bread," Elder Hughes cried. Elder Horace retrieved another piece and stuffed it into Martin's mouth.

"In the *name* of Jesus," Elder Hughes commanded, "leave this boy's body now, unclean spirit. Malachi is *not* his name. Martin is *not* your home. This house once was, but not this boy. Leave him now! *Now!* In the name of *Jesus*, I cast you *out!* There will be *no peace* for you in this body, evil spirit. *No peace* for Malachi. As long as you hold onto your residence here, I will not rest, I will not relent. I will *war* with you and torment you with the sacraments of the *body and blood of Christ!* I will force feed them to you until you can tolerate them no more. I will *make you leave* by the power of Christ!"

He grabbed another piece of bread and shoved it into Malachi's mouth.

"By the power of Christ, his body, and blood, I command you to leave now! *Now,* in the name of Jesus! *Now!*"

Elder Hughes's body began to jerk and twitch, but his hands stayed connected to Malachi's forehead and chin. Malachi began to convulse, overcome by a seizure. The other elders continued to pray without ceasing, even as the boy's whole body flopped like a fish out of water being electrocuted.

Debbie watched in horror and hope. The moment stretched out, as if dangling from a noose, but at last, Martin's body relaxed and became still. She stared at his chest, searching for the rise and fall that indicated he was still breathing. Her vision narrowed to nothing but Martin's torso, waiting, waiting.

She saw movement. Imperceptibly small, but there.

All the elders continued praying but moved back, allowing Debbie to get to her son. She rushed to his side and held her ear next to his mouth. The warmth of his breath tickled the inside of her ear and made her heart leap with joy. She scooped Martin into her arms and hugged him, burying her face in his neck as she cried.

The elders prayed on, praising God for his mercy and deliverance.

Nathan staggered into the kitchen where he grabbed a hand

towel and clutched it to his scalp, attempting to stop the bleeding.

Don't worry about me, he thought. *I'm just dandy.* He slid to a seated position on the floor, back to the wall. From there, he watched Debbie and Martin and waited for the encroaching blackness to recede and the sensation of being on a small boat in rough waters to finally pass.

Elder Hughes and his companions stayed for a while afterward.

Once Debbie was confident Martin would be fine, she laid him down on the couch and did her best to tend to Nathan's wounds. He left a trail of blood leading into the kitchen and a pool of it gathered around him. He lost a good amount from the numerous lacerations to his skull but not enough to be in any significant danger. The world tilted and wheeled occasionally from what was almost assuredly a concussion, but otherwise, he seemed fine. Elder Horace borrowed hydrogen peroxide and bandages from Debbie to tend to Elder Hughes's injuries. Elder Sophia was unsteady and complained of dizziness. She likely had a concussion as well but insisted on not leaving until the others were ready.

Elder Hughes wanted Nathan to go to the ER with Elder Sophia, but he refused.

"She can just say she fell," Nathan said, holding a gallon-size bag of ice to his head, "but I have no decent explanation for all the tiny bite marks on my head or the concussion." He shook his head. "I just can't. If I develop worse symptoms, Debbie can call nine-one-one, and we'll deal with it."

"I can't believe what we just saw," Elder Horace said to no one in particular, wiping his face and shaking his head. "I'd never have believed it in a million years if I didn't see it myself."

Elder Brown patted the young man on his shoulder. "Don't worry, you're not alone," he said to reassure him. "I've never seen anything like that in my entire life. And I've been around the world. Seen demonic possessions in India. Watched a man of God cast a devil out of a witch doctor in Africa. Seen men invite spirits into their bodies in Haiti and Indonesia. But I've never seen anything as crazy as what we just witnessed. Ever. That takes the cake, the blue ribbon, and the apple pie, son. I'm tellin' ya right now."

Elder Brown took a seat in one of the chairs and breathed a deep sigh while Elder Bryant flitted around getting drinks and towels and bandages or anything else any of them needed.

Once Elder Hughes was comfortable leaving Debbie, Nathan, and Martin alone, he gathered the elders together to say a final prayer. Afterward, he turned to Debbie.

"I'm leaving the holy water, a vial of the oil, and the remaining show bread," he advised her. "If something seems wrong, anoint the boy with the oil and holy water and feed him a piece of the bread. In the meantime," Elder Hughes pulled a piece of bread from the loaf, "let's tuck a piece under his pillow and keep it close to him."

Elder Hughes smiled.

"If you need anything, call me." He gave her a hug, then nodded at Nathan.

Elder Hughes took a step closer to the man. "Nathan," Elder Hughes said, "I understand you have issues with the Almighty, though Debbie did not reveal the source of such things. Whatever they are, I will likely wager they have more to do with hypocrites in the church than with God Himself, when you boil it all down. In my experience, that's generally the root of religious animosity. The problem of evil is difficult to answer with our limited point of view, but it is quite easy to see the glaring corruptions birthed in the hearts of God's servants throughout history. I would implore you to make peace with God. There are only two sides. Those with God and those not with Him, and hypocrites are certainly *not* with Him. Consider that. Your family needs your faith now. Martin needs your faith."

Elder Hughes perceived the rigidity in Nathan's face and neck, the hardness in his eyes.

"Very well," he relented. "If there's anything we can do, please call. Good night."

With that, the elders filed out, leaving Nathan and Debbie alone with their sleeping son. Nathan glanced at the clock. It was four a.m. He crawled into the living room, pulled himself up into his recliner, and leaned back. Debbie brewed a large cup of cappuccino and sat on the couch at Martin's feet next to Nathan, ready to keep watch over them both.

DECEMBER 24

Somewhere around seven a.m., Debbie nodded off. She dreamed of Martin, her Martin. Kind, gentle, funny. She held him and read to him, like she did before he outgrew it. It was a heavenly dream. Peaceful. Comforting. When she woke around nine o'clock later that morning, she felt refreshed despite the short duration of rest.

She checked on Nathan and Martin. Both were sleeping and breathing fine. She headed to the kitchen to clean up the blood and mess she had ignored the night before. Next, she cooked breakfast, hoping the smell of bacon, eggs, and pancakes would draw both her boys out of their slumber.

She prepared a large number of pancakes, scrambled a dozen eggs, and cooked two packages of bacon. She poured three glasses of orange juice and set the jug on the table. Everything was in place when she heard movement in the living room. Debbie hurried in there to find Martin sitting up, looking around, one hand touching the left side of his face. His cheek was bruised, a mottled discoloration of black, blue, and red hues. His right cheek had one single bruise the size of a man's thumb.

"Mom," he tried to speak, his voice weak and hoarse, "my throat hurts...and my face."

"Oh, baby," she said to him, "hold on one minute. I'll get you a painkiller pill and something for your throat."

Debbie hurried to the medicine cabinet, grabbed two ibuprofen, Chloroseptic spray, and a menthol cough drop. She returned with a glass of orange juice, plopped the pills into his open mouth, and handed him the glass. He sipped on it and swallowed the medicine. The act hurt, and he winced.

"Here," she said to him. "Open wide. This will help the pain."

Martin obeyed, and Debbie sprayed two pumps worth of the medicine into the back of his throat. Martin clucked his tongue and made a face at the horrible taste.

"Wait a couple minutes before you drink anything, baby. Then suck on this cough drop."

Martin took the cough drop in his other hand and held it, nodding in answer to his mother's instructions.

"I've got breakfast laid out on the table when you're ready," she said. Smiling big, she ruffled his hair and caressed his right cheek. "I love you, baby," she said. "I love you so much."

"Love you too, Mom," Martin said. He leaned forward and wrapped the arm holding the cough drop around her upper thigh and leaned his good cheek against her leg. "I missed you."

Debbie's heart melted. Her eyes oozed joyful tears.

"Oh, baby. I missed you too. So very, very much." She held his head to her with one hand and stood still, unwilling to move as long as he was willing to remain clutching her. Minutes later, Martin released her and leaned back on the couch. Debbie let his head go and watched him. He took a sip of orange juice and spoke.

"I'm ready to eat," he said and scooted to the edge of the couch. Debbie moved back. Martin stood and headed for the breakfast table.

Debbie turned her attention to Nathan. She rubbed his arm softly and spoke to him.

"Nathan. Na-than. Come on, honey, time to wake up. Breakfast is ready…and Martin is awake."

At his son's name, his face spasmed, a series of tics rippling across his flesh. Nathan opened his eyes and looked to his left, searching for Martin. Not seeing him, he looked at Debbie, concern wrinkling his brow.

"Where is he?" Nathan asked, sitting forward.

Debbie checked him with a hand on his shoulder.

"He's okay, Nathan." She smiled big, her face angelic, cherubic even, to Nathan. "He's at the breakfast table. He's fine. When you're ready, come join him."

Nathan put the footrest down on his recliner and started to sit up. He grimaced as he did so and squinted his eyes all but shut.

"Oh, mother of god," he said. "Why do I feel like a little person with a tiny golf club teed off on my head all night long?"

"Hmmm, well," Debbie began, "probably because that's not too far from the truth." She chuckled. "Let me get you something for the pain."

"I've got leftover Percocet in the medicine cabinet from a year ago when I hurt my knee," Nathan said. "Can you bring me one of those, please?"

Debbie nodded and headed off to retrieve it. She returned quickly and found Nathan standing up, though swaying slightly.

"C'mon. Let me help you to the table," she said. Once he was seated, she handed him the pill, and he swallowed it down with orange juice.

"Eat up," she told him, "then we need to talk."

"About what?" he asked, giving her an unsure and wary glance.

"About how soon we're moving the hell out of this house," she answered.

"Oh," he said and nodded. "I can answer that right now. Real damn soon. Before New Year's Eve. I don't care if we have to stay in a hotel until we can find something else or snag an apartment for a year. Whatever it takes to get out ASAP."

Debbie nodded and smiled, thankful they were in full agreement on a plan of action and the timeline.

Nathan turned his attention to Martin.

"Hey, buddy. How are you doing?"

Martin's mouth was full of bacon. He held up a finger, chewed, and swallowed.

"Good, Dad. But..." He paused to gulp down some orange juice. "What happened? Did we get in a car accident? My face and throat ache so much. And both you and Mom look like you are hurt too."

Nathan eyed Martin with indecision. He wasn't sure how to broach the subject at first. He decided to just ask questions.

"What do you remember, bud?"

Martin looked at his plate.

"Well, I remember dreaming about playing with all those cool toys in my closet. Malachi left and didn't come back. I was alone. It seemed like forever. I was so lonely. I missed you and Mom. Bad. I was sad. Really, really sad. And then the dream ended, and I dreamed of other stuff—Christmas morning, unwrapping gifts under the tree with y'all, eating cookies and candy and fudge. Stuff like that. Happy stuff. And then I woke up to the smell of breakfast, and Mom came in the room. That's pretty much it."

"Well, that's good. That's real good."

Nathan rubbed and pinched his mouth, thankful that Martin didn't remember all the bad things that had transpired while Malachi controlled his body.

"What happened to us...it's a long story, bud. It's complicated and a bit crazy. But Malachi is gone. And I don't want you to ever talk to him again or play with his toys either. Okay?"

Nathan's gaze was more pleading than demanding.

"Yeah. Sure thing, Dad. I don't need a friend like him."

Martin shoveled a forkful of pancake and syrup into his mouth and chewed.

Nathan and Debbie both sighed, thankful to have their son back. Their lives back. They had some obstacles to hurdle in the coming days: avoiding further legal problems while healing up, getting Martin cleared by the child psychologist, finding a new home and getting Martin back into school. Back to normal. But Debbie was confident they would make it happen.

It was eleven a.m. when Debbie answered her cell phone.

"Hello?" she said.

"Hi, Debbie?" the female voice asked. "This is Rachael. The librarian. We spoke a couple of days ago about the Barber family murders."

"Yes, yes," Debbie said. "I remember. What's up?"

"Well," Rachael began, "I've got the police reports...and so much more."

Debbie easily recognized the excitement in the girl's voice, but she thought she detected an additional sentiment—amazement. Amazement at the remarkable, the improbable. It made her uncomfortable, shaking the confidence she felt in their victory from the night before.

"What did you find, Rachael?"

"More than I could have ever imagined," she said. "I spoke with my father. I didn't even need to file a request for the reports with the city. My father had all the records."

"How?" Debbie interjected, incredulous.

"It turns out my father and the investigating officer, a Reginald Denning, were closer friends than I realized. According to my father, when Reggie got cancer and knew he wasn't going to beat it, he asked my father to make him a promise. You know how guys joke about having a friend who, when they die, is honor bound to go scrub their friend's computer of all porn and other perverted things before their wives can stumble onto it?"

"Um, yeah," Debbie answered, a little confused at this odd analogy heralding from the far end of left field.

"Well, Reggie asked my father to take possession of all his files on the Barber massacre. He didn't want his wife to see them. So, before he died, he gave all of it to my dad."

"Holy crap," Debbie said. "What kind of stuff is in there?"

"I'll get to that in a second," Rachael said, teasing Debbie's interest. "But here's the first thing that grabbed my attention by the throat. Reggie made my father promise to keep the files, not to burn them, and specifically made him promise *not* to give them to anyone, except the person he would give them to upon his own death, another protector whom he selected and designated in his will. He also instructed my father about something else. He told him he could never watch the films."

Rachael paused, letting that last tidbit of information hang in the air and twitch, much like a fisherman jiggling a lure with just the right wrist movement to make the bait dance.

"Films?" Debbie said, her mouth suddenly dry. "What kind of films?"

"Debbie, you need to come to my house. You have to see all this to believe it. I've read the files, the reports, the interviews and interrogations...and I've watched the films. Can you come over now?"

Debbie's head spun with ominous possibilities. She wanted to ignore Rachael and this threatening information, to just believe victory was theirs and no further problems would arise. But she knew she could not afford to be so naïve. She needed to gather all the information available in case something else happened.

"Yes. I can. What's your address? I'll be right over."

Rachael gave it to Debbie and hung up.

Debbie rushed over to Rachael's apartment, her mind a rollercoaster ride of fears and suppositions, wondering what revelations awaited her.

Rachael opened the door and ushered Debbie in right away. She forced a cup of hot tea into her visitor's hands and guided her to the living room. There was an old pull-down white screen set up on a tripod and a film projector positioned across from it. The blinds were lowered and the curtains pulled. The room felt like a cave, but the lights were on.

Sitting down on a loveseat and lowering her lips to the cup, Debbie detected the odor of alcoholic beverage in her drink. Her nose wrinkled at the potency.

"Is there whiskey in this?" she asked Rachael.

"No, rum and honey," she answered. "Drink it. You're going to need it. Trust me. I did." Rachael sipped from her own cup as she took a seat in the chair across from Debbie, a coffee table in between them.

"Okay," Rachael began, "here goes. I talked with my father, and I read the police reports Reggie gave to him." She patted multiple folders full of papers, stacked on top of each other on top of the coffee table. "There are numerous details in these reports that were never released to the public, though some aspects of it managed to creep out and became those rumors I told you about in the library. The truth is not far from the rumor, but it is far more complex, convoluted, and difficult to believe."

Rachael sipped her spiked drink twice, squeezing the cup in both hands, comforted by its warmth.

"I guess," she began speaking again, "the best place to start is with what the Barbers were involved in."

"What was that?" Debbie asked.

"Witchcraft," said Rachael.

"Witchcraft? What kind of witchcraft?"

"Well," Rachael elaborated, "in the beginning, their activities were fairly typical of the time period. Did you know that from the sixties to the mid-seventies, both in the UK and the US, major record labels, like Capital, produced records by proclaimed witches? These albums were primarily spoken, though some of them had music in the background. The albums included such things as an oral history of witchcraft and how to become a witch, but most of them focused on providing spells, incantations, prayers, chants, and conjurations for everything from becoming more wealthy or powerful, to gaining love, to even summoning spirits or demons. I did some hunting online and even found a few of them in their entirety on YouTube. One well-known album from the late sixties was even narrated by Vincent Price. Pretty wild and interesting, actually."

Rachael beamed with excitement for a moment but noticed Debbie did not seem to share her feelings.

"Anyway," Rachael continued, "the Barbers were part of a little hippie witches' coven here in town. Most of the members were just trying to increase their wealth and affluence and probably get off on all the orgies they took part in."

Debbie's eyebrows rose at the mention of orgies, Rachael noticed.

"Yeah, orgies, but we'll get to that shortly. The mayor and his wife back then were actually part of this. He went on to be involved with politics at the state level a few years after the murders. Apparently, he was seeking greater political influence through their rituals, and that's probably why the files were never released. It would have ruined his career.

"There's some film footage of their meetings," she informed Debbie. "Let me play a little for you."

Rachael stood, turned on the projector, and flipped the lights off.

Black-and-white images sprang to life, men and women gathered in what appeared to be a basement. It looked as if a sturdy pool table had been covered, perhaps with plywood and a red velvet sheet of sorts. Candles were placed at the four corners of the table as well as along two shelves mounted at head height on the wall across from where the camera was filming their activities. They wore black robes and masks but were naked otherwise. The men's masks looked like a goat's head with horns, and the women's masks appeared to be the face of an elven nymph or a faerie with pointed ears and rose-colored cheeks. They all carried candles and walked around the makeshift altar.

"Oh, spirits of the seven realms of the mortal world," they prayed together, "and spirits of the four dimensions of the witchcraft world, we beckon you unto us now. Hear our prayers and grant our desires that we may prosper and rule among the sons of Adam. Multiply our wealth."

They lifted their candles and chanted.

"Oh, spirits of the gray realm, hear us now. Hay–Yang–Hay–Yang, Sim–Ar–Us, Sim—I–Us, He–Bru–Done–Doe. "

Four times they repeated the words of power to the candles in their hands, then they lowered them. One of the men picked up a bell off the altar and rang it.

"Let us pay homage to Satan, Lucifer, the agent of power and pride who shapes chaos into control, the god within us all who teaches his students the way of might so we may exert our will and call our desired destinies into being."

He rang the bell again, and they all picked up another prayer.

"Oh, Father of the Night and Ruler of the Flame, Master of the Dark and Devious. Give us your strength and your wisdom, so we, too, may feel the power. Possess us. Give us prosperity.

Give us lust for the human flesh. Give us knowledge. Give us strength. Fill our desires and our needs. In return, we shall worship you all the days of our lives and of the hereafter."

The man rang the bell again, and they transitioned to their next supplication.

"Marbas, great and wise, hear our pleas. Show us the secret things, the hidden esoteric doctrines of your glory and art. Teach us the sacred paths and empower us to shape this world by mastery and might, to write our days upon this earth. By your wisdom, we control, we are the power. By your wisdom, we control, we are the power. By your wisdom, we control, we are the power."

As they prayed, a woman climbed atop the altar on hands and knees, her buttocks lowering to rest on her haunches. A man approached her, lifted her robe to reveal her naked backside.

"We ply our flesh in sacrifice to thee," the leader said. "We plow the furrows of lust and rut like beasts for thy pleasure."

The man behind the woman threw his own robe wide, exposing his priapic rigidity, then entered her and began thrusting diligently.

The rest of the participants continued walking about the altar, chanting.

"Oh, Marbas, the magnificent, our fleshly pleasures are for thee, grant us control of what daily will be."

Over and over, they invoked the greater demon's name and sought his favor.

After a short time, Debbie spoke up.

"Okay, this is just uncomfortable now. I feel like we're watching porn together, and we don't even know each other that well." She laughed, but it was an uncomfortable sound that did little to ease the tension.

"Oh my god," Rachael exclaimed. "I'm so sorry." She hopped up and moved behind the projector. "Let me move the film forward just a little further to something important you need to see."

Rachael advanced the film, started it back up, and stopped it, leaving a frame frozen on the screen. The man was still copulating with the lady like he was a dog and she was a bitch in heat. Debbie did not see what Rachael obviously wanted her to see. She glanced at Rachael.

"What am I looking for?"

Rachael moved to the screen and, using a ruler, pointed to a space in between two of the participants walking around the altar. It was something in the background, at the end of the room.

"Can you make that out?" she asked Debbie.

Debbie leaned forward, eyes squinting, scanning, doing her best to distinguish whatever it was from its surroundings. And then it struck her.

"Holy crap. Is that a kid squatting at the bottom of the staircase?"

"Yes!" said Rachael. "I believe it is. In fact, I believe it's Malachi, the Barbers' son."

Debbie's stomach did a barrel roll, as if gripped by some unseen force that now spun about in her abdomen.

"Ugh. They let the boy watch?" Debbie said with disgust.

"I don't know," Rachael admitted her ignorance. "Looks more like he snuck down and was spying on them, but who knows?"

She turned the light back on and turned the projector off, then sat back down and sipped her drink.

"So," she continued, "some weird shit for sure, but the rabbit hole goes deeper as far as the Barbers and their son go." She tapped the stack of files. "According to the interview transcripts in the police records, there were some interesting developments that eventually led to things going sideways."

"Okay, I'll bite," Debbie said. "What developments?"

"Well, Malachi got sick," Rachael said. "Leukemia, supposedly. Doctors couldn't do anything for it. The coven began to hold more services each week, and they spent more time praying to Marbas because, apparently, he's known for healing the sick and diseased. At least, that's what it says in the Goetia of Soloman's Lesser Key. But after months of prayers and ritual services, Malachi's health was still worsening. And according to the mayor, that's when the Barbers got desperate and everything went to hell in a handbasket."

Debbie cocked an eyebrow in curiosity. "What did they do?"

"They went to New Orleans and consulted with a woman known to be a voodoo priestess and practitioner of black magic. They returned with a new magic ritual, but one they only practiced in private at first. Eventually, the mayor insisted they allow the rest of the coven to perform it with them and permit him to film it."

"What was it?" Debbie inquired.

Rachael stood. "I'll show you," she said and switched the film reels on the projector. "This takes place on November first, early in the morning after Halloween night. Apparently, Marbas's strength is supposed to be strongest during the month of November, according to medieval literature. Oh, and I'll skip over the first part," she told Debbie, waving a hand in the air. "They engaged in a full-on orgy to 'gather' their energies for the ritual. Afterward, they brought Malachi in and placed him on their makeshift altar. It's still pretty damn weird, though, so be forewarned."

Debbie took a big swallow of her drink and then another. "Okay," she said to Rachael. "Let's do this."

"You'll notice," Rachael said, "as the ritual progresses, someone picks the camera up and moves it around this time. Beside the altar where Malachi is laid, there's a magic circle of sorts drawn on the basement floor. Part of the ritual takes place there as well. Also, according to the mayor, they gave Malachi something ahead of time to make him sleep. Good thing too. If he had been forced to watch, it would have been even more disgusting."

Rachael rolled the film.

Malachi laid across the altar on his back wearing nothing but a white linen loin cloth. Candles burned all around him, but he remained still as the others performed the ritual. They called out to Marbas, beseeching the demon's favor and healing power on Malachi's behalf. Natalie Barber held a doll made in the image of her son. She clutched it to her chest as she prayed.

"Oh, great and marvelous Marbas, who hears the call of those who worship him, we call on you now, I call on you, to heal my son, Malachi, and make him whole. Rid his body of this disease, this heinous leukemia. Purge his flesh and watch over him, protect him from disease and pestilence. Come forth in might and wisdom and remove this sickness, restore the flesh of my son. Come. Come. Come. Come and grant us power, grant us control that we may extend the days of his life. Hear our petition and appear. Hear our petition and appear. Hear our petition and appear. Appear. Appear. Appear."

Natalie laid the doll on the altar above Malachi's head, and the others placed quartz stones around about it.

"That's some form of protection vortex," Rachael informed Debbie, "according to the mayor in his interview."

Debbie nodded but did not speak.

Natalie and the others continued to chant praise and prayers to Marbas. The long hair of the women began to sway, then flutter. The candle flames moved as well, flickering and fading. Shadows danced across the room. Debbie was not sure whether they were natural or something one could not account for given the people and the light available. But whatever doubts she had vanished a moment later. The wind roared and gusted within the basement, the candle flames defying the natural order as they remained lit. The coven members raised their voices, shouting to the world beyond, their hair whipping as if assaulted from raging winds on every side.

"Appear! Appear! Appear! Appear! Appear! Appear!" Everyone joined Natalie in crying out for Marbas to manifest.

And then the lights sputtered and went out. There was a moment of silence, then the voice spoke. The sound was a deep baritone that vibrated and shook the world, shook the camera. Even the screen seemed to shudder before Debbie and Rachael. Debbie clutched her chest. It felt as if her heart quaked inside.

"What will you offer for his life?"

It was a single question. Nothing more.

Natalie spoke up at once.

"We commit our son to you, Marbas. Preserve him, and he is yours to influence and shape. I only wish that he may live."

Darkness and silence prevailed for several seconds before the voice spoke again.

"Seal the pact with blood and an offering of fleshly delights," Marbas commanded, and all the candles sprung to life once more.

Natalie and Richard Barber took a ceremonial blade from the altar and cut their hands. They dripped blood over the body of their son and walked over to the magic circle on the floor, though the cameraman focused more on them than the circle itself, which remained obscured. There, the husband and wife dripped blood into the circle and disrobed. Natalie lay on her back, and Richard crawled between her legs. The other coven members cut their hands as well and let their blood fall on Malachi.

Richard rutted away at his wife as she cried out in pleasure, giving a dramatic show of sexual exuberance for Marbas. The others chanted praise.

"Marbas the mighty. Marbas the wise. Marbas the revealer of secrets. Marbas the healer. Marbas, worthy of our adulation and service."

"What the fuck?" Debbie muttered, leaning forward in her seat to stare more closely at the screen.

Something was happening to Malachi's skin. She watched in disbelief as black pinprick dots appeared all over the boy's flesh and then grew. It was as if his body sweated great droplets of pitch while blackness oozed from the corners of his eyes. The cameraman zoomed in on it for several seconds, and then, the boy rose, his body levitating off the altar. His arms hung by his side, knuckles resting against the velvet-covered plywood.

Debbie's free hand clutched at her mouth, and she gasped.

The viscous black drops stretched toward the boy's feet. The cameraman panned in that direction until the magic circle came into view. Above Natalie and Richard Barber, a small black vortex opened up and spun. Its gravity suckled at the black liquid marching up off Malachi's skin, into the air and toward the vortex.

Debbie watched in horrified amazement as the fluid gathered above the vortex and began to swirl, congealing into a sphere, a black, shiny orb rotating faster and faster until it spun off toward the outer rim and raced around and around and down, like a roulette ball upon a wheel or a ship sinking into the maw of Charybdis. When the sphere vanished, the vortex collapsed upon itself and disappeared. Malachi's body lowered, and the candles flickered and extinguished as it thumped gently against the altar.

"It is finished," the voice of Marbas said.

One of the coven members scrambled in the dark to find the wall switch. The overhead lights came on.

"Mommy," Malachi cried, sitting up and looking around.

Natalie Barber scurried to her knees, wrapped a robe around her body, and moved out of the circle toward her son. Rachael stopped the film, turned the lights on, and sat back down.

Debbie looked away from the screen, flabbergasted. "Did it work?" she asked, staring at Rachael for an answer.

"As a matter of fact, according to the mayor's interview, the Barbers took Malachi to the oncologist, and after repeated testing, they confirmed Malachi no longer had leukemia. In fact, it was not just remission. It was as if the boy never had the disease at all. I found the medical records in the police file also."

Debbie's jaw hung slack. She took the last gulp of her drink and shook her head. "I've experienced some crazy shit here lately," she confessed, "beyond crazy, actually, but that video is still plain nuts. Cured of cancer? Good God."

"You see why I said you needed to come over, right?" Rachael asked. "You never would have believed me if I just told you over the phone."

Debbie nodded. "You're right. I wouldn't have. It's hard enough to believe it even after watching it." She stood and extended her cup to Rachael. "I need a refill," she said, "and don't hold back on the rum."

Rachael took it and proceeded to the kitchen to make another drink. Debbie continued to walk back in forth in the living room, staring at the screen, at the frozen image of Natalie Barber clutching her son Malachi much as Debbie herself did her son the night before.

"What I don't get," Debbie said, thinking out loud, "is how do you go from being cured of cancer to killing your parents in, what, less than two months?"

"Well, that's what we need to discuss next," Rachael said from behind the counter, stirring the tea and rum together. She returned to the living room, handed the drink to Debbie, and sat down. "According to the police reports, Malachi began showing dramatic behavioral changes within days after this ritual took place. He became different. His personality turned narcissistic. He lost all empathy for other people and even became violent with fellow students to get what he wanted. It was as if he had become a different person. A person free of moral constraints that most of us possess."

Debbie swallowed hard, feeling a lump in her throat that did not want to go away. This sounded *too* much like her son. "Was Malachi possessed?" she managed to ask.

"Not according to the mayor. Despite many things about Malachi having changed, there were others that remained the same. The mayor believed when Natalie offered Malachi to Marbas to influence and shape, that's exactly what the demon did. A portion of Marbas bled into Malachi's being, into his spirit, soul, and mind. Like an infection, it spread throughout his system, short circuiting all ethics and reducing his inhibitions. Ultimately, it led to Malachi killing his parents."

Debbie considered both the similarities and differences between Malachi and Martin, plus one other crucial question.

"So, how does this relate to the rumors?" she asked. "The ones that claim Mr. Barber rides around looking for another kid? Is there anything to that, based on the police report and the mayor's interview?"

"Good question," Rachael said. "I'm not completely sure. Depends on what you believe, I suppose, but the mayor said something in his interview that might shed light on it."

Debbie stared at Rachael, hungry for *any* speculation on this subject. Anything at all that might make sense of how her family ended up living in this horror story. "Well, spit it out," she told Rachael.

"I double-checked online, to see if what the mayor said was true, and what I found confirmed his statement. He claimed that Marbas was known for something else, something they had over-looked when they engaged in the ritual."

"What's that?" Debbie asked, dreading the answer even though she had no idea what it might be.

"Marbas was not just known for healing people," Rachael informed Debbie. "He was also known for *causing* diseases. The mayor believed the Barbers were manipulated by Marbas. First, he caused Malachi to fall ill with leukemia, and then the illness drove them to seek his favor and commit the child to him. Marbas stalked their son from the beginning." She sipped her drink. "And if that's true, who's to say that the influence of

Marbas is gone? Maybe he's mad that Mr. Barber screwed him out of a living vessel, a little boy to take as his own. Maybe he empowers Malachi's spirit and controls Mr. Barber, forcing him to search for another boy, the perfect boy for Malachi's spirit to possess so a piece of Marbas can have what he wanted to begin with, a living plaything to manipulate for an entire human lifetime and cause as much chaos as possible. That's what I think, anyway." She threw back the last of her lukewarm drink and swallowed. "The theory works for me," she finished.

The cogs were turning in Debbie's head, grinding, squealing, and screeching at her. Their vehicle died outside that house. It was Marbas's doing, and he chose Martin that day. The father's spirit was sent to take her daughter and then feed her fears by appearing to her off and on for months afterward, making her think she was crazy. She didn't want to believe it all, even though it made perfect sense of the insanity she had lived for six months now. It put all the pegs in the right holes. All of them except one detail. One question. How did she end up choosing *that* house? How did Marbas influence her, guarantee that's the place she would choose?

She turned the question over and over in her head, staring at the screen but seeing something else entirely.

Marbas, she thought. *How? How did you do it, Marbas?*

Something clicked into place. She envisioned her daughter's pendant. The backside with the weird symbols and the letters in a circle around the outer edge floated before her mind's eye.

"S M A R B A".

She watched herself hold the pendant in her thumb and forefinger and rotate it slightly counterclockwise.

The blood drained from Debbie's face. She felt light-headed, overwhelmed. Her arms fell slack at her sides.

"Oh my fucking God," she mumbled, eyes spinning off wildly as she turned away, reeling with shock.

"M A R B A S."

Debbie spoke the word with a croak.

"Marbas. Marbas drew me to that house."

"Debbie," Rachael asked, her tone full of concern, "are you okay?"

Debbie did not answer. She could not. She just shook her head back and forth. As she did so, she glanced up at the screen and saw something in the bottom corner obscured by the overhead lights. She stood and moved to inspect the screen closer.

"Kill the lights," she said to Rachael. "Kill the lights now, please!" Her voice was frantic.

Rachael had no idea why or what she was looking for, but she hurried to flip the switch and joined Debbie in front of the screen.

Debbie pointed at the bottom right corner of the screen. "Oh my God," she muttered. "I know that design, that symbol." She staggered back and turned to look at Rachael, eyes wide with shock. "Good God in Heaven, what is going on?" she asked.

"Debbie," Rachael said, "I'm not sure because I don't have much to go on. There's obviously something you haven't told me yet. Something you need to tell me. You can trust me. I've gone out of my way to help you by collecting all this information and sharing it with you, despite my father's protests. I know something bad is happening with you and your son. You won't talk about it with me, but I can tell something terrible is going on. You *need* to tell me about it. If you tell me, I might be able to offer more help. But if you won't tell me the details, there's nothing I can do."

Tears spilled down Debbie's pallid cheeks. Rachael stood, walked over, and sat down next to Debbie, gripping a hand in her own.

"Please, Debbie," Rachael pleaded with her. "Tell me. Let me help you."

Debbie bawled and wept great heaving cries of despair for

some time, but when she calmed at last, she told Rachael everything.

Every last detail.

Debbie recounted the life of her family, starting with their return trip from the lake cabin, continuing all the way up to that morning after the exorcism, and finally ending with the pendant and her revelation of when Marbas began to influence her and draw her family to the house. When finished, she sat still, her body and emotions spent from the effort. She was drained.

Rachael had fixed a second drink for herself about halfway through and was already finished with it. She set the cup down on the coffee table with a clink.

"Holy mother of God," she said. "How have you maintained your sanity? I'm sure I would have lost it by now if I were in your shoes."

"I'm desperate to save my son," Debbie stated, matter of fact. She saw no need to elaborate.

"I get it," Rachael said. "The old mama bear spirit. It doesn't want to give up or let go."

"Yeah," Debbie agreed, a slight smile appearing on her face. "I guess that's it."

"There's one thing I want to confirm with you, though," Rachael said. "The pendant and the symbols on the back with the letters MARBAS. I think what you're describing and what you saw in the film is a sigil. Numerous demons and devils recorded in medieval literature are said to have sigils that represent them, and these sigils can hold the entity's power or act as a link through which their power can operate."

Rachael typed away on her smartphone while talking. She pinched and pulled the screen, then held it up for Debbie to see.

"Is this what the symbol on the back of Bella's pendant looks like?"

"Yes," Debbie said, almost breathless. "Where did you find that?"

"Oh, Wikipedia," Rachael said and chuckled. "I'm sure I could find it in a hundred other locations, but that's the easiest one to pull up quick." She shivered and looked back down at her phone, quickly reading the short entry on Marbas. "Oh, wow," she said, jaw dropping for a moment. "This is too freaky. You know what else it says here about Marbas?" she asked Debbie.

"What?" Debbie responded, gulping as a palpable dread spread across her face.

"It says Marbas is depicted as a great lion who can also take the shape of a man."

"Oh my God!" Debbie exclaimed. "Th-That explains the drawings with a lion…the lion in my dream and the lion threatening Bella in Martin's drawing!" She spoke the words in a near panic, pointing her finger at Rachael. "Oh my God. The lion is Marbas!"

Rachael stood and went to her. Squatting down in front of her, she took both Debbie's hands in her own and looked the distraught woman in the eye. "Yes," she said. "Yes, it's likely true, just like all of this you're experiencing is likely true. I don't doubt the truth of it one bit. I can assure you of that." She paused and squeezed Debbie's hands firmly. "And that's why you have to take what I say next dead serious."

The earnestness in Rachael's eyes refused to be ignored. "Two things," she began, holding up index and middle fingers. "First, you have to get rid of that pendant. Get it out of your house, out of your yard, out of your vehicles. Get it as far away from you and your family as possible."

Rachael could see the pain in Debbie's eyes at the mere thought of throwing that piece of her daughter away. "I know," she said, trying to identify with Debbie's anguish, "I know. It's one of the only things left that connects you with your daughter, but it's tainted, Debbie. It bears the sigil of Marbas and may act as a conduit of his power. There's something dark and deadly at work in it now, and you can't risk keeping it near you or your family. Promise me you'll get rid of it when you get home."

Rachael stared at Debbie, her eyes demanding an answer.

"I-I don't know, Rachael," Debbie said.

"Debbie! You must!" Rachael was emphatic and uncompromising on this point.

"Okay," Debbie said without conviction. "Okay. Okay. I'll do it."

"All right," Rachael continued. "That also means you need to get rid of Marbas's sigil in that room under the carpet. Eradicate it. Take a sander to it, or a screwdriver or hammer. Whatever it takes. Remove it from the boards of your house. Okay?"

Debbie nodded.

"Now, second, and just as important," Rachael said, "you *cannot* let your guard down. Do not believe the exorcism cured your son."

Debbie's face scrunched up in a what-the-hell expression, but before she could object, Rachael elaborated.

"You cannot trust Martin yet. He needs to prove he is himself and only him over several days, maybe even weeks. You need to be vigilant and figure out a way to keep each other safe in case Malachi isn't gone."

"But..." Debbie started to speak. "You're telling me to think the worst right now, to act as if nothing we did made a difference. That's acting like there's no hope. I don't think I'm strong enough to do that. I *need* hope...desperately. It's the only source of encouragement my husband and I have."

"I get it, Debbie," Rachael said. "It sucks thinking the people you love may be lost to you, or that they may act against you, even try to hurt you, but it's necessary for your survival. You have to look at Martin like he's a possible wolf in sheep's clothing or a fox hidden in the hen house waiting for his opportunity to strike. Don't let Marbas and Malachi catch you unprepared. After all you and your family have been through, don't let your struggles go to waste. Stay vigilant. If the change is real, it will last. Make sure there are no aberrations of any kind in Martin's behavior."

Debbie hung her head and shook it slowly.

"I'll do my best," she told Rachael, then looked around to find a clock. "Oh my god," she said. "It's going on four p.m. I have to get home."

She thanked Rachael for all her help and a listening ear that did not judge. They said goodbye, Rachael telling her to call if she needed anything, and Debbie left for home. During the ride, she considered Rachael's parting advice and whether she could honestly follow through on either one. She felt as if the very acts would be a form of betrayal to each of her children, and she did *not* have the stomach for that.

DEBBIE ARRIVED HOME TO FIND BOTH HER BOYS ASLEEP on the couch. A new Christmas movie was playing on the TV. *Christmas Chronicles* with Kurt Russell. She stood there long enough to realize it was almost over, then headed out to the garage where she grabbed a piece of coarse sandpaper and a large flathead screwdriver. She proceeded upstairs to Martin's room first and entered the secret room. Debbie pulled the carpet back and removed the portfolio, exposing the sigil of Marbas.

She dug the screwdriver into the wood and twisted it. The movement tore a chunk of wood out. She repeated the process over and over until there was nothing of the sigil left intact. Debbie wiped the bits away and scrubbed the area with the sandpaper vigorously until she was satisfied her efforts had scoured the demon's identity from the floorboards. She put the portfolio back and crawled out of the small room, shutting the door behind her.

Debbie was gone by the time a glowing light shown from beneath the carpet and an unknown force burned the sigil of Marbas back into the sanded area she had worked so hard to cleanse of evil. Had she given it much thought, the idea that the evil in her house could be removed so easily might have seemed preposterous, but she was exhausted beyond measure and struggling to maintain hope.

Oblivious to what transpired behind her, Debbie went into her and Nathan's bedroom. There, she opened the top drawer of her dresser and found Bella's pendant. She slipped it in her pocket and went back downstairs. She told herself she would hop in the minivan and drive to the little backroad bridge that passed over a creek near their house. She would throw it in the water there.

But when she reached the first floor, she felt overcome with an emotional fatigue at the mere thought. She made coffee and told herself to leave, to walk out the door, to fulfill her promise and rid their house of this dangerous power, but it was a feeble command.

Martin stirred and called her name, asked her to come lie with him and Daddy. She could not resist that simple earthly delight. The hope it offered. The hope she longed for. She curled up with them and turned on the movie *Santa Clause* with Tim Allen.

They napped off and on the rest of the day in the living room, watching one Christmas movie after another together—*Santa Clause, How the Grinch Stole Christmas, Jingle All the Way*, and *It's a Wonderful Life*. Nate had ordered multiple pizzas from Domino's earlier in the day while Debbie was gone, so they didn't have to go out or cook anything.

Around ten p.m., Debbie and Nathan nodded off in the middle

of *It's A Wonderful Life*. Martin had already fallen asleep an hour before they did, his face tranquil and serene.

DEBBIE HEARD A NOISE IN HER SLEEP, DISTANT, muffled through walls. But she knew right away it was wrong. There was something unnatural about it. It dragged her from a peaceful slumber, her motherly instincts refusing to allow her to remain unconscious.

Coming to, she looked for Martin next to her on the couch, and when he wasn't there, she continued scanning the room for him. Nothing. Debbie leaped to her feet and almost blacked out from standing up too fast. She bent over, lowering her head below her waist, and waited for the black to part and retreat.

Feeling more stable, she began walking through the house, searching for Martin and listening for the sound that woke her. She checked the dining room, kitchen, den, living room, and laundry room, looking everywhere for her son. No Martin.

Debbie headed for the stairs and began her ascent.

Once on the stairs, the noise drifted to her ears again, but she was unable to place it. It was guttural and faint, an attempt at words but a failed one. She followed the sounds to Martin's room. When she walked through the door, Debbie's legs gave out and she hit the hardwood floor, sprawling toward her son where he lay next to the closet door, arms splayed out crooked, one in front and one behind him. His body jerked and twitched. He stared vacantly in her direction, his mouth limp, one side of his face slack, syllables gargling in his throat, unable to reach his lips much less be properly pronounced.

"*Nnnnnnrrrrrrg…oooooooaaaarrrrrraaaooooooaaarrrerg…mmmmmmm-mmmmmoooooooooooo…gug gug gug gug.*"

Martin's eyes blinked, then moved at a snail's pace until they came to rest on Debbie and fixated on her eyes. She watched his throat work, constricting and relaxing in pulses of effort, defeat, and effort again.

"Mmmmmmmmmaaaahhhhhhhhhhmmmmmmmmmmm…"

It was all he could say, but his eyes pleaded with her to save him. Help him. Make everything better again.

"Naaaaate!"

The shrill scream erupted from Debbie's throat like a siren rising in volume. Terror filled her belly with a fiery death, threatening to melt her bowels.

Nathan jumped out of the chair before he was fully awake and hit the floor stumbling and lurching toward the sound that jerked him from sleep. That sound injected horror into his heart. He clawed at furniture for support as the room swayed and spun around him like a Tilt-a-Whirl. He almost fell but caught himself, hugging the newel with both hands, the bannisters stretching up the staircase before him.

"Naaaate!"

Debbie's scream reached his ears again, and he forced himself to drop down and take the stairs on all fours. He slapped the steps and dug his fingernails into the wood, pulling himself upward.

Debbie regained her strength and scrambled across the floor to Martin, pulling him onto her lap and rocking him. He was limp, like a puppet with its strings cut.

"Oh God, oh God, oh God," she said. "Martin. Martin, baby. Talk to me. Wake up." She shook him gently, but his head only joggled as if at sea. "No, no, no, no, no, no. C'mon, baby! Wake up!"

Nathan clambered through the doorway and zeroed in on Debbie's voice. He saw his son, the boy's body flaccid and paralyzed, but his eyes full of fear. The sight struck Nathan in the gut, knocking what little vigor he possessed out of him. Along with any hope.

Debbie met his gaze. *"Do something!"* her eyes commanded him, but he didn't know what to do, nor did he possess the strength to act in that moment. His body drooped, muscles deflated and impotent, much like his faith. Nathan possessed no weapons to battle the evil at hand, and he knew it.

"He's...coming..." Martin said.

Just two words. Two words of warning. Words loaded with an awful, panic-inducing dread. It seized Debbie's heart and squeezed, enveloped her with a claustrophobic grip of inescapable horror. Those two words prophesied doom. Like a trumpet sounding the end of days, those two words announced the unleashing of a devil from the abyss, arising with no other purpose than to take her son and destroy her world.

Debbie imagined the lion from the pictures and her dream, the beast stalking forward to seize her family like gazelles and feed.

A light appeared about the frame of Martin's closet entrance, growing in brightness by the second. A mist seeped out from the crack under his door. Debbie and Nathan heard an audible click as they watched the doorknob turn. The door opened, creaking at a speed of centimeters per second, multiplying their apprehension to unbearable levels. When the door stood open at last, the fog rolled and roiled, bellowing out from within and hiding what waited inside. They both held their breath and watched the closet door. Seconds dragged out, the moment strangling them like a noose. When their bodies finally screamed for breath and inhaled of their own accord, a form appeared out of the fog, no more than two feet from Debbie and Martin.

It was Stretch Monster, his green, scaly skin pliable and alive. He curled his upper lip and snarled at them.

"No," Debbie said and moaned. It wasn't a lion, but the dread was no less potent. In fact, it seemed more intimidating, evil veiled in something so childish. "No," she whispered.

Stretch Monster took a step forward. But instead of exerting greater intimidation, the creature might as well have stepped on a landmine, triggering Debbie into action. She roared like a momma bear.

"*No!* You can't have my son!" Debbie reached up, grabbed the closet door, and slammed it shut, knocking Stretch Monster back inside. Without hesitating, she set Martin down, stood to grab his desk chair, and wedged the back of it under the closet doorknob. She scooped Martin back up and headed toward the staircase.

"C'mon, Nathan!" she yelled over her shoulder.

Nathan heard her feet pounding down the stairs at warp speed. He turned and began crawling behind her. The sound of little fists pounding on the wooden door with far more force than they should have been capable of followed him as he descended the staircase on hands and knees.

Debbie passed him, coming back up the stairs as he was going down, something in her hands he couldn't make out. He paused to ask her what she was doing, but she cut him off.

"Get down there and stay with Martin!" she barked and continued up, taking stairs two at a time.

Nathan obeyed without question. She was in far better condition to act on their behalf right now than he was.

Debbie skidded sideways into Martin's room, turning to face the closet door before she stopped moving. Her sock feet nearly slid out from under her as she tried to gain forward traction. She paused, caught her balance, and stepped to within a few feet of the door. Popping the cap on the lighter fluid she held, she brought it up and squeezed hard and long, covering the entire closet door and up to the ceiling. She sprayed more of it under the door. The hinges rattled as the Stretch Monster slammed against it, causing small cracks to appear.

She drew a trail of the volatile fluid along the floor to the door, then tossed the bottle on Martin's bed. She pulled out a box of matches, produced one, lit it, and dropped it on the puddle in front of her. It lit, flared into bright yellow flames that sprinted for the closet door and up the wall.

"Fuck you, Malachi!" she shouted in defiance. "Try to destroy my world? I'll destroy your *fucking* home!" She flipped double birds toward the closet door and ran out of the room.

Debbie leaped off the bottom stair and hit the ground running. She slid into the kitchen, grabbed her shoes, and slipped them on. She gathered the car keys, her wallet, phone, and the items Elder Hughes left behind and slipped them all into her purse. She grabbed a jacket for each of them, put on hers, and threw the purse over her shoulder as she hurried into the living room with a pair of Nathan's shoes in one hand. She tossed them at Nathan along with his jacket.

"Put them on and get out of the house. I'm taking Martin to the car."

Nathan saw the fury in her face.

"What did you do, Deb?" he asked.

"I'm burning this fucking house down, babe. Now hurry the fuck up!"

She didn't wait for Nathan to say anything. She picked up Martin, sat him on her hip, clutched him tight to her body, then opened the door and hurried out, car keys in hand. She hit the unlock button as she half ran along the driveway. She put Martin in the backseat and belted him in. He had recovered a small amount of function, enough to hold himself upright against the seat, but little more. She opened her purse, dug inside, and withdrew the bottle of holy water. Debbie popped the cork out, poured it in Martin's mouth, and made him swallow. Then she took the vial of oil and smeared some on his forehead just like she saw the elders do. Lastly, she ripped off a piece of the bread, stuck it in Martin's mouth, and told him to chew.

Debbie stuffed everything back into her purse, jumped in the driver's seat, started the vehicle, and backed up as close to the front porch as possible. She hopped back out. Nathan was crawling out the front door. She looked up. Flames were visible through the window to Martin's room. She met Nathan at the stairs, helped him stand, and assisted him in walking to their vehicle and getting in the front passenger seat.

"Buckle up, dear," she said. "We're getting the hell out of here."

She clicked her own seatbelt in, slammed the gearshift into drive, and punched the gas. She glanced in the rearview mirror just once and smiled at the flames peeling out of Martin's bedroom window.

CHRISTMAS DAY

Debbie drove for a solid three hours before hopping off the interstate to check into a motel at 2:48 a.m. She spoke with the clerk with her hood up. He ran her credit card and gave her two room keys. Room 313.

She retrieved Martin and Nathan. Martin was doing much better. About an hour after they left, he was able to talk. Debbie wasn't sure whether it was the holy water, oil, and bread, the growing distance from the house, or the fact that the house was most certainly burned down by now—or at least severely damaged. Maybe it was a combination of all those factors. Debbie wasn't sure and didn't really care. Her son was looking and sounding much better, and when she opened the vehicle door, he got out on his own and walked.

Debbie slapped a ball cap on Nathan's head to hide his worst injuries and helped him maneuver through the back door, into the elevator, and up to their room. Once inside, Nathan took off his jacket and bloody shirt. He wiped off his upper body with a wet rag in the bathroom, then collapsed onto the king-size bed. Slipping off his shoes, he slid under the covers. Martin crawled in bed with him.

Debbie stepped out onto the balcony and closed the sliding glass door behind her. She pulled out her cellphone and dialed Rachael's number. After four rings, Rachael picked up.

"Debbie?" she asked, her voice quiet and wavering.

"Yes," Debbie answered, "it's me. I need to talk to you."

"Umm…okay," Rachael assured her. "What can I do?"

Debbie informed Rachael of what had transpired, then gave her their hotel name, address, and room number.

"If I don't call you tomorrow by three p.m., call the police and tell them to come here and do a welfare check," Debbie instructed Rachael. "Can you do that for me?"

"Yeah, absolutely. But remember," she urged Debbie, "do not trust your son. I don't care how much better you think he is now that you're far away from the house. Do not let your guard down."

Debbie squeezed her eyes shut.

"I don't think I have a choice right now, Rachael," she said. "I've been running on adrenaline since I saw Martin crumpled on his bedroom floor. I'm coming down hard and fast. I need to hang up and go back inside before I collapse out here in the cold. I can't stay awake. Just, please, do as I asked, if need be."

"Okay," Rachael said, wishing she was there to watch Debbie's back.

"Thank you," Debbie answered. "I'll talk to you later. I gotta go right now. Bye."

Debbie thumbed the end button as she pulled the door open, then went inside and closed it behind her. She kicked off her shoes and removed the hoodie, tossing it on the floor, then got under the covers, sandwiching Martin between her and Nathan.

Sleep came moments later.

A FEELING OF IMMINENT DANGER STRUCK RACHAEL the moment she hung up with Debbie. It filled her with a terrible fear that prophesied a dreadful end for Debbie and her family. It gnawed at her belly like a pack of rabid rats. It was certain. Undeniable. And she could not bear it.

Rachael dressed in a flash, grabbed her purse, and rushed out the door. Jumping into her car, she punched the address for Debbie's motel into her maps app. She shivered at the cold while her engine warmed up but began driving right away.

She sped along the highway, determined to arrive at the motel as quickly as possible without killing herself or someone else.

MARTIN FELT DEATHLY COLD. HIS LIMBS NUMB. HIS torso heavy and lethargic. He could barely lift his head. He had the sensation of a heavy weight lodged in his diaphragm, restricting his breathing. He managed to open his eyes and look toward the foot of the bed.

The light from the bathroom enabled him to see Stretch Monster there, staring at him, arms elongated so he stood like a gorilla, fists supporting him as well as his feet.

The beast spoke.

"It's me, Martin. Malachi. You can't escape me. You can never escape me. Marbas has granted me power over you. A piece of him lives within me, and now in you as well."

Malachi paused and stared at him with the inhuman yellow eyes of the Stretch Monster.

"You know who Marbas is, Martin." It was a statement, not a question. "You know the lion."

Martin nodded, the movement of his head almost imperceptible.

"Because of him, you cannot resist me. You cannot hurt me. But I can hurt you. I can torment you. Every day. All day. Do you understand, Martin? Blink your eyes if you understand."

His eyes were the only thing Martin could control now. He blinked.

"Good," Malachi said. "Good. It's important we're on the same page. That you are fully aware of what is at stake. I can drive you insane, a prisoner in your own body. Do things you will find revolting. Disgusting. And you'll be powerless to stop me. Or I might lock your mind away in that room with the toys for years on end and do as I please. You think you were lonely before. That was just a week. I'm talking years." The creature smiled and laughed, its big canine teeth shaking at him, it seemed.

"Or…" Malachi drew the word out. "Or you can do what I want you to do, and I won't torture you so god damned much."

Malachi leered at Martin for a long moment.

"So, what's it going to be? Do you want to hear what I want from you?"

Martin blinked.

"Ah. Good. Glad to see you recognize the agony in store for you if you refuse me. But enough of that. What I want is very simple."

Malachi remained silent, dragging the moment out, making Martin's little chest tighten up in anxious suspense.

"I want you to kill your parents, Martin. That's all."

Martin's eyes dilated with pure horror. The very idea was detestable to him. Loathsome. Inconceivable.

He strained to shake his head side to side, if only a minute amount. Tears streamed down his cheeks.

"Ah. Poor baby boy. You love your mom and dad, huh? Well, too fucking bad. Your mom's a stubborn bitch and your daddy's gotta go too. Now, mind you, it is *going* to happen. They are *going* to die. In just a minute, actually. So it's really just a matter of whether *you* do it and you suffer very, very little or you *refuse* me, and I make you suffer terribly for the rest of your life, *every single day*. Either way, Marbas will torment your sister and your parents and feast on their terror-filled bowels for years to come. You can join them if you like, but I'd flee for the proverbial hills myself. But, of course, it's up to you."

Fear washed through Martin's eyes, and more tears flowed, but they remained wide open, almost vibrating side to side. That simple movement gave Malachi his answer.

"You sure about this?" Malachi asked Martin.

Martin blinked.

"Hmph. You're no fun at all," Malachi said with distaste and a disappointed tone. "Very well. I'll do it myself."

Stretch Monster's hands took Martin's left hand. The last thing he felt was something cool and metallic against his skin. The world became black as he watched Stretch Monster turn and walk away, dropping off the end of the bed.

"Night, night, Martin," he heard Malachi say in his head, and suddenly he was in the small room beyond his old closet, surrounded by all the old toys. All alone. He looked around for a door, but there was none.

MALACHI FLEXED MARTIN'S FINGERS AND WIGGLED HIS toes. He gripped the object in his left hand with affection. He looked to his right. Debbie lay there next to him, sound asleep. He looked to his left. Nathan lay there, dead to the world. Martin's frown got turned upside down into Malachi's smile. The boy lifted the item in front of him with his left hand, pinched a portion of it with his right hand, and opened it. The blade gleamed silver in the light, the words Old Timer inscribed along the wooden inlay handle.

He turned to Debbie first. Nathan would be easy. She was the strongest of the two right now.

It was just a quick poke. Right between the larynx and the muscle stretching down from jaw to clavicle on her left side. Just like he did to his mother and his father so many years ago. The carotid artery pierced, blood gushed and spurted. The sharp pain woke Debbie up. Malachi rolled over and poked Nathan too, then twisted it all about for good measure before pulling the blade out of his throat.

Just like the Hokie Pokie, Malachi thought and giggled.

Debbie's left hand flew up and pressed the wound on her neck. She removed it and looked at it. Seeing the bright red blood covering her palm, she reapplied pressure and frantically looked around. Martin was climbing down off the bed. She looked after him, confused. From next to her came gurgling noises. She turned to see what was happening.

Nathan gripped his throat with both hands, eyes wide like an animal caught in a snare. His mouth opened and closed, trying to breathe. Blood and red foam bubbled up over his lips.

"Nate," Debbie managed to say in a panic. "What's going on? What happened?"

"Me," a voice said. It was Martin's voice, but it sneered at her. Debbie turned to look at her son. He stood at the foot of the bed. One little hand waved at her, four fingers rising and falling together. She saw the eyes and knew it was Malachi.

"No," she said in a strained whisper.

"Yup. I happened. Gotcha, bitch."

Malachi winked at her and made a shooting sign with thumb and index finger. "Just like I got my parents."

Debbie's head spun and tilted. Nathan was nearing the end of his tailspin plummet, weak from blood loss, his injury more severe than Debbie's. He gurgled and made wet wheezing noises as he laid back on the pillow, hands still clutching his throat as he stared at the ceiling.

Debbie tried to crawl toward the end of the bed with one arm, but it collapsed beneath her. She faceplanted into the comforter and skidded forward until her head hung over the edge. Blood pulsed and spurted between her fingers.

Malachi cocked his head as if he were listening to something.

"What's that, Mom?" he asked. "Oh, I know. It's the fat lady singing. Your time is done. And you know, it's a right tragic ending. Cause you know, it *didn't* have to end like this. You could have lived. You and Dad here, both. We could have been a happy little family. All you had to do was *do* what I said. Give me what I wanted. That's all. But noooo. Not you. Just like that bitch of a mother that gave birth to me. Is it *so* much to ask that a parent make their child happy? That's all you idiots have to do. Make us happy. Give us what we want. Do what we say, what we ask. But that's okay. I'll enjoy this body without you around just as well. I'm gonna make your little boy suffer. I'll do horrible things with this body and make him watch. It'll be *exquisitely fun*."

The world was narrowing, constricting, the black abyss encroaching on all sides. Debbie wanted to curse and rail and flail out at Malachi, but her body would not listen to her commands. It lost all volition, all animus. At last, it wilted, like a dead flower bowing toward the earth from which it sprung.

Malachi climbed off the bed. He dug around in Debbie's purse, withdrew two pens and a pencil, and walked over to the wall, where he set about drawing his masterpiece. He had been at work for a while when a knock at the door drew Malachi's attention away from his art. He cocked his head for a moment.

"The zealous friend," he said, then turned and headed for the door, a knowing look upon his face, the knife gripped in his little hand. He opened the door.

Rachael's face filled with surprise at the sight of a boy answering the door but even more so when the child dove at her leg, head low beneath her knee cap, free hand cupping her heel with a strength no eight-year-old should possess while the blade severed her Achilles tendon. The leg gave out, and she fell, the back of her skull smacking the hallway floor. The world went dark, wobbled, and spun around and around. A moment later, she had the distinct feeling of being dragged. She heard the door click shut and sensed the light from outside the room disappear. A little hand covered her mouth just before she felt a stinging pain at her throat and something warm flowing down the side of her neck. She tried to resist, to struggle, but the grip was powerful even as her own strength fled her body by the second.

"You know too much," Malachi said to Rachael. "Can't have that. Nope. Can't have that at all."

When Rachael's heart stopped beating, Malachi left her on the floor and returned to his work. He spent the next few minutes putting the final touches on it and borrowed Debbie's blood to add some color. Once he was happy with the end product, he returned the pens and pencil to Debbie's purse and climbed up on the bed.

There, he dragged Debbie up to her pillow and positioned her head on it next to Nathan. When he had them both arranged just so, Malachi pulled the covers up to their chins. Afterward, he picked up the phone and dialed 911, set it down on the counter, and crawled back in bed between them and snuggled in.

THE FIRST TWO OFFICERS ON SCENE SPOTTED A GOUT of blood staining the hallway carpet in front of the door to room 313. They drew their guns and knocked hard three times. When there was no immediate answer, they kicked the door open and barged in, flashlights dancing over the carnage. The first one tripped over Rachael's corpse and nearly fell onto the bed. The second swept his light around the room to make sure there was no immediate threat. Once satisfied, he proceeded to turn on the lights.

Both officers scrutinized the scene, struggling to make sense out of the brutality laid before them along with the dreadful drawing on the wall. They thought everyone was dead at first, but then their eyes fell on the boy and observed he was gripping a bloody pocketknife in his hand. He was alive and breathing and looked at peace. His innocent appearance was disarming, but there was no doubt in the officers' minds.

This boy was guilty and headed for the looney bin.

DECEMBER 26

Martin awoke in a white room with padded bracelets strapping his wrists and ankles to the metal bars along each side of the bed he lay on. A doctor stood next to him, a nurse at the foot of his bed.

"Well, he's awake again," the doctor said. "Can you tell me what your name is, son?"

"Umm, my name is Martin Loch, sir."

He tugged against the restraints, looked around, and realized where he was. He'd met this doctor before.

"Where are my parents?" he asked.

The doctor pursed his lips and squinted at Martin. A skeptical look.

"I think you know where your parents are, Martin," the doctor said.

"No," he bleated like a lost sheep. "Where are they? I want my momma."

"You know where they are, Martin," the doctor insisted. "Think."

Martin cried.

"Oh, no," he said, recognition dawning in his brain. "No. Please, no. Are they dead?"

"You know they are, Martin. You killed them."

"It wasn't me," Martin said, tears flowing down his cheeks. "It wasn't me. It wasn't me. It was Malachi. He did it. He did it."

Martin bawled and sobbed. The doctor looked on with detached suspicion. He was not fully convinced Martin's assertions were true after reading the police report.

"And did Malachi draw this image on the wall in your motel room as well, Martin?"

Martin looked at the 8"x10" photo the doctor held up for him to see. He clamped his eyes shut in terror.

"Not me!" he shouted. "Not me! Not me!"

Martin wept. For his family, for their souls, and for his own life. After a minute, the crying subsided and then stopped without warning. The boy's face underwent a transformation. He lost all appearance of weakness, sorrow, remorse. His eyes hardened and glinted beneath the lights with the coldness of a predator.

The doctor took a step back, alarmed at the sudden change.

"Hello?" he asked the boy on the bed. "What's your name, son?"

"Malachi," the boy answered and looked at the picture still held out by the doctor. "My name's Malachi. Martin is too weak to hang around. I'm in charge. You can talk to me. I killed our parents."

Malachi smiled and looked at the doctor, then the nurse, then back at the photo to admire his work.

Against a wall were three figures huddled together. A little girl with blond hair and wearing a white sundress clung to a lady. A man hugged both of them tight. Red spattered the grownups' throats and sat in thick splotches on the little girl's dress. Their faces were caricatures full of horrific fear. Beside them squatted a small boy with black hair. He cried over the rest of his family but was not able to touch them it seemed. Across from the family stood another young boy with black hair. Beside him walked a great lion. Blackness bled from its eyes, and from one paw extended two leashes behind the beast to wrap around the necks of another man and woman it held in tow. Naked, their heads hung, chins to chests, bodies bruised.

"You like it, Doc?" Malachi asked. "I think it's one of my best pieces yet."

The doctor strained to hide his disgust at the boy's words. Rubbing his chin, he motioned to the nurse to join him in the hall.

"Okay, Malachi. I'll be right back. Just one minute."

Malachi smirked as they left the room.

Outside, the doctor spoke with the nurse.

"Well, I was doubtful initially, but it appears we have a genuine case of Dissociative Identity Disorder here. We'll have to question him further and run tests, but I've got a strong suspicion that's what we're dealing with here."

The nurse agreed with him.

"The good kid in there is probably tormented by what he did. Who knows if he'll ever come back out?"

Martin heard every word said, saw everything through his own eyes as Malachi controlled his body. A puppet on strings.

In that moment, he wished desperately for the secret room, the toys…and the solitude.

Instead, he heard the sound of purring, the low, rumbling motor sound of a cat, well fed and content, except it was far too loud to be a mere cat. It permeated the air, vibrating his skin, his bones, until it filled his mind with a growling thunder, reverberating all around, surrounding him with its presence.

"Marbas approaches now, little one," Martin heard Malachi whisper in his ear, in his mind. "Whimper and moan, it will do you no good." A laugh echoed all around Martin but was soon eclipsed.

The gentle footsteps of stealth amidst the grasslands of the savannah were no longer a part of the game. They were replaced now with the thudding sounds of a mighty beast striding forth in glory. Confident. Fearless. An undisputed apex predator of Hell and Earth. No human could stand against him or escape. The room swelled to gigantic proportions to accommodate Marbas as he entered. A colossal lion padded into sight. Its golden-red mane gleamed like burnished bronze, and its eyes burned with sulfur and brimstone while darkness bled from the corners.

Marbas dipped his head and moved closer, one corner of its mouth rising slightly in amusement at Martin's terror. Martin shook and trembled without control. Marbas eased closer and closer, drawing out the moment, until he was nearly nose to nose with Martin. The stench of the beast's breath filled Martin's nostrils—a fetid odor full of death and sex and putrefaction.

Without warning, Marbas licked Martin's face from chin to forehead, hundreds of spines arrayed like soldiers in a phalanx across the tongue tugging at his flesh, pulling it up until they relinquished their hold and dragged roughly across his skin, tasting the fear oozing from the boy's pores.

"Mmmmmm," the beast groaned in pleasure, then spoke. "I have such plans for you, Martin…and for your family. Your mother will make a wonderful whore in Hell, and your father, oh, that tragic, pitiable soul shall bring me much satisfaction. I shall make a whipping boy of sorts out of him. The torments I will inflict upon your father shall remind him daily of the foul hubris which brought him low and delivered all of you into my grasp. His disbelief in gods and devils and all the other grotesque things that go bump in the night. His willing ignorance and refusal to act in defense of his family was your undoing. His afflictions will cry out, 'Guilty!' with every abuse and injury. But worst of all, I will allow him to watch you grow up with myself and Malachi at the helm, allow him to gaze into the murderous dark that will fill your eyes, my son. From the day we leave this institution, you and your father will watch as I teach Malachi the art of killing, the appetites of the flesh, and empower him to never be caught. All the days of your physical life, you shall know nothing but death. You will long for peace, but the hunt will be your world. And who knows? Maybe one day I will corrupt you as I did Malachi. One day your heart may grow to look with fondness on our deviant pleasures, as so many of my children do."

Marbas waved a paw, and Martin saw a horde of people—men, women, and children—standing behind him. Those like his sister and parents and Malachi's parents, who were clearly down-trodden and forlorn, were the minority. Surrounding them was a vast multitude of souls whose eyes bled darkness, just like Marbas, and whose mouths leered with savage hunger and bris-tled with rows of sharpened teeth.

"My children are voracious eaters, young boy," Marbas said. "They long for the tender flesh of youth most of all, just like their father."

Marbas smiled and pawed at Martin's face, feigning a tender touch.

"Yes, boy," Marbas continued, "your flesh shall serve me well. The delights I shall initiate you and young Malachi into shall be *sumptuous*, indeed! *Glorious,* even!"

Martin felt dizzy. The world began to spin, and he diminished within it. Malachi ascended the throne of his consciousness once more, with Marbas at the reins to guide him. Martin was merely a passenger now, paralyzed, powerless, and bereft of any promise of good tidings or great joy in this Christmas season, or ever again. Darkness and woe were his inheritance now. Nothing more awaited him.

He thought of the secret room full of toys again and wished

earnestly for it. He tried to imagine a safe place, a little slice of heaven to hide away from the hell Marbas and Malachi had prepared for him and his family.

But it was a fool's dream to hope, a folly and fantasy which would bring only grief.

THE END

Join the Crystal Lake community today!

Subscribe to our Newsletter!
(Scan the QR code or click if eBook)

Subscribe to our Patreon!
(Scan the QR code or click if eBook)

Visit our Linktree for
all social media sites!
(Scan the QR code or click if eBook)

Download our catalog!
(Scan the QR code or click if eBook)

ABOUT THE AUTHOR

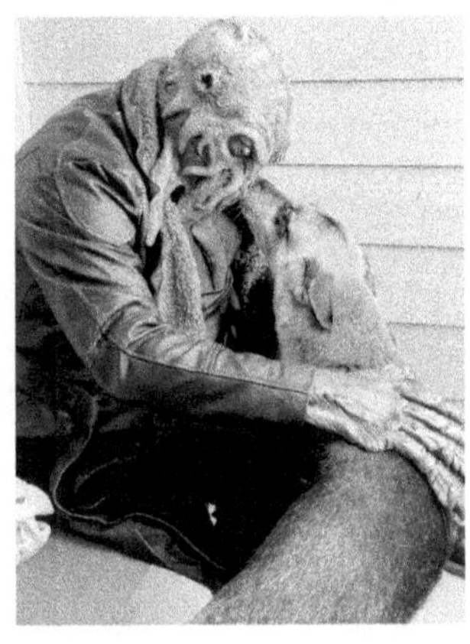

For the last sixteen years Mike has taught Military, Law Enforcement and Bodyguards high speed, tactical and off-road driving as well as hand to hand Combatives. He's practiced various martial arts since 1989. Filipino blade arts are his current favorite. Since he was a teenager he's loved reading, writing, and watching movies, particularly in the horror and sci-fi genre. He has a beautiful, supportive wife and a son and daughter who have both graduated high school and moved out. His babies now are his German Shepherd, Ziva, a Daddy's girl who loves to play, and a Border Collie named Joey "The Bandit". Mike is a lover of music, and it is an integral part of his writing ritual.

Mike writes an eclectic mix of horror stories, exploring dark supernatural entities, cosmic terrors, and natural monstrosities along with the wicked deeds of the human heart. He's skilled at provoking a significant response from his readers – whether shock, terror, dread, an uneasy sense of empathy, Heebie Jeebie crawlies, or surprise at unexpected twists. Mike will *make* you feel while reading. As one reviewer said, when you read a Mike Duke book you don't just read about an experience, you *have* an experience.